I0686017

Asher's Mark

by
Amy Durham

Asher's Mark
Copyright © 2014 Amy Durham
Print Edition

Published By Amy Durham
ISBN: 9780985070687

Editor: Taylor K's Editing Service
Cover Artist: Tracy Stewart (www.simplybookish.com)
Original Artwork on cover by: Teresa Reasor (www.teresareasor.com)
Formatter: BB eBooks (www.bbebooksthailand.com)
Beta Readers & Proofreaders: Dawn Laurent Bourgeois, Teresa Reasor,
Barry Blakeman, & Cheryl Blakeman

Contact Information: amybdurham@gmail.com

All rights reserved. Without limiting the rights under copyright reserved above, no part of this publication may be reproduced, stored in or introduced into a retrieval system, or transmitted, in any form, or by any means (electronic, mechanical, photocopying, recording, or otherwise) without the prior written permission of both the copyright owner and the above publisher of this book.

This is a work of fiction. Names, characters, places, brands, media, and incidents are either the product of the author's imagination or are used fictitiously. The author acknowledges the trademarked status and trademark owners of various products referenced in this work of fiction, which have been used without permission. The publication/use of these trademarks is not authorized, associated with, or sponsored by the trademark owners.

This ebook is licensed for your personal enjoyment only. This ebook may not be re-sold or given away to other people. If you would like to share this book with another person, please purchase an additional copy for each person you share it with. If you are reading this ebook and did not purchase it, or it was not purchased for your use only, please purchase your own copy. Thank you for respecting the author's work.

Other Books by Amy Durham

Once Again (Sky Cove #1)

For Once: A Sky Cove Short Story (Sky Cove #1.5)
~ free ebook

Once And For All (Sky Cove #2)

Dusk

Dedication

To Cayce

Asher found his some of his best, most enduring friendships, at work. So did I. I can't begin to tell you how grateful I am for the past six years or how deeply and profoundly you have enriched my life. There is no one like you in the entire world, and I'm so fortunate to be able to call you *friend*. I love you dearly. Here's to many more years of being BFFs!

Acknowledgements

Every book is a group effort, and with each book I write I'm more and more aware of all the people who help me bring these stories to fruition.

Thank you to Tracy Stewart at Simply Bookish for the absolutely gorgeous cover for this book. You brought Asher and Grace to life in the most spectacular way!

Thank you to Teresa Reasor for the beautiful original artwork you created for the cover. That amazing ship tattoo on Asher's arm? Teresa drew that, especially for his arm, and it looks amazing!

Taylor Kent, thank you for careful and insightful editing, and for helping me make Asher's Mark the best it could be.

To my beta readers and proofreaders – Dawn Laurent-Bourgeois, Teresa Reasor, Barry Blakeman, and Cheryl Blakeman – thanks for expert eyes and belief in my stories.

As always, thanks to Glenda Edwards for all kinds of brainstorming and plotting help, and for answering my occasional legal questions.

To Dustin Quillen of Bodean's Tattoo in Campbellsville, KY, thanks for answering my questions about tattooing and for reading sections of the book to make sure I got it right.

To Paul Salvette and the team at BB eBooks, thank you for always making my books look great with your outstanding formatting!

Prologue

June 10, 2014

Grace

I STAND IN front of the casket, a tidal wave of emotion washing over me.

Sadness. Anger. Regret. Confusion. Nothing about this scenario is right or good or fair.

A wonderful young man with so much potential is dead. Gone forever. An enormous hole now gapes wide and bottomless in the middle of all our lives.

Next to me stands Asher. Straight and stoic, bathed in the light of the strange pink lamps on either side of the casket, he looks down at the body. His blank expression does nothing to mask his fury and grief. It only underscores it. The muscles of his jaw clench tight and his throat tenses as he tries in vain to hold back his sorrow. He's lost so much more than I have, and yet he still tries to comfort me. His hand moves a fraction of an inch until his pinky finger wraps around mine, squeezing lightly in a silent show of support.

Asher is touching me.

My insides quiver. My heart betrays me.

Asher, who is sensitive and kind, strong when he needs to be, talented and driven, and completely misunderstood. Asher, who I'd first loved. Who I loved still. Asher, whose brother, Adam, is in the casket.

Adam, who was my boyfriend.

Chapter 1

Two years earlier...
April 25, 2012

Grace

TONY ADKINS GIVES new meaning to the word bully.

Not only does he litter the hallways of Greyson High School with comments about the desirability or undesirability of girls' backsides and waltz to the front of the lunch line each day like he has every right to cut in front of everyone else, but he also picks on Kyle Martin. Mercilessly.

Kyle is a seventeen-year-old with Down's Syndrome. He's happy and friendly, and everyone loves him. Which is probably why Tony takes great pleasure in torturing him.

Even though the school year is almost over, I still feel like a lowly underclassman. My school isn't huge, but it isn't small either, so it still manages to be intimidating for an introvert like me. That's why I often ask to be excused from class a few minutes early in order to get in and out of the restroom before the general population. Today, as I come around the corner of the cafeteria, heading to the bathroom, Tony has Kyle cornered and appears to be tormenting him. It infuriates me. I want to intervene so badly, but I'm completely frozen in my spot.

"Come on, Kyle," Tony coaxes, his voice slimy and deceitful. "You know you want to."

Kyle shakes his head. "No. It isn't right. I can't do that."

"Girls are used to it," Tony continues. "You just go up to her, grab her chest, and squeeze."

I have no idea who *her* is, but Tony's maniacal laughter makes my stomach turn.

"But she'll be mad at me." Kyle's voice shakes and he sounds on the verge of tears.

"Nah. Girls like it," Tony says. "Trust me."

Tony's bullying is already bad enough, but it takes a special kind of nasty to be so awful to Kyle, who's never been anything but sweet and helpful and has no real way to defend himself against Tony's deviousness. I have to do something. I don't know what, but it's time to stop being such a chicken. Maybe if I make my presence known, Tony will back off. I'm just about to step forward when Asher Howell barrels out of the bathroom.

Asher is an imposing figure. I'm not a good judge of height, but I know he's at least six feet tall. Probably more. At eighteen, or close to it, he isn't overly bulky like a football player. Instead, he's slender and lean. Dressed in his standard ripped jeans that I'm certain don't meet the school dress code, worn out Converse Chucks, and a plaid button-up with the sleeves rolled to the elbows, he looks every bit the rebel running counter to the high school norm.

He is absolutely gorgeous.

Asher lets the bathroom door slam behind him and shoves Tony hard enough that he stumbles back against the concrete block wall. Fury seethes across Asher's expression, and his fists clench at his sides. Apparently, he heard the whole thing too, because his dark brown eyes blaze with outrage.

"What the hell, Asher!" Tony shouts as his head smacks against the wall, bouncing against the black and yellow hawk, our school mascot.

Asher says nothing, just steps forward and puts his body between Kyle and Tony, glaring at the scumbag like he wants to wipe the floor with him. I don't know if either of them see me or not, but Kyle does, so I motion for him to come stand beside me and out of the line of fire.

"What is wrong with you, you little punk?" Asher says, his tone hushed but no less intense.

"Watch your mouth, Howell," Tony fires back, pushing off the wall. "It's none of your damn business."

The words are barely out of Tony's mouth when Asher punches him right in the face. Tony's head snaps back, and Kyle and I jump, scrambling to get out of the way. I've seen fights before, but never this close up. And never when I actually wanted to cheer for a particular side.

The bell to signal class change rings, and I hear the rumble of students as they pour out of the classrooms. Tony starts to right himself, but doesn't get a chance because Asher hits him again, this time uppercutting him in the chin. Tony hits the floor, landing on his butt before winding up flat on his back.

If this continues, the white tiled floor is going to be splattered with Tony's blood, because Asher shows no signs of backing down.

I grab Kyle's arm and pull him further back, out of the way of the approaching footsteps. Asher stands directly over Tony, as if daring him to try and get up. Tony's face looks misshapen already, I assume from the swelling caused by Asher's fist. A group of girls round the corner, heading for the bathroom. As soon as they see Tony on the floor and Asher hulking above him, fists ready to strike again, they scream like... well... little girls.

After that, everything seems to happen at once, yet at the same time it feels like slow motion. Mr. Wiggins, a forty-something man with male-pattern baldness that he tries to cover-up with a very unfortunate comb-around, comes running out of his classroom door, shouting at everyone. Mr. Bledsoe, the principal, shows up moments later, attempting to disperse the crowd by ordering everyone back to class. Very few people pay attention to him. Asher and Tony are both ushered toward the office, and, with nothing else to see, students finally begin to leave.

I spot Margo Edwards, who's in my next class, and a thought occurs to me.

"Kyle, stay right here, okay?" I ask.

Kyle nods.

I catch up with Margo just before she turns the corner.

"Hey, tell Mrs. Garcia that I'll be late," I say. "I saw what happened and I need to tell Mr. Bledsoe."

I don't wait for a response before walking back toward Kyle.

"Kyle, listen to me," I say, looking him directly in the eye. "We need to tell Mr. Bledsoe what happened. We need to tell him what Tony was trying to get you to do."

Kyle shakes his head. I know it'll be really embarrassing for him to talk about.

"Don't worry. I'll be there with you. I'll even do all the talking. But if we don't tell Mr. Bledsoe, Asher's going to get in big trouble for hitting Tony."

"Asher stuck up for me," Kyle says.

"Yes, he did."

Taking charge of a situation isn't something I regularly do, but despite how strange it feels, I take Kyle by the hand and together we walk toward the office.

✧   ✧   ✧

ASHER SITS IN a conference room separated from the main office by a windowed wall. I see him slouched in one of the standard chairs, upholstered in the same boring green as the rest of the office furniture. His dark hair, cut short and close in the back, is long enough in the front to hang across his forehead and hide his eyes as he waits for whatever punishment is about to be delivered. His eyebrow piercing twinkles from between strands of dark, chocolate colored hair. I'd never thought of myself as particularly fond of facial piercings, but on Asher... yeah.

I don't see Tony, but I figure he's with the nurse getting his face iced down. He's lucky he doesn't need stitches.

Kyle fidgets beside me. I take his hand in mine and say, "It's okay. Don't be nervous."

"You're nice, Grace," he whispers. "I'm glad you're helping me."

How Tony could be so mean to Kyle is something I'll never understand.

Mr. Bledsoe opens his office door and waves us in. Closing it behind us, he cuts right to the chase. "I understand you witnessed the fight between Asher Howell and Tony Adkins."

"I witnessed more than that, Mr. Bledsoe." I have no idea where all this courage is coming from, but I'm not about to back down. "Just before I turned the corner toward the bathroom, I heard Tony talking to Kyle. He wasn't being very nice."

"Is that true, Kyle?" Mr. Bledsoe asks.

Kyle nods but doesn't say anything.

"What exactly was Tony saying to you?"

Kyle stares at the floor and shifts his weight back and forth between his feet.

"You didn't do anything wrong, Kyle," I say. I look at Mr. Bledsoe, taking note of his graying hair and wrinkled forehead. Being a school administrator must've taken its toll. "He's really embarrassed. Is it okay if I tell you what was going on?"

"Of course." Mr. Bledsoe crosses his arms over his chest.

I take a deep breath. "I heard Tony trying to get Kyle to grab a girl's chest."

Kyle's face flames with embarrassment. "It's not your fault, Kyle."

"Are you sure that's what Tony was doing?" Mr. Bledsoe asks, as if he couldn't believe such an upstanding student was capable of being so awful.

"Yes, sir," I answer, my voice as firm as I can make it. "Kyle was obviously upset and uncomfortable. I didn't get there in time to hear her name, but I heard Kyle say 'No, I can't do that. It's not right. She'll be mad at me.' But Tony just kept on. He told him girls were used to it and he should just go up, grab her chest, and squeeze. That's when I knew he was trying to get Kyle to grab some poor girl's breasts. I was just about to say something and try to put a stop to it when Asher came out of the boys' bathroom. He must've overheard the entire thing as well."

"Is this true, Kyle? Was Tony attempting to get you to do something inappropriate?"

I want to point out to Mr. Bledsoe that not only is it inappropriate, it's also probably illegal, but I figured I should just keep my mouth shut for the time being.

Kyle looks up, summoning all his bravery, and says, "Yes, sir."

"Who was the girl?" Bledsoe asks. "The one Tony was telling you to touch."

"Jessica Torres." Kyle's voice comes out as a whisper. He's so embarrassed it my makes my heart hurt. And naturally, Tony chose one of the most popular girls in school, which would just maximize Kyle's humiliation if he'd followed Tony's instructions.

"And what precipitated Asher hitting Tony?" Mr. Bledsoe asks. "I need to know who used physical violence first."

Oh crap. How do I tell the truth and not get Asher into more trouble?

"When Asher stepped out of the restroom, the first thing he did was push Tony to get him away from Kyle." I intentionally leave out the amount of force Asher used.

"And how did Tony respond?"

"He cussed at Asher," I say. "Then he pushed off the wall and came at him."

"So Tony hit first?"

I swallow hard. "No. Asher did, but in a kind of

preemptive way. It looked like Tony was about to attack him."

"When someone hits first, he can't claim self-defense." He says this like he's a freaking prosecuting attorney. I wonder if it would do any good for me to object.

"Mr. Bledsoe, Tony is a menace. A bully. He makes sexually explicit comments to every girl he passes in the hall. But his favorite target is Kyle. He's mean enough to the rest of us, but the way he treats Kyle is so much worse. It's bullying and harassment, Mr. Bledsoe."

"Even so, Asher did not have cause to hit him. To put a stop to the behavior, yes. To use physical violence, no." Mr. Bledsoe opens his office door and gestures for us to leave. "We'll handle any reports of bullying through the office."

And we've been dismissed.

Kyle and I exit the office, and I do my best not to let him see how angry I am.

"Did we help?" Kyle asks, once we were in the hallway.

"We told the truth," I say. "And that's the most important thing."

"I won't forget how you helped me," Kyle says. "Or how Asher stood up for me."

I walk Kyle back to his classroom but can't bring myself to go to my own. I decide it isn't exactly skipping since Mrs. Garcia knows I'd witnessed a fight and went to the office. So instead of returning to class,

I head back toward the office, hoping to catch Asher once Mr. Bledsoe finishes with him.

I manage to stay unnoticed as I loiter near the front office. I have no idea how long it takes for Mr. Bledsoe to decide on a punishment and officially bestow it, but I'm determined to speak to Asher.

Before today, he'd been nothing more than a cute guy two grades ahead of me. I've noticed him mainly because he doesn't dress in the same preppy style as a lot of the boys at Greyson High. But today, he's a champion of the underdog, and that makes him infinitely more attractive.

Mr. Bledsoe steps toward the glass door of the office, and I shrink back toward the main hallway. Only a handful of students move through the hall since most everyone is still in fourth period. Peering around the edge of a row of lockers, I watch as Asher leaves the office, head held high, and turns in my direction.

Luckily, Mr. Bledsoe doesn't accompany him. Asher heads toward the section of the hallway where most of the seniors have their lockers. Mustering every ounce of bravery I possess, I speak.

"Asher," I say, causing him to stop and look directly at me. "I'm so sorry."

His eyes narrow and he tilts his head, like he's trying to figure out who I am.

"I tried to help, but I'm afraid I just made things worse because I had to tell Mr. Bledsoe that you hit first."

One side of his mouth lifts. It's not so much a smile as it is an acknowledgement of irony. "You didn't make things worse," he says. "I told him the same thing. I hit Tony first."

"What did he do to you?" I ask, hoping that somehow Mr. Bledsoe had done the right thing and left Asher alone.

Asher shrugs one shoulder. "Called my mom and suspended me for three days."

"Seriously!" I say it loud enough that I'm afraid I've disturbed one of the classrooms near us. I lower my voice. "After what Tony did, *you* get suspended?"

"I doubt Tony's escaping unpunished," Asher says. "You and Kyle confirmed what I'd already told Mr. Bledsoe about Tony. Maybe he'll at least get punished for picking on Kyle."

"I just can't believe he suspended you." I can't remember the last time I'd been so pissed. "You're a hero. You should get some credit for it."

This time Asher does smile, like maybe he's enjoying having someone upset on his behalf. He steps toward me, closing the distance until only a foot remains between us. My heartbeat speeds up.

"What's your name?" he asks, his voice soft and deep.

"Grace Ballard." I marvel that my voice doesn't squeak.

"I'm no hero, Grace," he whispers. "And I didn't do it for credit. I did it because somebody had to, and because sometimes it's just not enough to tell an asshole like Tony to shut up."

He's so wrong. He is definitely a hero.

Chapter 2

Asher

THE PETITE, AUBURN-HEADED girl in front of me is a walking contradiction. One second she's all meek and apologetic over something that's not her fault, and the next she's all kinds of pissed that I got suspended for knocking the shit out of Tony. Those hazel green eyes of hers waffle back and forth between indignation and uncertainty.

Her name is Grace, and she thinks I'm a hero.

I find myself really digging contradictions right at the moment.

"I'm no hero, Grace," I whisper. "And I didn't do it for credit. I did it because somebody had to, and because sometimes it's just not enough to tell an asshole like Tony to shut up."

Her eyes drop to the floor, like I totally deflated the hero balloon she's imagined around me. For about half a second I almost feel bad, but then she looks at me again and the ability to form rational thought abandons me. In her eyes is everything I never knew I wanted, every feeling I never imagined but now want more than I want my next breath.

"That just makes you more of a hero," she says. "Kyle will never forget how you stood up for him. Neither will I."

Good grief, this girl is destroying me. Looking at me like that, like she has all kinds of faith and confidence in me, just about sends me to my knees. If I never move from this spot I won't complain. Mr. Bledsoe gave me fifteen minutes to get my stuff and leave, but his time limit means nothing at the moment. All I care about right now is Grace.

"Are you a sophomore?" I ask, pretty sure she's the same age as my brother.

She blushes. Holy cow. A pink flush against that auburn hair. My gut screams at me to get closer to her.

"Is it that obvious I'm an underclassman?" she replies, a bit of meekness flashing in her eyes.

I shake my head. "That's not an insult or anything. I just thought I'd seen you in some of Adam's classes, so I sort of figured you were the same age."

"Adam?"

"My brother," I say. And man, I hope Adam hasn't messed her over. Even though he just got his license last month, my brother's been hopping from one girl to the next for so long I've stopped trying to keep up. He's fast developing a reputation as a player, and the thought that he might've toyed with Grace's heart leaves a sour taste in my mouth.

"Adam Howell?" she asks, though I can tell she doesn't expect an answer. "I never put two and two together."

"You know Adam?" I hold my breath and wait.

"This school isn't huge, so yeah, I know him. We have a couple of classes together, but I've never really talked to him outside of class."

I take that to mean my brother hasn't flirted or made advances, then dropped her like a hot potato. Adam's reputation hasn't ruined things for me before I even get a chance with this girl. Relief washes through me.

"So yeah," she says, pushing a strand of hair behind her ear, which naturally makes me imagine putting my lips right there on that tender spot below her ear. "Sophomore. And you're a senior, right?"

I drag my thoughts out of the gutter and nod.

So she's probably sixteen. I wonder if her parents let her date yet. If not, I'll figure something out. I need to get her number so we don't lose contact.

"Hey, can I –"

"Grace, what are you doing out of class?" Brian Ballard stalks toward us.

Greyson, Arizona's golden boy, who's heading to Stanford on a full tuition scholarship because of his astronomical SAT score. And yeah, Mr. Perfect also happens to be Grace's brother.

And he's clearly not happy to find his sister alone in the hallway with Asher Howell.

I know what I look like. I know the long bangs hanging in my face and the silver hoop in my eyebrow make people think I don't give a damn about stuff like people and grades. I don't brag about my 4.0 GPA, but it exists.

I don't care that people make assumptions about me. But knowing what's probably going through Brian Ballard's mind as he watches me talking to his sister… that bothers me.

It bothers me even more seeing Grace shrink right in front of my eyes, the brightness and vibrancy sliding away as her brother approaches.

"Grace was just being helpful," I say, looking straight at Brian. His perfectly styled hair and light blue polo shirt annoy the heck out of me. I really hope he lets it drop. I don't want to get into an argument with him right in front of Grace.

"Sometimes Grace is too nice for her own good." Brian comes to a stop right behind his sister. I don't miss the disapproval in his voice.

God, what a piece of crap.

"I'm *right here*, Brian." She whirls around to face him. "Don't talk about me like I'm not here."

And there's her feistiness. I can't help the smile that crosses my face. Brian's eyes never leave mine, and his message is obvious. *Stay away from my sister.*

Much as I want to point out that his sister is more than smart enough to make her own judgments, I don't want to cause Grace any problems. I can't alienate her brother if I want to get to know her better. I figure I'll let it go for now and reconnect with her when my suspension is over.

"I've got to grab my stuff and head out anyway," I say. She turns back around and pins me with those green eyes. I'll never get tired of looking at her. "Thanks again, Grace. I'll see you later."

Walking away is about the hardest thing I've ever done, but arguing with her brother is no way to endear myself. If I want to pursue things with Grace, I have to be careful. Move slowly.

No one's ever looked at me and really *seen* me. I've always been the guy who's a little different, kind of introverted, liked well enough but never part of the popular elite. And that's been fine. I've never craved approval from the people I go to school with. I have a few buddies, and I get along with my teachers. High school is just the connecting road between childhood and the start of my life.

But the way Grace's eyes took me in, the way her smile seemed to reach out and grab me by the heart… it's like finally someone *saw* me. The *real* me.

And now that I've felt it, there's no way I can let that feeling go. There's something about this girl that I can't explain, and deep down I know that I need to get to know her. So I'll pace myself, and not hurry things.

I'm pretty sure she's worth the wait.

Chapter 3

Grace

LEAVE IT TO Brian to ruin everything and make me look like a stupid child, completely unworthy of Asher's attention.

Ignoring my brother, I watch Asher walk all the way down the hall, noticing the easy way he moves and the sway of his arms as he makes his way to his locker. He slings a well-worn backpack over one shoulder, closes his locker, and turns back to look at me. I can almost feel the condemnation pouring off Brian as Asher nods his head and smiles before heading out of the building.

"Seriously Brian?" I don't even turn around to look at him.

"Are you skipping class?" he asks, sounding like the freaking hallway police.

"No." I offer no further explanation.

"Then why were you out here with him?" The sarcasm is so thick on the word *him* I figure he probably tastes it.

"You know Brian," I say, finally spinning around to face him. "Sometimes I leave class to go the restroom. Sometimes a teacher sends me on an errand. Sometimes I have to get something from my locker. There are all kinds of reasons I might be out of class, so why do you automatically assume I was skipping?"

"Were you?" he asks again.

"I know I'm not perfect like you, but have I ever done anything to make you think I'd intentionally ditch class?"

"I've never seen you hanging out with questionable people before, so when I see you practically nose to nose with Asher Howell what am I supposed to think?"

"Asher's *questionable?*"

"He's weird, Grace," Brian says. "Never socializes with any of the rest of us. Hangs out in the art room all the time. And you saw the piercing in his eyebrow."

"You're absolutely right, Brian. Something would definitely have to be wrong with a person who wouldn't want to hang out with you. And who could ever trust someone who enjoys art? I can't believe I was so stupid."

"You're so naive," he sneers. "You know his brother is a total man whore, right? Surely you've heard the talk about Adam Howell."

I haven't, but I don't necessarily think that *not* hearing gossip is anything to be ashamed of. "Asher isn't like brother."

"They live together," Brian says. "They can't be all

that different."

"You and I live together and we are nothing alike."
I glare at him. "And thank God for that."

✧   ✧   ✧

MY LAST CLASS of the day is biology. It isn't my
favorite, but I've been dying to get here since the
moment Asher walked out of school to serve his
suspension.

Adam Howell sits two rows over from me. I've
never really paid much attention to him, but today I
will. He's Asher's brother, and I want any and all
information I can learn about Asher.

At first glance you wouldn't guess they were brothers. Adam has on khaki cargo shorts and a graphic tee
shirt from one of those trendy stores at the mall. His
hair, a lighter brown than Asher's, is short and gelled
with some kind of product to maintain that messy look.
He dresses to fit in. To look like everyone else.

But with a closer look at his deep brown eyes and
tan complexion, I can see the similarities.

It would be totally stupid to strike up a conversation with him given that we aren't exactly buddies, so
instead I listen to the back and forth between Adam
and Jordan Green.

"Dude, your brother knocked Tony Adkins on his
ass!" Jordan clasps hands with Adam as if they're
celebrating some huge success.

Which I suppose they are. Even though I know

they're probably only excited because there's been a fight, I have to admit that Asher taking Tony down the way he did feels like a major accomplishment.

"I heard, man," Adam says, dropping into the seat behind Jordan. "I wish I'd seen it. Tony's such a douche. That prick's had it coming for a long time."

Yes, yes he has.

"I came out of Wiggins' class and there Tony was, sprawled on the floor with Asher standing over him like damn enforcer. I was like *hell yeah!*"

It *had* been impressive.

"Tony got suspended, too," Adam says. "But only for the rest of today and tomorrow. I can't wait to talk to Ash and find out what Tony did to set him off."

"I know," I say, and then immediately regret it when Adam, Jordan, and everyone else in the classroom turns to look at me.

"How do you know?" asks Sydney, one of my good friends who sits next to me.

"I saw the whole thing."

"No shit!" Adam says. "Well tell us!"

Thankfully, Mrs. Wells, our teacher, is still in the hallway. I don't exactly want to relay the whole story in front of an adult. "I overheard Tony talking to Kyle Martin. He was picking on him, like usual, trying to get him to do something really inappropriate. Asher was in the bathroom and overheard the whole thing. He came out and put a stop to it."

"I bet he did!" Adam exclaims. "Ash gets totally

jacked up when somebody's being picked on."

Well, Adam might be a man whore like Brian said, but at least he sees the stupidity of Tony's actions. And the heroism in Asher's.

"Asher doesn't seem like the type to fight," Sydney says.

I just shrug. I haven't been around Asher enough to form an opinion before today, but when he came out of that bathroom, eyes blazing and trained on Tony, I wouldn't have bet against him.

"He's not much with the ladies." Adam lowers his voice as Mrs. Wells steps in the room, but his comment still sparks laughter from Jordan and a couple other guys. "But bother somebody who doesn't deserve it and you better stay out of his way."

Asher wasn't much with the ladies? Well, that's fine because he is *plenty* as far as I'm concerned.

Chapter 4

Asher

"HEARD YOU SMACKED down with Tony Adkins." Adam busts into my bedroom as soon as he gets home. Mom had taken my cell phone for the duration of my suspension, but I'm sure Adam had blown it up with texts once he heard about it.

"I didn't really smack down *with* him. It was more like I smacked down *on* him." I probably take a little too much pride in that admission. I close my physics book and turn my chair away from the desk and toward Adam. No sense trying to do homework while he's in the room.

Adam falls down laughing on my bed. We might be completely different when it comes to school, girls, and practically everything else, but there is one thing we agree on. We hate bullies.

"Jordan was in Wiggins' room and saw the end result. How many punches you throw?"

"Two."

"What about him?"

"Zero."

"Dang, Asher," Adam says. "You can be such a badass. You could freaking own that school if you were like that all the time."

And here is the difference between my brother and me. Adam's consumed with fitting in and being popular. He succeeds nicely. Me? I couldn't care less.

"You know that's not why I flattened him."

"Yeah, I heard he was picking on Kyle Martin." Adam sits up and scoots to the edge of the mattress. "What the hell is wrong with him?"

"Lack of brain cells?" I suggest.

"No doubt," Adam says. "Grace said you definitely put a stop to it, though."

"You talked to Grace?" Everything inside me lights up and my heart takes off like a jackhammer.

"Yeah, she's in my last class. Jordan was talking about it and she told us what she saw."

"You talk to her much?" I hope I sound casual enough. No way do I want my brother realizing I have a thing for this girl. He'd never shut up about it. Heck, he might even go to school tomorrow and tell her.

"Nah, not much," he answers. "You?"

I let out the breath I'd been holding. "Not until today. She took Kyle to the office and talked to Mr. Bledsoe after the fight. I ran into her in the hall when I was getting my stuff. She was mad I'd gotten suspended for sticking up for Kyle."

"That does suck majorly."

I shrug my shoulders. "It was nice she tried to help."

"She does seem nice, now that you mention it," Adam says. I watch the wheels turning in his head and my stomach sinks. "And pretty, too."

Oh *hell* no.

"Don't go there, Adam." I get up from my seat and drop onto the bed beside him. "Seriously, don't even try."

"What's the matter, Ash?" he teases, elbowing me in the ribs. "You got dibs?"

Do I ever. But I'm not about to tell him that.

"You know who her brother is?" I ask.

Adam shakes his head.

"Brian Ballard."

"Boy Genius?"

"That's right," I say. "He happened to see me talking to her after I left Mr. Bledsoe's office, and let's just say he wasn't happy. I get the sense the overprotective big brother syndrome is in full swing."

"You don't think he'd approve of me?" Adam's laughter tells me it isn't an actual question.

"I don't think he'd approve of anyone," I reply. "But let's face it. Your reputation with girls isn't stellar."

"Whatever," Adam says, pushing up off the bed. "Plenty of ladies to fill my time with. No need to get Boy Genius riled up."

I want to shout in relief.

Adam reaches for the doorknob just as a knock sounds from the other side. Mom must be home early.

When she steps into the room she still has that *I can't believe you got into a fight at school* look on her face.

"Come on, Mom. Don't bust his balls over this," Adam says, seeing her expression and leaping to my defense. "He was sticking up for a special needs kid."

Mom rolls her eyes. "Honestly, Adam? Your choice of words is awful." She hates it when he makes reference to genitals.

Adam just laughs. One corner of Mom's mouth turns up, and I can't help but laugh too.

"Fighting at school is never a good thing," she says, tossing my cell phone at me. "You're eighteen years old. Taking your cell phone was a knee-jerk reaction. You're still grounded until your suspension is over." She narrows her eyes at me and sighs. "But I am glad you defended that young man."

"That's Asher." Adam plops back down beside me on the bed. "He's like Batman or some crap like that."

"I didn't come in here to talk about Asher's new penchant for violence." She pulls out my desk chair and sits down. "We accepted an offer on the house today."

Our house has been on the market for two years, ever since Mom and Dad split. This house is too much, both financially and in terms of space, for the three of us, so as a part of their divorce settlement, they've been trying to sell it.

We'd known it was coming, but I still feel kind of shocked.

"Where will we go?" Adam asks.

"The realtor found a rent-to-own not far from here," she answers. "It's just the right size for us, and it's vacant."

"We won't have to move schools will we?" Adam sounds panicked.

I hadn't thought of that. With just over a month to go before graduation, I don't think I'd have to transfer even if we do move out of the area, but for Adam that would be a big deal.

Mom shakes her head. "No, it's the same district."

"Thank God," Adam says. "I'd have hated to break the hearts of all the girls at Greyson High."

This time I'm the one rolling my eyes.

"When do we have to be out of here?" I ask. I'd already begun getting rid of some old stuff, minimizing things in order to make my move to Flagstaff for college easier, but the thought of packing it all up twice kind of sucks.

"We'll get the keys to the rental at the end of the week," she says. "So we can start moving things over then. We need to be out of here in four weeks."

"That's quick," I say.

"I know the timing's not great for you, but you won't have to unpack all of it when we get to the new house. Some things can just keep boxed up for your move to college."

"I don't have to share a room with this buttwipe, do I?" Adam asks, smacking me on the back of my head. At least he didn't say ass in front of Mom. This time.

"Language, Adam." Apparently, Mom thinks butt is a bad word. That or she knows he really meant ass and just hadn't said it. "No, there are three bedrooms, so you'll each have your own. Not that Asher will be in his long."

"When he's gone, can I turn his room into my man cave?"

"You have to actually *be* a man to have a man cave," I say.

He smacks me on the head again. I grab his arm and yank him down into a headlock. He pretends to choke. I just laugh.

"I'm sure Asher will come home sometimes," Mom says. "Holidays. Maybe a weekend here and there. He'll have to have somewhere to sleep."

"He can take the couch."

I tighten my arm around Adam's neck.

Grace's face pops into my mind, like it has been all day, her green eyes looking at me like I'd hung the moon. If things go the way I hope with her, I'll be home as often as I can.

Chapter 5

May 3, 2012

Grace

A SHER HAS BEEN back at school for three days. I've become an expert on spotting him in the hallway. Given our two-year age difference, our schedules don't exactly match up, but in the chaos between classes, I have no problem finding his dark brown hair and slender form in the crowds.

I really want to talk to him, but other than the day of the fight, we don't just randomly bump into each other, and I can't come up with a decent reason to seek him out.

And even if I do, he'll probably think I'm an idiot.

I see girls talk to boys they like all the time. I even watched Sydney flirt with Jordan Green in biology yesterday. But for the life of me, I have no idea how they do it without making fools out of themselves.

No doubt if I manage to get another moment alone with Asher that's exactly what I'll do.

I study myself in the bathroom mirror, hurrying

through my hand washing so I can be in the hallway during class change and maybe catch a glimpse of him. Part of me feels pitiful for the enormous crush I have on him, but another part of me believes this is part of every girl's high school experience. Crushing on an older guy.

I pull my reddish-brown hair into a low, side pony-tail that hangs over my left shoulder. Like most red heads, I have a few freckles dotting my face. I don't make much of an attempt to cover them with make-up. It's basically a futile effort, and they don't bother me that much anyway.

I smooth the wrinkles on my purple tunic that I have over brown leggings, then swipe a bit of pink gloss on my lips. You know… just in case.

Swinging the tote bag I use to carry stuff from class to class over my shoulder, I push open the door.

And see Asher leaning against the opposite wall.

"Asher." My voice is breathy, and his name feels sweet on my lips.

"Grace." A slight smile plays on his face and his eyes don't leave mine.

Okay, now I'm thankful for the primping I just did.

As he pushes off the wall and walks toward me I let my eyes take him in. A Metallica tee shirt that's seen its better days, faded jeans that sit low on hips, studded belt, and black Chucks that long ago paled to gray.

My. Mouth. Waters.

"Last time you saw me here I wasn't exactly at my best," he says, pushing his hands into his pockets as he comes to a stop right in front of me.

"I thought you were pretty amazing last time I saw you here," I answer, lowering my eyelids.

Did I just flirt? Without even trying? Maybe that's the key. You say things that are true and just lace them with meaning.

Asher shrugs. "Not exactly the first impression I would've chosen, but I wouldn't take it back even if I could. Tony deserved it."

"I'm just sorry I couldn't be more help and that you got suspended."

He smiles and tilts his head, causing his long bangs to sweep sideways across his forehead. He's changed his piercing since the last time I saw him. Instead of a hoop through his eyebrow, today there's a silver barbell.

And, yep. Just as hot as the hoop.

"I feel like we've had this conversation before," he says.

I'm not exactly sure what to say beyond what we've already covered, so I just smile.

"Any chance your brother's going to show up?" he asks with a chuckle.

I laugh as well, but good grief, I hope not. No one kills a mood more than Brian. "Doubt it. He's way too conscientious to leave class early, unless the building was on fire."

"I've been hanging here the past couple of days,

hoping to run in to you."

I swear my soul starts singing. "You have?"

"At the risk of repeating myself, I wanted to thank you again," he says. He pulls a piece of paper from his pocket and hands it to me. "That's my phone number. If Tony says anything to you about you talking to Mr. Bledsoe, I want you to tell me."

I look at the paper. His phone number. Oh my.

Asher goes on. "I doubt he'll start crap with you, especially since he's already on Bledsoe's radar, but if he does, I want to know."

I'm stunned. I have his phone number. This is better than winning the lottery.

"Not that I think you couldn't handle yourself," he adds. "But if he causes you problems because you helped me, well, I want to know."

It occurs to me that I haven't said anything. What I really want to do is squeal and turn in circles, but I don't think that will send the right message. Instead, I settle for, "Okay. Thanks."

I drop the paper – now my most priceless possession – into my tote bag. Lifting my eyes to meet his, I try to come up with something to say.

But I have nothing. Absolutely nothing. Except that I want to spend an eternity staring into those dark brown eyes.

"If you text me, I'll save your number," Asher says.

I nod, unable to form words. What? Had I turned mute all of a sudden? I order myself to get it together and act like I have some sense.

"Thank you," I say. "For being concerned about me."

And honestly, it is super sweet. He doesn't want Tony giving me a hard time for telling Mr. Bledsoe what I'd witnessed. Adam might think Asher isn't *much with the ladies*, but it looks to me like Adam and every other guy at Greyson High can learn a thing or two from Asher.

BEFORE MRS. GARCIA begins class, I discreetly enter Asher's phone number into my contact list. Just in case someone, namely my nosy big brother, gets a hold of my phone, I list him only as *A*.

I fire off a text after saving his number.

Me This is Grace. Thanks again.
A: No problem. Keep in touch.
Me: Will do

Much to my disappointment, that's the end of my texting with Asher Howell for the foreseeable future.

Chapter 6

May 26, 2012

Grace

I APPEARS WE'RE getting new neighbors.

I've seen a woman coming and going over the past few days, dropping boxes off, but today a moving van arrives. From my bedroom, I have a direct view across the driveway. With nothing better to do on a Saturday morning, I sit on the small love seat in my room and watch as movers unload furniture.

My phone buzzes with a text. Asher hasn't been exactly chatty, so I've stopped jumping with excitement each time a text message comes. I've given up hope that he'll keep in touch, even though he's the one who suggested it. I have, however, managed to restrain myself from texting him like a desperate lunatic.

I decide it must be a girl thing. We take things seriously, even when they're only meant as polite conversation.

The text is from Sydney.

Sydney: *What's up?*

Me: *Watching the new neighbors move in.*

Sydney: *Anybody you know?*

Me: *I don't think so.*

Sydney: *If it's a hot guy you gotta introduce your-self!*

Me: *Riiiiight.*

A black car turns in, pulling in on the other side of the moving van. I hear two doors open and close and keep my eyes glued to the house, hoping to see who's moving in.

From my seat inside my room, I see two pairs of feet moving around on the far side of the moving van. The faded black Chucks make my heart stop. All the breath leaves my lungs. Leaving my cell on the love seat, I stand and walk quickly to the door that leads out of my room and into the side yard. I open the door to get a better view and completely ignore the incoming text message. I watch the feet move about between the van and the car and notice the frayed ends of the jeans against the shoes.

I step outside, not having a clue what I'll say or do if what I suspect turns out to be true. I have no ideas, no plans. I just stand there like a statue, eyes never leaving the driveway.

Their voices are masked by the noise of the movers, but when a pair of cargo shorts walks out from behind the van, there's no more question.

"Adam?" I say, more to myself than him.

"No way!" he exclaims, turning and directing his

next words back toward the car. "You'll never guess who lives next door."

I don't move. I watch the Chucks move toward Adam and I'm not sure whether to shout for joy or cringe with awkwardness when he comes into sight.

Asher.

His eyes widen and he stares. I stare. The wind blows, gentle and easy, but neither one of us moves. Time sort of stops in that moment. It's like we're connected by some weird, cosmic vibe. I can't decide if destiny has engineered this to put us closer to each other, or if it's fate playing some kind of cruel joke.

"Grace?" Asher's voice breaks the silence.

"Hi." It's the best I can do at the moment, and I don't think I could keep the longing out of my voice for all the money in the world.

"You live here?" he asks, eyes still locked on mine.

I nod. "Looks like you do too. Or you're about to."

"Yeah."

And he keeps on staring. Strands of hair blow across my face as the wind picks up, but I do nothing to stop them.

"You two just gonna look at each other all day?" Adam says, laughing. "You act like long lost lovers or some shit."

Good lord. Am I that obvious? I shake my head, pushing my hair behind my ears, and force myself to act like a regular human being.

"Just surprised to see you two," I say, walking toward them.

Act normal. Act normal.

"You're stuck with us now." Adam grabs me in some kind of bear hug, lifting my feet off the ground, which is very weird considering we've had approximately two conversations prior to this one. "Or at least me. Ash is moving to Flagstaff later this summer for college."

He sits my feet back on the ground, and somehow I keep my balance.

The shock of Adam's hug barely registers as his words sink in. Asher is moving away. Of course he is. Why hadn't I considered that? I know he's graduating. Panic claws its way up my throat.

"Flagstaff?" I ask, telling myself not to freak out. It's only an hour and a half away. I turn toward Asher, who looks ready to take someone's head off.

"NAU," Adam answers.

Asher still just looks at me, so I look back and smile, noticing how his breathing slows and his arms relax.

Calm down, I order myself. It's Flagstaff, not New York City.

The movers continue their activity, unloading what looks like a kitchen table and chairs. The blue sedan I'd seen earlier in the week pulls in behind the black car that I assume belongs to Asher.

The same short, broad-shouldered lady I saw a few days ago emerges from behind the moving van, carting a huge plastic tub. Her raven-colored hair, pulled into a long ponytail, hangs several inches past her shoulders. Must be their mom.

"Adam, there's another one of these in the trunk," she calls. "Go grab it!"

"Mom, look! It's Grace!" Like she has any idea who I am. Adam sounds way too excited about my presence. I'm quickly figuring out that full steam ahead is Adam's go-to personality trait.

The two of them disappear inside the house with the plastic tubs, leaving me standing on the lawn with just Asher.

"I'll introduce you to Mom when she comes back out." He moves a step closer, pushing a hand through the dark hair that sweeps across his forehead.

Today's shirt is a short sleeve, brown snap-up. If there was a name patch sewn on one side of the chest, it would look exactly like one of those shirts mechanics wear when they slide underneath a car. The silver barbell is still present in his eyebrow. Both knees show through huge holes in his jeans. Nothing about him conforms to the majority, and he fascinates me more every time I see him.

"My folks have been divorced for a couple of years," he goes on. "You may see Dad around from time to time, but it's just Mom and us who are moving in."

All at once reality descends. *Asher is moving in next door.* Right next door. To me. And even though he's leaving for college, I have all summer to get to know him better.

"What are you studying at NAU?" I ask, hoping to get a handle on what his life will be like once he leaves. And if I can figure out a way to stay a part of it.

"Art education," he says with a sigh, causing me to wonder if he's certain about his choice.

"I've seen your drawings hanging in the art room window." I take a step closer because I just can't stop myself. The truth is, after the day of the fight, I'd purposely gone by the art display window on a regular basis, looking for his work. "You're so talented."

He shrugs. "They say you should study what you're passionate about."

Just hearing the word *passionate* come out of his mouth sends my pulse pounding. I know from looking at his drawings that he's passionate about art. It almost scares me how much I want him to feel a similar passion for me.

"Well, you'll be great." And he will. He'll be a success at anything he puts his mind to.

He smiles, small and lopsided, but a smile nonetheless. It does amazing and beautiful things to my heart.

Adam barrels out of the house, followed by their mom. They head straight for us.

"Grace, this is –" Adam starts, but gets cut off by Asher.

"Mom, this is Grace Ballard." He puts his hand on my shoulder, sending shivers down the length of my body. It's a simple gesture, a common thing to do when introducing someone, but it's the very first time he's touched me, and I'm nearly undone by it. "She's the one who went to bat for me with Mr. Bledsoe last month."

"Grace," she says, reaching out to shake my hand. "Thank you so much."

"This is my mom, Stella Howell." Asher finishes making the introduction but doesn't take his hand off my shoulder. I say a silent prayer of thanks.

"It's nice to meet you, Ms. Howell."

"Call me Stella," she says. "I hear Ms. Howell and I think of my former mother-in-law."

Her skin is a shade darker than Asher's, and though her sons have hair in two different shades of brown, hers is jet black. The wide cheek bones and tear-drop shaped, turquoise earrings make me think perhaps she's Navajo.

Growing up in Northern Arizona, I've been around the Navajo culture all my life. I've always loved the sense of tradition that the Navajo are steeped in. I make a mental note to ask Asher about his mom's heritage.

"Grace is in my biology class," Adam pipes up. "And I think Jordan's got a thing for her friend, Sydney."

Well, Sydney will certainly be happy to hear that.

"I'll let you all get back to your moving," I say. "I didn't mean to interrupt. I just recognized Asher and Adam and wanted to say hello."

"So glad you did," Stella says. "You're welcome at

our place anytime."

She and Adam begin walking toward the moving van, but Asher hangs back. Though it makes me nervous, I take it as a good sign that he wants another moment with me.

"It's really cool that you live next door." He tilts his head and lifts one corner of his mouth. "I guess we'll be running into each other."

Giddiness bubbles inside me at the thought. And is completely doused as Brian comes out the front door. It's too much to hope that he'll go straight to his car and head to whatever lame thing he's doing this morning without noticing Asher and me in the side yard.

Like he has some kind of kill-Grace's-good-fortune radar, he heads right for us. The look on his face says he's about to make fools out of both of us.

Asher straightens, pulling his shoulders square and setting his jaw as if tensing for a confrontation. Which, I suppose, he is.

I jump into action before Brian can launch into whatever nonsense he's about to spew.

"Brian, I thought you were headed out." He doesn't slow his pace. He just keeps stalking. "Asher and his family are moving in next door." That stops him, but his glare is still noticeable even from six feet away. "I've just met his mother, who is a very nice lady. She and Adam took some boxes inside, but I'm sure they'll be right back out if you'd like to meet her, too."

Brian is far too straight-laced to be rude in front of an adult, and I recognize the moment he gives up on the tough-guy act he'd been about to unleash. Turning his attention from Asher and me, he walks toward the neighbor's house just as Stella and Adam come out. I watch as he politely introduces himself, most certainly impressing Stella with his impeccable manners.

"Wow," Asher says, moving so close that his arm brushes my shoulder. "I bet you've never had so much as a skinned knee with him around to protect you."

I want to laugh, but can't. Though he's exaggerating, Asher has totally nailed the dynamic between my brother and me.

"Not only that," I whisper, my eyes following Brian as he gets in his car and backs out onto the street. "But it's impossible for anything I do to measure up. Not when he's already set the standard so high."

Asher turns to face me. I can't identify the expression on his face. One second it looks like fury, the next compassion. For a moment I think he's going to say something, and I hold my breath, waiting for what it might be.

"Asher!" his mom calls from the driveway. "Come grab some boxes. You can visit all summer!"

He lifts one shoulder in what looks like an apology. I can't help but smile.

"Welcome to the neighborhood, Asher."

Chapter 7

June 4, 2012

Asher

WE'VE BEEN MOVED in for a little over a week. Graduation has come and gone, and I'm spending the summer working as part-time manual labor at the hospital – unloading deliveries and unpacking boxes. Dad works as one of the head accountants, or whatever they're called, at Greyson Area Medical Center, and he pulled some strings to get me the job.

I guess I'm grateful for the job, but at the moment I'm more grateful that it's my day off. And that I have the house to myself. Adam is at Jordan's, which seems to be where he spends most of his time, and Mom works full-time as a dental hygienist.

I grab my headphones and pull up a playlist on my phone, then pick up my sketchpad and pencils, and head out to the back deck. I sink down onto one of the patio loungers, pulling my knees up to create a place to work. Like always, I lose myself in the drawing, in the way I feel when I make images appear on paper. Time passes, and I pay no attention. As a result, I'm totally unaware of Grace's presence until she touches my shoulder.

I pull the headphones from my ears and look up into her green eyes. Elation soars through me, and for a moment I wonder for a moment if I've imagined her.

"Hi." Just one word, but her voice is like a song, welcoming and enticing.

"Grace." I scramble to my feet, tossing my supplies onto the seat I just vacated. "I didn't hear you."

She doesn't have make up on which highlights the dusting of freckles across her nose and cheeks. She's so pretty that I feel dizzy just looking at her.

"You looked pretty absorbed," she says, nodding toward the paper and pencils. "I'm sorry if I disturbed you."

I shake my head. "No. No way. You aren't bothering me at all."

I glance over toward her driveway. This couldn't be more perfect. Brian's car is nowhere to be seen. Mom and Adam are both gone. We're alone.

"I saw you out here when I got home from work and just thought I'd say hello."

"Where do you work?" I ask, wondering how she got home since she didn't appear to have a car.

"I work mornings at the day care a couple of blocks from here," she answers. "I get off at noon, so when it's not raining, I walk home."

A thought pops into my head and I go with it. "Have you had lunch?"

She shakes her head and smiles. For the first time I notice what she has on. White shorts that hit her mid-thigh, just short enough to be amazing, but not so short they're indecent, and a navy blue tank top that hugs her form in ways that make my insides tremble. The fact that she seems to have no idea how gorgeous she is makes her even more irresistible.

"I was just about to order a pizza." It's not exactly a lie. I would've ordered a pizza once I realized it was lunch time. "You want to join me?"

It'll *almost* be like a date. We'll eat together. Talk. Laugh. And with no one else around, I'll have her all to myself. No overbearing big brother to give me the evil eye. No Adam grabbing her up and hugging her while I fight the urge to punch him in the throat.

"Okay." Her smile lights up her face and I want nothing more than to make her look like that every day of my life.

"I usually order pepperoni and mushrooms, but I'll get whatever you like. I'm not picky." I pick up my cell and scroll until I find the number for the closest pizza joint.

"That sounds fine," she says. "Mushrooms are my favorite."

"Great. I'll call it in and grab some drinks from the fridge." I move toward the door that leads into the kitchen, telling myself not to skip and dance around and give away how freaking excited I am. "Don't go anywhere."

A minute later, I'm about to step back onto the patio with a couple cans of soda and two plates. Grace has taken a seat at the table. Her back is to me, and she's pulled her auburn hair over one shoulder, leaving the other shoulder and the long expanse of her neck exposed.

I nearly swallow my tongue. Her skin glows as the sun spills across it, and I can't remember ever wanting anything more than I want to run my fingers down her neck.

Get yourself under control. The last thing I want to do is come on too strong and scare her off. I remind myself I've already decided I should move slow, give it time to develop, and give her brother time to get the stick out of his ass. It's the whole reason I haven't texted her every day since she gave me her number.

With a deep breath, I push open the door and join her, taking the seat next to her.

"Should be here in about twenty minutes," I say, putting the drinks and plates on the table.

"What were you drawing when I walked up?" she asks, pointing at the lounger where my sketchpad and pencils are.

I shrug. "Just some random sketches." I'm not super private about my drawings like some people are, but I don't exactly know how to tell her what my plans are for the one she saw.

"Can I see?" she asks, her voice dropping to a near whisper.

"Sure." I reach over, pick up the pad, and hand it to her, surprised by how happy it makes me to share my art with her. Somehow it feels intimate, like we're connecting in a way neither of us has ever connected with another person.

She takes the sketchpad from me, cradling it in her arms like it's something valuable and precious. Before she looks down at it, her eyes lock on mine and she smiles.

"Thank you."

As her eyes drop to the drawing on the page, something shifts in my heart, and I know I'll never be quite the same.

Chapter 8

Grace

THE SHIP ON the paper looks like it could sail right out of the sketchbook and onto the patio. I feel certain I'd be able to feel the water move against my fingers if I reach out to touch the choppy waves. Everywhere I look I see movement and emotion.

The things displayed at school had been wonderful. But this... this is so much more.

"Asher." I breathe his name with reverence. "Wow."

"It's not finished yet," he says. "I'll add some clouds, maybe some rain."

"I'd say it's beautiful, but that wouldn't do it justice." I want to run my finger along the sails that rise triumphantly from the ship, but I'm afraid of smudging the lines and shading he's done with such care. "I can almost feel the anxiety of being tossed around by those waves."

Asher's eyes widen, like I've surprised him with that statement. "That's exactly what I was trying to accomplish," he says. "Sometimes I wonder if I'm creating any kind of emotional landscape, or if I'm just drawing pictures that are nice to look at."

No words can describe how it feels to be able to validate what is obviously so important to him. I feel like I could fly across the Grand Canyon at this moment.

"You've succeeded." I lock eyes with him. "No question."

The smile that spreads across his face takes my breath away. I've seen him smile before, but not like this. Not with a joy and brilliance that seems to come from some place deep inside him.

He's so beautiful I want to weep.

"Now the challenge becomes how to create a contrasting emotion in the same picture." He sits up straighter and turns his chair to directly face mine. Talking about his art seems to bring him even more to life. "So that at the same time you're feeling all the tension and fear of being on a ship during a storm, you also feel some sense of happiness or peace."

"Something tells me you'll figure out a way to do it."

The sound of a car in the driveway signals the pizza delivery. Asher heads around the side of the house to pick it up. Just before disappearing around the corner, he looks back. "You can look through the rest of the sketchpad if you want to."

Oh man.

With gentleness and enormous respect, I turn through the pages of his drawings. I'm so in awe of his talent and his willingness to share it with me. Happiness seems ready to burst out of me at any second.

I hear the pizza delivery guy back out of the driveway just as my eyes land on a page full of four swirling circles, each in a different color. This one isn't so much a picture as it is an explosion. His other drawings have all been in pencil or black ink. This one looks like colored pencils. Black, white, turquoise, and yellow vortexes overlap in the center and seem to pull me into their whirlpool of color.

Asher sits the pizza box on the table and drops back into his chair as my gaze lingers on the picture.

"I don't usually use a lot of color," he says, opening the pizza and placing a slice on each plate. "But that one's different."

I take the plate from him and sit the sketchpad on an empty chair, out of the way of soda and dripping tomato sauce.

"Can you tell me about that one?" I ask.

"Those are the colors of the sacred mountains on the Navajo Nation flag," he answers, taking a bite of pizza.

"I wondered if your family was part Navajo." I take a bite, settle back in my seat, and wait for him to continue.

"My mom is Navajo," he explains. "But she didn't grow up on the reservation. My grandparents moved off res when they got married because my grandfather got a job in Flagstaff. They live in Sedona now. Most of what I know about the Navajo is from the stories my grandparents told me."

"Your dad's not Navajo?"

Asher shakes his head. "Nah. He's Anglo. He and Mom met in college."

I wonder what caused the split between his parents, but I don't think it's my place to ask. Instead, I refocus on the drawing. "So those colors are important to the Navajo?"

He nods, grabbing a second slice of pizza from the box, first for me, then for himself. "The four colors pop up pretty often in Navajo legends. My grandfather told me they represent certain things in the Navajo story of creation."

"Really?"

"Yeah. The legend says that the world started as this big black island that was just floating around. And above the island there were these four clouds. One black, one white, one blue, and one yellow. The black was supposedly the female one, where all life was held. The white cloud was said to be the male. And when the two clouds met, all the different life forms began."

"What were the other two clouds?" I ask, reaching for my drink.

"The blue cloud was home to birds. My grandfather said especially bluebirds and other blue-colored birds. When the new lifeforms came to their world, they left and went to the yellow cloud. But the yellow cloud was a huge flood, which is another thing that pops up pretty often in Navajo legends. So the birds and all the lifeforms went to the white cloud, which was empty. Man planted seeds there, and then all life moved on to the fifth world – this one."

"Fascinating."

"The original Navajo homeland was between four mountains. That's why there are four sacred mountains on the flag."

"And each mountain is one of those colors?" I ask, pointing to the drawing.

"That's right." He grabs a third piece of pizza and offers it to me. I shake my head, so he drops it on his own plate.

I finish my drink while he starts in on his third slice. I wonder how many of his drawings have themes from the Navajo culture.

"Do you use a lot of Navajo stories in your artwork?"

"Sometimes." He shrugs, gesturing to the open sketchpad. "That one for sure. I like the way the colors represent specific things. But most of the time it's not so literal. The Navajo legends are so full of symbolism, and every story my grandfather ever told me was so... I don't know... *visual.* I think the symbolism and visual aspect to the stories just sort of push me to create."

"I wish someone had explained art and creativity to me in that way," I say. "You're going to be an awesome art teacher."

"Maybe." He finishes his pizza and stacks both our plates on the table. "I guess I'm still not sure about that. I just know that art is important, on a gut level, and I want to help people understand that."

"You've convinced me," I whisper.

"Thanks." He leans toward me, his dark chocolate eyes warming me from the inside. "I think I needed to hear that."

His face is so close I can feel his breath on my cheek. I tilt my head, angling so our gazes connected. I have no experience or intuition where boys are concerned, but I swear he's about to kiss me.

"Ash!" Adam yells from inside the house.

Asher and I spring apart. Not that we'd been connected at the lips or anything. Adam came home just in time to screw that up. Apparently, Asher and I had been so caught up in our conversation that we didn't even hear his brother arrive.

Adam may've ruined the moment, but I know I'm never going to be the same. I don't even know how to explain what it means to me that Asher shared himself with me so freely. There's a kind of security in knowing he trusts me enough to open up that makes me feel safe and protected. That probably sounds crazy, but it's the truth. Everything about Asher makes me feel safe. He defended Kyle, who couldn't defend himself, and didn't complain or raise any sort of fuss about the punishment he received. And yet that fierceness is balanced by the tender and careful way he creates his art. It's a potent combination that wraps me in an enormous sense of warmth and protection.

As much as I've always thought teenagers were stupid for saying how *in love* they were with their boyfriends or girlfriends, in my soul I'm certain, without a doubt, that I love Asher Howell.

Chapter 9

July 31, 2012

Asher

TEXTING WITH GRACE is awesome. Not quite as satisfying as being alone with her, but still awesome. When we text, and we've been texting a *lot,* we don't have to worry about Adam's interruptions or Brian's disapproving looks.

And Brian *does* disapprove of our friendship.

I met Grace's parents not long after our patio lunch, and they seem okay with the fact that we occasionally hang out in the backyard. Naturally, we rarely have time to ourselves since Brian makes it a point to lurk around. Not to mention that if Adam's in the vicinity, he's the center of attention. Of course, her parents might change their tune if things between us move beyond friendly neighbors, and I have no doubt Brian will be there to fuel the fire if and when that happens.

Which makes texting the safest way for us to communicate. Not only does it afford us privacy, but I'm also not tempted to kiss her senseless like I almost did that day on the patio.

I still don't know if I'm more upset with Adam for interrupting us before I sealed the deal, or for not showing up sooner, so things never got to that point.

Not that I don't want to kiss Grace. Most days I want to kiss her more than I want to draw. But I can't rush this. It's too important.

But yeah, texting is safe. So, as I find a spot in the hospital cafeteria to spend my lunch break, I pull out my phone and send one.

Me: How was work?

She's on her way home from work by now. It's one of my favorite times to talk to her. I like to imagine her walking home from the day care, her beautiful auburn hair moving with the breeze, and her smile just for me.

Her response is quick.

Grace: Good. You?
Me: Same old. On my lunch break now.

Which isn't exactly news since we go through this same routine almost every day. But I'm not tired of it. Not by a long shot.

Grace: Drawn any more masterpieces lately?
Me: Still tweaking the ship.
Grace: You should draw me something.

I'd thought about it. I really want to, but I'm not

sure how to give it to her without giving myself and my feelings away.

> **Me:** *Really?*
>
> **Grace:** *I'll put it in my room & think of you when you're in Flagstaff.*

Well, that settles it. I'll definitely draw something special for her.

> **Me:** *Ok. I'll give it some thought & draw you something nice.*

She responds with a string of smiley faces. Emoticons used to get on my nerves, but when Grace uses them to express happiness, I actually love them.

I imagine one of my drawings hanging in her bedroom. Imagine her looking at it and thinking about me while I'm away at college. It makes me happy that she wants to remember me, wants a small part of me with her. But it also makes me sad, knowing we won't be across the yard from each other.

Not only that, but my life is changing. Drastically. I'm heading to college, to the beginning of my adult life. Logically I know that maintaining any sort of relationship, even a friendship, will be difficult. I know in my heart that Grace is worth the effort, but I want things to be exactly right. I want to settle into college life and start building my reputation in Flagstaff. I want to make a place in my life that Grace can easily slip into. A place where she won't have to worry or feel any hint of insecurity.

Though I never want to cause conflict between her and her brother and her parents, I don't feel the need to prove myself to anyone but her. People can make assumptions about me all they want based on how I dress or how I wear my hair. That I don't care about. But I want to prove myself to her. I want her to always be sure of who I am and how I feel for her.

So, I'll draw her something. Something that will encompass all I feel and illustrate how seamlessly she's melded into my life. A picture that expresses all my hopes and dreams. I'll bleed myself into the drawing for her. And someday soon, when the time is right, I'll tell her what it all means. I'll give her all the thoughts and feelings that inspired her drawing.

And she'll know that I've loved her from the beginning.

Chapter 10

August 22, 2012

Grace

A SHER IS LEAVING tomorrow.

Adam and I have been back in school for over a week, our junior year of high school underway. In many ways, this summer has been a huge success. Asher and I got to know one another in a really profound way. I confided in him about the self-doubt I've always experienced growing up in Brian's shadow. He knows all about how I have no idea what I want to do with my life, because instead of figuring out who I want to be, I've spent years chasing after Brian's lofty example and failing miserably. Asher shared his art with me. He gave me an understanding and love of creativity. He's shown me so much about his Navajo heritage and let me know that part of him.

Moments alone have been few and far between, but we've made up for that with near constant, enthusiastic texting. It's given us the chance to get to know each other without all the stress and anxiety of dating.

We're friends. *Best friends.*

And that's all.

I tell myself it's enough. It's the foundation we need. Somewhere in my brain I know that being such close friends will only make us stronger as a couple.

But we aren't a couple yet.

And he's leaving for Flagstaff in the morning.

I don't want to dwell on it tonight. Stella has planned a celebration in his honor, and the last thing I want to do is drag the mood down.

Mom, Dad, and Brian have been invited as well, and being a polite neighbor, Mom accepted and volunteered to bring an appetizer. So, the four of us stand on the front porch and ring the bell, a plate full of finger sandwiches in Mom's arms.

Adam answers the door, opening it wide and stepping back to let us in. "Since when do you ring the front doorbell, Grace?" he says with a laugh. "Usually you just stick your head in the back door and ask if anyone's home."

I consider slapping him. I love Adam. I really do. He might be a total player with the girls, but he's a genuinely nice and lovable guy. Right now, though, I want him to zip it before Brian and my parents begin to wonder just how much time I've spent over here this summer.

"Didn't seem appropriate this time," I answer, shooting him a look that says *shut up or die.*

Brian has worked full time at the public library all

summer, which made it easy for him to take three online college courses in the process. Dad's an accountant – an appropriately boring job for him – and Mom is his secretary. They've owned and run the business together since they got married. Translation... none of them were home in the afternoons when I got off work. And I spent many of those afternoons on the sofa with Adam and Asher, learning how to beat them both at *Call of Duty* and *Injustice*.

And a good chunk of the rest of my spare time I spent texting with Asher.

Speaking of Asher, I see him across the living room talking to a man in a suit and tie. His hair is light brown, the same shade as Adam's, but his jaw is square and distinct, just like Asher's. He's got to be their father.

His eyes find mine and I swear they darken with emotion as our gazes collide. Even from across the room, with a bunch of people between us, there's a connection... a sense of belonging. From the look in his eyes, I'm sure I'm not the only one who feels it. I imagine sprinting across the room and into his arms, not surprised by how much I want that vision to be a reality.

"Where should I set this, Adam?" Mom asks, her voice yanking me from my visual admiration of Asher in a pair of non-ripped jeans and a plain white button down shirt, untucked. Seriously drool-worthy. I figure that's about as dressed up as he ever gets, which is just fine with me.

"The kitchen," Adam says, pointing toward the back of the house. "Through there."

We make our way in that direction, the four of us still moving together, which is stupid since there's no reason for all of us to crowd in the kitchen.

At the stove, Stella talks with a guest I don't recognize, but gives me a smile and a wave when she sees us. Mom sits her dish on the counter with all the other food, and once again, the four of us move in unison back toward the living room.

Asher catches us as soon as we return. Across the room, he'd looked amazing. Up close, he is absolutely breathtaking. My heart goes crazy, hammering away inside my chest, and my breathing becomes shallow. By now I should be used to my reaction to him, but the intensity of his presence takes me by surprise every single time.

"Mr. and Mrs. Ballard, I'd like to introduce you to my father, Dave Howell," Asher begins. I smile at his impeccable manners, cutting my eyes toward Brian. He looks a little baffled that the guy with an eyebrow ring can be so polite.

With Mom and Dad occupied shaking hands and exchanging the normal pleasantries with Mr. Howell, I glance at Asher. Brian stands slightly behind him, unable to see his face. Asher takes the opportunity to wink, the silver hoop in his eyebrow glinting in the light as he moves. My stomach turns over, and I fight the urge to smile like a mad woman, knowing Brian would notice.

"And this is their son, Brian," Asher continues, once the hand shaking ceases.

"Ah, yes," Mr. Howell says. "You're headed to Stanford right?"

Of course, at the mention of his astronomical academic success, Brian begins running off at the mouth. "That's right," Brian says. "I leave the day after tomorrow." I don't even feel bad that I can't wait for him to go. He carries on with Mr. Howell, acting like a well-mannered gentleman, when in truth, he's only layering his long list of accomplishments into his introduction.

Asher shoots me a look, and I roll my eyes. He mouths the word *sorry,* aware of how much I dislike being Brian's runner-up.

"Dad," Asher says, smoothly interrupting Brian's soliloquy. "This is Grace Ballard. She and Adam are in the same class."

"It's nice to meet you, Mr. Howell." Making sure to make eye contact, I shake his hand, my grip firm and sure. This is Asher's father after all, and I need to make a good impression.

His eyes narrow, but not in a judgmental way. It's like he's studying me. Maybe he notices something between Asher and me. I'd like to think I'm not that obvious, but maybe fathers have some kind of intuition when it comes to their sons.

After a moment, he gives me a quick nod and says, "Very nice to meet you, Grace."

I feel like I just passed the biggest test of my life.

The front door opens and a couple of Asher's buddies from the art department come in. He excuses himself to go greet them, and my parents and Brian step away to mingle with the other guests. Asher turns back and catches my eye, a huge grin on his face.

I do my best to interact with people, but making small talk is not my strong suit. However, I don't want to be forced to hang around my parents or Brian all evening, so I make the effort. No surprise, I find it easiest to talk with Adam or help Stella with the food.

Also no surprise, I keep one eye on Asher at all times, stealing smiles as often as I can.

As the guests begin to slow down on trips to the appetizer bar, Stella and I clear some of the empty plates. Alone in the kitchen, Stella takes me by the arm. "I have a surprise for Asher. Give me five minutes, and then you and Adam get everyone into the hallway. It'll be a tight squeeze, but it won't take too long."

I nod, excited for whatever Stella has planned, then head to the living room to find Adam.

Five minutes later, Adam and I usher Asher into the hall, followed by the other guests. My breath catches as I see the pictures hanging on the wall behind Stella.

Asher's artwork.

"We haven't lived in this house long," she begins. "And I know you're headed off to college tomorrow, but this house wouldn't be a home without your work hanging on the walls."

"Mom," Asher whispers, his voice heavy with emotion.

"The other day when you thought you'd misplaced your sketchbook, I had taken it to the print shop to have these made."

Three huge prints hang behind her, framed in simple, brown wooden frames, allowing the beauty of his work to shine through. I recognize each one from the day I looked through his sketchpad, but the one in the center draws my attention the same way it did the first time.

The overlapping circles of turquoise, yellow, black, and white. The four colors of the Navajo sacred mountains.

"I had one of these made for your grandparents," Stella says, pointing toward the center print. "I had it shipped to Sedona yesterday."

Asher hugs his mom, clearly overwhelmed and speechless. All around there's applause and lots of oohing over his talent. Mr. Howell steps forward and pats Asher on the back.

"I'm sure NAU is a great school for art education," Brian says. I recognize his comment for what it was – a slap at the university and Asher's major. Because everyone knows that NAU is no Stanford. When did my brother turn into suck a jerk?

"It is," Asher says, looking at Brian with an expression that says *I couldn't care less what you think of me.* "And the scholarship I got for my 4.0 GPA is also really nice."

Bam! I have to bite the inside of my cheek to keep from laughing out loud. Asher just shut my brother up with one sentence. Brian's face turns red from embarrassment, but I'm the only one who notices.

I enjoy every second of it.

From there, the party begins to die down, and when my parents decide it's time to head home, I have no effective strategy for staying behind. So we say our goodbyes and walk back home.

I've just flopped down on the love seat in my room when my cell phone buzzes in my pocket.

A: *Side yard. Midnight. Can you make it?*

Yes! I *so* can make it. I care not that tomorrow is a school day.

Me: *Sure.*
A: *Can't wait.*

I dance around my room like a giddy schoolgirl and am not ashamed at all.

Chapter 11

Midnight, August 23, 2012

Grace

T HE HOUSE IS dark and quiet a few minutes before
midnight. My parents have to work in the
morning, and Brian has never been a night owl.

At one time, long before we moved into this house,
my room had been a screened in porch. The previous
owners decided to wall it up and create another room,
and left the outside door with access to the side yard.
The room isn't huge, which was why Brian hadn't
wanted it when we moved here. But even at the age of
nine, something told me the outside door would
someday come in handy.

The moon lights the night sky just enough that I
see when Asher pushes open the patio door and steps
outside. Silently, I slip out my door and meet him
halfway.

"Hi." I'm not sure why I'm whispering since we're
far enough away from either house that no one's going
to hear us, but it just seems that whispering fits the

mood.

"Hey." From behind his back, he produces a rolled up piece of paper and hands it to me.

"What's this?"

"It's your drawing," he says. "I didn't want to give it to you in front of everyone at the party."

A wave of euphoria sweeps through me, enough to warm me against the chilly night air. I hadn't forgotten about asking him to draw something for me, but that conversation had been so jovial that I'd wondered if maybe he thought I was just joking.

I take the drawing from him, knowing without even looking that it is the most precious gift I've ever been given.

Because Asher created something just for me.

My heart tumbles and expands and just about consumes me.

"Aren't you going to look at it?" he asks, one corner of his mouth turning up.

I nod, carefully unrolling the thick paper to reveal his creation.

A clicking noise sounds, and I look over to see that Asher has a small flashlight pointed at the paper.

The night air is still. It just sort of hangs in the space around us, cool and thick. I feel the warmth from Asher's body as he steps so close behind me that my shoulder touches his chest. I want more than anything to sink back into him, to press my back to his chest and feel him against me.

But I don't move.

He shines the beam over my shoulder, toward the line of trees behind our houses, so that no one in either of our homes could see the light. The picture reveals itself slowly, and as the last edge unrolls, it's all my eyes can do to take in the beauty of it.

"Asher," I say softly, my lungs struggling to take in enough oxygen. "Wow."

It's me. The entire left side of the drawing is me. He captured me from the shoulders up, my face turned to the side. My gaze is fixed on something far away... something I long for... something I love. It's the exact way I feel in my heart every time I look at Asher.

And he's captured it perfectly, even though he knows none of what I feel.

In the picture, my hair blows out and away from my body, one long strand of my red locks curling into what looks like some kind of Navajo weaving. The circular pattern is white and black, some small triangular shapes pointing toward the center. Around the inner circle of triangles is a red stripe that's formed by the piece of my hair that has somehow become entwined in the weave.

He's not only drawn me. He's combined me with something from his heritage. With a part of himself.

Love, deep and exquisite, courses through me.

"This is breathtaking, Asher." This time I whisper not for fear of waking my parents, but because that's all the sound my vocal cords are capable of. His talent and his heart have rendered me practically speechless.

"And that's a Navajo basket," he continues, pointing toward the weaving that my hair had become a part of. "I wanted to illustrate how two people who are different, like you and me, can build a strong friendship."

I try not to cringe at the word friendship, reminding myself that what exists between us is so much more than most kids our age experience when they date. Besides, being friends will make our eventual relationship unshakeable.

And I *do* believe that we will eventually be together.

Nevertheless, I want desperately to be more than just his friend.

"Thank you." I turn to face him. Even in the dark, with the moon barely illuminating his face, the deep pools of his brown eyes draw me in. "No one's ever given me something this special before."

"Well, that's a shame," he says, taking a step closer and turning off the flashlight. "Because you're very special."

My entire being surges with happiness. Thousands of words flood my mind, jumbling and rolling until I can't form a coherent thought. For lack of anything brilliant and profound to say, I throw my arms around him.

The drawing clutched in one hand, I tiptoe until I can nestle my face into the crook of his neck. His arms come around my waist, hugging me close. Everything inside me cries out in relief because finally... *finally*... I am in his embrace.

It feels like home.

"I'm going to miss you so much," I whisper against his neck.

"Me too," he says. "But I'll be back. As often as I can. I promise."

I believe him.

Chapter 12

Two years later…. June 16, 2014

Grace

ASHER NEVER CAME back like he'd promised. Not really.

I stare out my bedroom window at the patio where I'd spent so much time with him… and his brother. Two boys so different, yet both so amazing. I've been privileged to know them both, to love them both, although in vastly different ways.

We buried Adam almost a week ago. Inside I feel ripped in half. One part of my heart feels nothing but loathing at the fact that I still pine for Asher this way, while the other part simply cannot help the love that never went away.

Knowing there's no reconciling the two parts of my heart, I give into the melancholy.

For a while after he went to Flagstaff, Asher texted me regularly. He even called me a few times. I knew his class schedule, his roommate's name and major. I even knew when he applied for a job at a coffee shop.

But in October of that year, his contact with me became sporadic. Days went by with no communication of any kind. I told myself it was because he was busy with school and work, but deep down I knew the truth.

Asher was totally out of my league and he'd finally realized it.

He didn't come home until Thanksgiving, and even then he avoided me. He didn't even stay for the whole weekend. I knew this because I sulked in my room the entire evening after our family's turkey dinner, and then cried with a grief I'd never imagined as I watched him load his car that same night and leave.

By Christmas, I gave up all hope. I began to wonder if he'd started using drugs or something. Even though that might've explained his hurtful behavior, I could never convince myself that Asher would do something so reckless.

But then he came home for the holidays and announced to his family that he'd dropped out of school to become a tattoo apprentice. His parents, obviously, were more than a little pissed off.

Not that Asher himself had told me. Adam had. If Asher had bothered to talk to me about it, he would've found the one person who didn't think he'd completely lost his mind.

I snap my mind back to the present, reminding myself that I decided a long time ago not to be angry with Asher. Two years ago our lives were in opposite places and I had no right to expect anything from him.

And now is no time to lose myself in the memories that still cut so deep.

Adam is dead. Bright, beautiful Adam, who filled each day with sunshine. Stupid aneurysm. Some crazy, freak thing and suddenly he's just gone. He'll never again burst into a room and draw every eye to him. He'll never throw another baseball. He won't head to Tucson to the University of Arizona.

Everyone expects me to be devastated. And I am. My heart grieves, honestly and intensely, but not in the way people think. Not because the love of my life is gone. Not because my life has been suddenly thrown wildly off track. But how can I tell people the truth without sounding awful?

The phone clutched in my hand vibrates with an incoming text. I stopped reading and answering most texts the day Adam died. I simply can't deal with all the sympathy messages. I know people mean well, but I just can't read the same thing over and over again five hundred times.

And I don't dare go near my Facebook profile. I know it's just more of the same.

If not for my parents and Brian, who's finally growing out of his jerk behavior and has been surprisingly kind throughout everything, I'd have turned the phone off completely.

Glancing down at the screen, I promise myself that if it's some friendly *I'm thinking of you* message I'll shut the phone off for the night. It's almost nine o'clock anyway, so I might as well get ready for bed and try to go to sleep. Well, lie down in my bed and stare at the dark ceiling while pretending to sleep is more like it.

My breath catches in my throat when I see the contact initial attached to the text.

A.

Asher.

I never deleted his contact information, although I'd been tempted to many times. He's still listed as just *A,* exactly the way I entered his name the day he gave me his number. I know he's still in town. I've noticed his car in his mom's driveway every day since the funeral.

Admitting that I look first thing each morning is a tough pill to swallow.

Slowing my breathing, I look down again and read the text.

A: *Wanna talk?*

Something uncomfortably familiar slides around inside me. Something I haven't felt in almost two years. I'm almost ashamed when I realize what it is.

Joy.

How can I feel joy at a time like this?

The shame and guilt and confusion pulse inside me, but the spark of joy does not dim.

I pick up my phone and text him back.

Me: *OMG yes.*

Chapter 13

Asher

WHY THE HECK did I send that text?

Yeah, sure I want to talk to Grace. About Adam and life and so much else that I can't give voice to. But seriously? Did I really just text my brother's girlfriend?

Yes, I did.

I can't stand knowing she's just across the driveway. So close, yet so very far away. And that's my fault. I haven't seen her since Adam's funeral. I tell myself I should keep my distance. Apparently I'm unable to listen to my own good sense.

I told Mom I'd stay with her for a few weeks. I'm glad to be here. Honestly, I am. Being here with her is the right thing to do, for both of us, even though Flagstaff is home for me now. I'll be back there before long, tattooing full time again at Resolution Ink.

I have a life there. One I'm proud of. I'll get back to it soon enough. For now, Mom needs me and I need her.

And yeah… Grace is here.

So I have a tough time wishing to be in Flagstaff instead of Greyson.

She texts back, and I hold my breath.

Grace: OMG yes.

Any possible objection to seeing her flees my mind immediately.

Slipping quietly out the back door, I make my way down the patio steps and over to the door I knew leads to Grace's bedroom. I know she's still up because I saw the soft glow of the lamp in her window before I texted her.

I have no idea what's going on in the rest of the house, so I tap super quiet on the door. She pulls it open after three taps and stands across the threshold from me. Her body language says *exhaustion,* but something in her expression says *happiness.*

It takes me by surprise that she can look both sad and happy at the same time, but she does.

And then it happens.

She smiles at me. It's small, but it's there.

And I'm done for.

"Hi Asher." She whispers my name the way I've heard her say it so many times before, and I'm not prepared for the delight that radiates through me. She's wearing a black, long sleeve tee that reads *Greyson High School Class of 2014*and a pair of pink pajama bottoms. Her auburn hair hangs loose around her shoulders, and her face is scrubbed free of make-up. She's never been more beautiful. "It's good to see you."

Shouldn't she appear more down in the dumps? I mean, not that I want her to be miserably depressed or anything, but her boyfriend just died. For that matter, shouldn't I be filled with gloomy despair instead of feeling crazy happy to be standing in Grace's doorway?

God, how messed up is this? I'm grieving for my brother, who I love, but at the same time I'm drooling over his girlfriend? And somehow happy that she doesn't seem completely devastated?

"Hey." I shove my hands in my pockets and try, without success, to come up with something to explain my presence.

Grace saves me from the awkward silence. "You want to come in?"

I nod. She takes a step back to give me room to walk through the door.

To keep form staring at her, I take note of her small bedroom. It's pretty. Not overly girly. A double bed with a white comforter, unmade but not a total mess. A dresser with a huge mirror attached. Bulletin board full of pictures by the light switch, one of which is of her and Adam. Quickly, I look at something else. Mint green love seat beside the window. Though I try really hard to focus on the particulars of the room, one thought keeps echoing through my mind.

I. Am. In. Grace's. Bedroom.

"Are you here all summer?" Her question yanks my

thoughts back to the moment.

"For the next few weeks," I answer. "Mom needs me, and I want to be here for her."

"What about your job?"

I wondered how long it would be before that came up. I figure people in Greyson probably think I'm going to set up shop and ink people from the kitchen table in my mom's house.

"My boss is cool. He gave me some personal leave for a while," I say. "Dad got me my old job at the hospital. Temporarily, of course. That way I can pay my rent and keep my apartment in Flagstaff."

Grace nods. For a moment we just look at each other. Her eyes are tired but intense. I have no idea what she's thinking or feeling, but for me, every feeling I had for her two years ago comes rushing to the surface, drowning me in thoughts of what could've been.

What *should've*been.

"Sit down?" she asks, gesturing to the love seat.

"Okay."

I step toward the love seat and she follows. I sit on the side closest to the window and watch as she lowers herself beside me. My heart goes ballistic. After all this time, she's so close.

Her thigh brushes mine and I freeze. Electricity zings under my skin. How can I still feel this way after two years? It's like no time has passed and nothing ever kept us apart. I feel like an idiot. She's never been mine.

She was my brother's girlfriend for the past ten months, until last week. How is it I still want her to be mine so bad?

I feel the guilt, swift and strong, but it's nothing compared to the feelings Grace inspires in me.

"I heard you're tattooing full time now," she says, turning her body slightly so she's facing me.

"I bet you did." I'm sure she got the full dissertation on how I'm throwing my life away. "But yeah. Since February. Right after I was home for Adam's birthday."

In the two years I'd been gone, I'd tried to stay away as much as possible. That sounds awful, but it's true. Making the decision to drop out of school was absolutely the right thing for me. I knew as soon as I started college that teaching art was not for me; especially once I found a way to use my abilities another way. Convincing my mom and dad had not been so easy. And truthfully, they still aren't fully on board.

But worst of all was how I'd pulled away from Grace, telling myself I was in no place to offer her anything. Back then, I'd been an almost-nineteen-year-old working part-time in a coffee shop, barely able to pay my bills, and spending every other moment apprenticing at Resolution Ink.

While I'm grateful to Bing – and always will be – for the chance he gave me, I'll always kind of hate myself for the chasm I let it create between Grace and me.

"I know your parents were pissed that you didn't go back to school," she goes on. "They were hoping it was some kind of phase and you'd realize your mistake."

I look over at her, hoping to gauge what she thinks about my decision, and see her roll her eyes when she talks about my parents' reaction.

I can't help the small grin that tugs at my lips. Does she really think my folks overreacted? "They thought I was throwing my life away."

She nods. "They just didn't understand."

She turns toward me more and tilts her head. That gorgeous auburn hair I'd always adored falls away from her shoulder, exposing the silky skin of her neck. Longing so deep I can taste it rears up inside me.

"You seem happy," she whispers. "Well, I mean considering what your family's been through."

"You've been through it, too," I say, tearing my eyes from the long column of her throat. "You lost him, too."

She shrugs and shakes her head. "It's not the same. He's your brother."

Yeah, he is. And I'm sitting here with his girl. And even as the disgrace swims through my veins, I can't stop myself.

"Let's change the subject," I suggest. "I want to think about happier things."

Which is true. I just leave out that talking about Adam makes the guilt that much worse.

Chapter 14

Grace

ASHER IS IN my bedroom.

I know it should feel weird, but it doesn't. I can't even find a shred of the hostility I felt for the way he just dropped me all those months ago. Instead, I just feel warmth.

Of course, it doesn't help that he looks all kinds of wonderful. While the front of his hair still sweeps across his forehead, occasionally obscuring one eye, he no longer keeps the back cut short. Instead, his dark brown hair is thick against his neck, the ends laying in every possible direction. It should look shaggy, but on him it just looks hot. I almost smile when I take note of the silver hoop through his eyebrow. I've always liked his piercing. His clothes are much the same as always, except the red, high top Chucks look pretty new. A gray hoodie hangs unzipped on his shoulders, revealing what looks like a vintage Route 66 tee shirt.

I wonder if he keeps his arms covered while he's home because his tattoos are a sore spot for his parents.

Not that I've seen his tattoos. But I really, really want to.

"Tell me about your job," I say, figuring that's as safe a topic as any. When he looks at me with raised eyebrows, like he thinks I'm just trying to appease him, I continue. "No seriously. I want to know."

And I do. I've always wanted to be brave enough to go my own way and figure out who I am. Growing up in the shadow of the proverbial overachiever didn't exactly make it easy to be an individual. I know my mom and dad don't quite understand my choice to skip college and go to cosmetology school, but they didn't fight me on it. In their words... *at least it's a viable career.*

Asher narrows his eyes, as if thinking how to word his answer. After a long moment, he begins. "School wasn't for me. I know that sounds crazy, since I always had good grades and I had a scholarship, but I knew from almost the beginning that I couldn't stay."

"You never told me," I whisper, thinking back on those first weeks after he'd gone to Flagstaff. He told me practically everything. Or at least that's what I thought.

"I know." He drops his eyes to the floor. "I didn't know how to."

Did he think I would've been disappointed in him? Surely he knew me better than that. But then again, we'd only known each other for a matter of months. His parents had been with him all his life and they disapproved. What reason did he have to think I'd feel differently?

I want to say something... *anything*... so he'll know I would never judge him, but before I can form a thought, he goes on.

"I'd been saving money for a tattoo for a while. Since before I left for Flagstaff. It was going to be my big rebellion." He chuckles under his breath, keeping his head down and his gaze on the tan carpet on my bedroom floor. "I asked around and found a shop that had a really good reputation. I made an appointment for early October."

October. The same time he began distancing himself from me.

"Bing, the guy that did my tattoo, was amazing. I just sat there in awe and watched him. I didn't even pay attention to the sting of the needle." He lifts his face and looks straight at me, like he wants me to hear his next words more than anything. "With every bit of the picture that came alive on my skin, I was more and more certain what I wanted to do."

"I know what it's like to not meet everyone's expectations," I say, barely resisting the urge to reach for his hand.

"Yeah, I guess you do." He smiles. It's the first genuine smile I've seen from him since he's been back. And something beautiful cracks wide open inside me.

When he'd dropped out of college, Stella kept hoping he'd see the error of his ways and go back. But he never did. Adam said Asher just always had his own ideas and didn't care too much what other people thought. He'd made it sound like Asher dropped out just to spite his parents. But I never got that vibe from him. I always knew he cared about his parents' feelings. But Asher had always been different... in a good way. He'd never fit into anyone's idea of a common stereotype.

I like that about him.

In fact, I love that about him.

"So what are your plans now that high school's over?" he asks.

"Adam never told you?" I ask, surprised by the revelation. I just figured he already knew.

Asher shakes his head. "We didn't talk a lot about things here."

Adam never mentioned that his relationship with his brother was strained, but I suppose since their parents were still upset over Asher's career decision, maybe they just steered away from talking about family and friends in Greyson.

I hate to think that things may've been less than perfect between the two of them in the months before Adam's death.

"Cosmetology school," I answer, leaving out the other details of my plans. Since Adam hadn't told him, I don't think now is the moment to disclose it all.

"That suits you," he says, nudging me gently with his shoulder. The gesture reminds me so much of the

Asher I'd known two years ago that it causes a lump to form in my throat.

I can't do this. I can't let myself get wrapped up in him again. I search my mind for something to say that will bring the conversation back to a neutral place.

"So, your job," I say, returning to our original topic.

"Yeah, my job." He goes back to looking at the floor. "Bing, the guy that did my ink that day, is actually the owner of the shop. A couple weeks after I got the tat done, I went back in with my portfolio and asked about the apprenticeship process. He said he wasn't in the market for an apprentice, but he took a look at my work anyway."

"Let me guess. He loved it."

Asher smiles. "Yeah. He offered me the chance to apprentice with him, so I took the rest of the semester to find an apartment and a roommate. I already had the job at the coffee shop, so I told them I'd need more hours after the first of the year."

That had been eighteen months ago. Eighteen months of a brand new life he didn't want me to be a part of. The thought of it makes my heart ache. Although I'd seen him a handful of time since then – the occasional holiday or birthday, and the week or so he'd come home before Adam and I started our senior year – we hadn't talked. Not until tonight.

How many times had I wished for an opportunity just like this? And now that I have the chance, circumstances keep me silent. If I could've gotten him alone for five minutes last summer, I would've confessed every feeling I had for him and let the chips fall. Instead, he'd avoided me the entire time he'd been home, and when Adam asked me to go to the back to school party with him the day after Asher went back to Flagstaff, I'd said yes.

After that, I stayed away every time Asher came home to visit. And there hadn't been that many times. It was just too hard, being with Adam but loving Asher. Fortunately, Adam hadn't pushed me to join them for their family events. Our relationship had never been like that anyway.

"Where'd you go?" Asher asks, his voice soft and questioning.

I'd completely zoned out for a moment. I shake my head to clear the fog. "Just wondering how long the apprenticeship process takes."

"It's different for every artist. Mine took about a year." I can't help but notice how his eyes light up when he talks about his job. "You don't make any money apprenticing, so I kept my job at the coffee shop. The whole year was a grind, working as many hours as I could at my paying job, then spending even more time at the shop. I did a lot of sweeping and dusting. Cleaned the bathrooms more times than I want to remember. But I loved it. It's all part of learning the business. And I learned so much from Bing."

"And he gave you a job there when you finished?"

"Yeah. That wasn't a guarantee, so I'd started putting out feelers at other shops. But just before I finished the apprenticeship, one of the other guys got married and moved to Phoenix. Bing offered me his spot."

"I'm not surprised," I say. "You're so talented."

One side of his mouth lifts into that lopsided grin I've always loved. "Thanks. I'm not making a lot of money yet, but it's enough that I don't have to work at the coffee shop anymore."

Just like that my emotions swing back in the other direction and I want nothing more than to just be close to him again. I have no idea how... or even *if* that's possible, but my heart never really let him go, and I can't ignore it. Will he share himself with me? Just a little bit? I figure it wouldn't hurt to ask.

"Will you show me your tattoos?"

I hold my breath while I wait for his answer.

Chapter 15

Asher

"REALLY?" GRACE IS the first person here who hasn't made me feel like a total loser for quitting college. I don't know why that surprises me. She's always been the kindest, most non-judgmental person I've ever known.

"I mean, only if you don't mind." Her voice holds a hint of shyness, like she isn't certain how I'll react. "And obviously, if you have ink in some place indecent, keep it to yourself."

Her smile ignites something inside me, something I desperately want to hold on to. I just have no idea how to hang on to it after everything that's happened.

For now, I figure the best way to start is to show her what she asked to see. With my right hand, I push up the left sleeve of my jacket, revealing the most recent piece of art on my body. I turn my hand over so she can see the inside of my wrist, where it looks like a paintbrush loaded with black paint has made random brushstrokes across my skin.

"Oh my gosh." Her eyes widen and she leans in to get a closer look. I wish she'd just take my hand in hers and pull it to her. "It's so realistic."

"Bing did it," I say. "He's done all my work. I'm right handed, so this is the hand I paint and draw with."

"It's beautiful," she breathes, her voice no more than a whisper.

"It means a lot to hear you say that." I can't stop the honesty from bubbling out of me. And I don't want to. Before this moment, I didn't have any idea just how much I craved validation from her.

Her eyes catch mine and she smiles again. God, I've missed her.

"I guess a lot of people still think tattoos are trashy. Or that people who have them must have criminal tendencies," I say. "But that's crap. Art comes in lots of forms. Tattoos are one."

"You told me once that you knew art was important, on a gut level, and you wanted to help other people understand that." Hearing her repeat those words, knowing she'd remembered them all this time, does something to my heart, like a potent mix of excitement and approval. "I think that's exactly what you're doing. You just found a different way to go about it."

And just like that, I know. Time hasn't dimmed my feelings for her at all. She's still exactly what I want... what I've *always* wanted.

But she's still Adam's. Even though he's dead. In fact, now it feels like she'll *always* be Adam's. How colossally unfair is that?

I feel immediately guilty for that thought.

"I know you must have other tattoos," she says, her eyes narrowing in what looks a lot like mischief. "Aren't tattoo artists supposed to be all inked up?"

I love this playful side of her. It surprises me a bit that she can seem lighthearted, considering the fact that we just buried Adam a week ago, but maybe enough of what we shared two years ago remains that she can relax with me.

"I'm working on it," I answer, just as my phone buzzes in my pocket. I ignore the phone without a second thought. "I have a large piece on my back, across the shoulders. And my right arm is covered from shoulder to elbow. Eventually it'll be a full sleeve."

"Well, I'd love to see them some time, if you feel like showing me."

I'm just about to get rid of my hoodie so she can see my right arm when my phone goes off again.

Reaching in the back pocket of my jeans, I pull out my phone and glance at the screen.

Mom: Will you be home soon?

"Everything okay?" Grace asks.

"Yeah." I scrub my hands down my face out of frustration and am reminded I haven't shaved in a couple of days. "Mom's been smothering me a little. I understand, but it's still difficult to go from being on my own to having to report in with her every hour."

"She's just hurting." Grace's voice sounds a million miles away. "I guess we all are."

"I know." I shove the phone back in my pocket and stand up. "I should get back over there and hang out with her for a few before she goes to bed."

"Give her a hug for me?"

I nod, wishing I could hug Grace myself, just because I want to.

She stands and walks with me toward the door, and with every step, the dread of leaving punches me harder in the pit of my stomach. Her presence is soothing and warm, and I just want to soak in it.

I put my hand on the doorknob and turn back toward her. I can't leave without making plans to see her again. I'll be here for another few weeks, and I want to spend them with her.

"You want to hang out again tomorrow?" I ask. "I could use some time out of the house, and Mom needs some time without me underfoot, even if she doesn't realize it."

Grace nods, dropping her eyes and tilting her face toward the ground. I figure she doesn't want me to see the way her mouth curves into a grin. But I see it. And my heart soars.

"I'll text you," I say, stepping out the door and pulling it closed behind me.

God, I love her.

Chapter 16

Grace

ASHER IS COMING back tomorrow. He's coming back! I very nearly squeal and dance with glee, but manage to keep myself in check. After all, Asher told me once before that he'd be back, and he didn't make good on that promise.

I silently scold myself for that thought. Tonight, he gave me a small glimpse into what went wrong between us. He hadn't known how to tell me that college wasn't for him… that he wasn't going to stay in school. And when even his family hadn't been supportive, he'd done the only thing he knew to do. He'd relied solely on himself.

It still hurt, but at least I had some clue about what had gone through his mind back then.

Besides, if tonight is any indication, maybe he's ready to let me back in. He'd been so open with me, so ready to share stories about his life and his job. He showed me one of his tattoos, and if Stella hadn't texted, I feel certain he was about to remove his jacket to show me the ink on his left arm.

A thought occurs to me and my eyes dart around my room, making a mental list of any Adam memorabilia that is in plain sight. Reconnecting with Asher will be a complicated process, and I know it'll be even more difficult with pictures of Adam staring at us each time we're in this room together.

And please, dear Lord, let us be in this room together a lot. Or anywhere else together. A lot.

Walking to the bulletin board that hangs just above my light switch, I scan the multitude of pictures tacked up there. Most are snapshots of Sydney and me, even a few of the kids at the daycare where I work during the summers. But in the center is a large shot of Adam and me that Stella took back in March, on my eighteenth birthday. His arm is slung around my shoulder, and I'm holding two fingers up behind his head as bunny ears. We both have huge smiles as we pose for the camera.

I smile at the memory. It had been a good night. Stella and Adam had joined my parents and me at Saucy Salsa for Mexican food and fried ice cream, followed by a loud, off-key rendition of *Feliz Cumpleaños.* I remember feeling happy that night, enjoying the company, while at the same time wishing for something I couldn't put my finger on.

Stella enlarged the picture and gave me a copy the next week.

Reaching up, I remove the tack from the top of the

picture and carefully lay it on my dresser. With the eight-by-ten picture gone from my bulletin board, I can see a large part of the picture it had hidden. Not a snapshot. A drawing.

Asher's drawing.

I never had the heart to take it down, so I covered it up with other pictures. As I move the candid shots to the corners of the board so that the bulk of his drawing shows, I note the way I'd been so cautious to not let another tack stick through his creation. I'd pinned other pictures all around the drawing, letting them overlap and conceal his creation, but the corners of his drawing, where I first pinned it up, were the only places that had been touched by a push pin.

I realize at once that the two pictures are a metaphor for my heart. I covered Asher up with Adam, but Asher had always been there, right under the surface.

As non-serious as my relationship with Adam had been, I'd still been unfair to him. I couldn't help but wonder if he knew.

On my nightstand is a small, framed picture of Adam, one of his formal senior portraits. His hair, lighter brown than Asher's, and his dark brown eyes remind me what a strikingly handsome young man he'd been. My heart aches for what we've all lost... what the world has lost.

From the top of my closet I retrieve an empty shoebox. I place both pictures of Adam, along with the necklace he'd given me for Christmas inside. I leave the box of keepsakes open on my dresser. It seems appropriate, as if I'm somehow acknowledging how important Adam had been while at the same time signifying my desire to go forward.

I just hope I can find a way to go forward without the guilt. Because despite what had always been in my heart for Asher, Adam had fulfilled something significant in my life. However, if I have to play the grieving widow with Asher, the way I've had to with all our classmates over the past week, I might lose my mind.

Plopping down on my bed and falling back against the pillows, I let my mind return to the day Adam first stepped into my life in *that* way.

Ten months ago, just before Adam and I began our senior year of high school, Asher had come home for a week. He hadn't wanted to, but Stella had begged, and apparently Dave had guilted him, and he'd finally relented.

I remember how badly I'd wanted to talk to him, to tell him everything in my heart, but he'd made it impossible to get a moment alone with him. Finally, I'd been forced to accept that I had no chance. Seriously, Asher's the kind of guy that college girls would fall all over themselves for. I knew he had them lined up around the block, drooling for him to tattoo them. I'd watched him throw his bag in the backseat of his car, then slide into the driver's seat, and I almost went over to stop him. But what good would it have done?

So, I'd watched him drive away. Again.

It had been later that night when Adam came to my door.

"There's a back to school party out at Jordan's Friday night," he'd said. "There's supposed to be a bonfire. Do you want to go with me?"

"Not really my thing." I figured he was only asking out of some kind of pity, which sucked. Not only that, but Adam was known as the life of the party, especially with girls. I didn't want any part of that.

"It's not that kind of party," Adam had countered. "His parents are throwing it for him since it's the start of our senior year. They'll be there, which means no booze or random hook-ups."

"You must be disappointed." I'd laughed when I said it, not meaning it as an insult. For all his cavorting, Adam really was a lovable guy. It was hard not to like him.

"Nah. I'm kind of tired of that scene."

"Seriously? Greyson High's very own lothario is hanging up his hat?" I'd joked.

"I guess I'm growing up, but don't tell anybody," he'd said, causing us both to laugh. "I just want a date that I can have fun with, someone I can trust. That's why I'm asking you. No pressure and no expectations, Grace."

He'd seemed almost meek, which was a switch for Adam. And it was that meekness that had me accepting his invitation. It would be nice to have a date, especially one as sought-after as Adam. The fact that we knew each other and genuinely liked each other was another plus.

"Okay," I whispered, and what I thought would be a fun date to kick off our senior year of high school turned into ten months of dating.

And here I am, mourning Adam's loss with my heart lodged firmly in my throat over his brother, Asher.

Chapter 17

June 17, 2014

Asher

I CAN'T BELIEVE how nervous I am.

I never worry about what I wear. Normally all that matters is that my clothes are clean and don't look slept in. But tonight, I dig through my duffel bag as if the perfect shirt is going to jump out and smack me.

I feel like a freaking girl.

But yeah, I like girls. *This* girl in particular, so I figure I better not complain too much about their attention to fashion.

I pull on a long sleeve button-up over my tee shirt and roll the cuffs halfway up my forearms. I'll take it off when I get to Grace's so she can see the tattoo on my left arm if she wants, but I don't want to deal with Mom's eye-rolling on my way out the door. The wrist tattoo is visible, but it's small. Besides, it's not like Mom doesn't know I have ink in several places.

I lace up my Converse and run a comb through my hair, eyeing the tiny hole in the left side of my bottom lip and the barely noticeable clear plastic retainer. I've been hiding my lip piercing since I came home, the same way I did when I came home for Adam's graduation a couple weeks ago, because I know Mom won't like it. But a big part of me wants to put it back in tonight. Something tells me Grace will think it's cool.

So, I wash my hands and retrieve the small plastic bag that holds the plain silver ring. I like my two piercings, but I don't have the desire for a lot of flash. I pull open the segment of the ring, hold it secure with my right hand, and slide it easily into place.

I don't spend a lot of time studying myself in the mirror, but as my reflection stares back and me, I feel like myself for the first time since I've been back in Greyson. Not that the lip ring is such a big deal or anything. It's just that I'm not hiding anything anymore.

Pulling my phone from my back pocket, I shoot Grace a text.

Me: *Okay to come over now? Or should I wait a while?*

She answers a few seconds later.

Grace: *Now's fine. See you soon.*

I notice the empty spot on my home screen where the Facebook app used to be. For about half a second I consider re-installing it, but then remember the reason

I deleted it in the first place. The day Adam died, my phone practically blew up with texts and Facebook notifications. I couldn't handle it, so I deleted the app and turned off my phone. Thankfully the texts have slowed down since the funeral, but I still have no desire to wade through the wall posts and inbox messages on my Facebook profile.

I have way better things to do tonight anyway.

Dropping my phone in my pocket, I turn right to head to the kitchen and out the back door, not realizing that Mom is on the back patio.

"You're going to Grace's again." It's a statement, not a question.

I stop but don't turn around to look at her. "Yes."

"It's good the two of you can share your grief," she says.

My heart constricts and the taste of guilt coats my tongue. While Mom is right, that's only part of the reason I want to see Grace.

I have no idea how to even plant the seed that perhaps there's more to it. Don't even know if I should. After a moment, I decide a small bit of truth won't hurt.

"Grace and I used to be really close." I sit down in the chair next to her.

"Yes, I know." Her hands rest on her lap, clasped together, and she keeps her gaze there.

"I'm glad to be here with you, Mom," I say. "There's nowhere I'd rather be right now. But it's good for both of us to have some time apart. Eventually I'm going to back to Flagstaff."

She nods. "Be careful with Grace, Asher. She's been hurt a lot."

And I'm responsible for some of that hurt. The knowledge cuts me deep. "I don't want to see her hurt anymore."

Mom looks up at me then, her eyes landing on my lip ring. "I wondered when you were going to put that in your lip."

"You knew?" I ask.

"I know I've had a million things on my mind since you've been home, but I did notice the hole in your lip." She smiles, but it doesn't reach her eyes. "I appreciate you leaving it out during the funeral."

"I knew you'd rather people not see the tattoos, so I figured the new piercing wouldn't be your favorite either."

"I just don't see why you need all the embellishments. You're such a beautiful young man."

"It's just self-expression, Mom," I say, reaching out to squeeze her hand. "I'm still the same me."

"I guess so." She takes a deep breath. "Tell Grace to come by some time. I think it might help to start talking about Adam." Her voice cracks and she waits a beat before continuing. "To start remembering."

"I love you, Mom." I have no other words at the moment, so I lean over and kiss her cheek, then stand up to head across the driveway toward Grace's house.

The sadness of Adam's absence is a permanent fixture in my life, but there's a lightness to my step as I approach her door.

I feel like I'm going to see my girl. And even though I know that's not the case, I pray that somehow, some way, I can make it true.

Chapter 18

Grace

IT'S COMPLETELY UNFAIR the way my heart flutters when I see Asher at my door. And it's not because he looks great, although he really does. Tonight he's wearing a plain black tee shirt under an unbuttoned red and black plaid shirt. With the sleeves folded up, I can see the edges of the wrist tattoo he showed me last night.

I'm immediately glad I took the time to put on a nice pair of jeans and flowery tank top.

The hoodie he had on last night hid the fact that his body has filled out since high school. I'd still describe him as lean, but there's no denying that his shoulders and arms are more muscular than before.

And then my eyes land on the lip ring. That hadn't been there last night. I'm as fascinated by it as I was by the eyebrow piercing two years ago. I wonder what it would feel like to...

"You going to invite me in or just stare at my lip ring all night?" Laughter laces his voice, and I feel the blush begin to creep up my neck.

"Sorry," I say, stepping back to let him in. "It just surprised me."

"I got it a few months ago and Mom hadn't seen it," he explains. "Since she's not a big fan of my body art, I didn't want to spring in on her too quick. I didn't wear it at your graduation ceremony, either."

I knew he'd been there the night of graduation, but I hadn't seen him. Adam and I had celebrated with our own families. And I'm sure that Asher went back to Flagstaff before Adam's party was even over.

"How is your mom?" I ask, moving to the love seat and gesturing for him to join me. "I've thought about going over, but –"

"She'd like that." He takes his spot next to me. "She told me to tell you she'd like it if you stopped by. She's ready to start remembering."

I nod, knowing the hurt will never truly go away, but that remembering the good times is the first step to being able to move on from the pain. "I'll try to go over soon. I start back at the daycare tomorrow, but I'll find time to visit her in the next day or so."

"Mom hasn't gone back to Dr. Young's office yet," he says. "She's supposed to start back next week. He told her he'd let her ease back in as she felt ready."

"How's your dad?" I ask. Over the course of the past couple of years, as I got to know Asher, Adam, and Stella, I'd only been around Dave Howell a handful of times. I'd seen him at the funeral, of course, but I hadn't spoken to him.

Asher shrugs. "Sad. Staying busy. It's his way of coping, I guess. You know he's getting married again, right?"

"Yeah. Adam told me last month after the engagement." I shift on the love seat to face him, surprised that the mention of Adam's name doesn't feel difficult or uncomfortable. Asher seems unfazed by it as well. "Is it awkward?"

"Nah, it's all amicable. He and Mom have been divorced four years. We knew it would happen someday."

"Nice that he could get you temporary work at the hospital while you're in town."

Asher takes a deep breath. "Yeah, I'm grateful for that. Otherwise I wouldn't be able to pay my rent and my roommate would have to find someone else to move in. But I forgot how much I hate this job."

"I don't think we're supposed to love our high school summer jobs," I say. "Especially once we're out of high school."

"Not loving the daycare these days?" he asks, a smile tugging at the corners of his lips.

"Just hard to feel enthusiastic about it when I know cosmetology school is right around the corner."

"I always knew you were a creative at heart," Asher says, reaching over to gently pull on the end of my ponytail. "You just needed to step out of Brian's shadow."

"I guess I have you to thank for that."

"How so?"

"Remember when you told me the story about the four colors in the Navajo flag?" When he nods, I go on. "You told me that the stories your grandfather told you made you want to create because there was something so visual about all of them. After that, I started looking at things differently. I wanted to find ways to see creativity in everything. And I discovered that even the most ordinary, mundane things could be canvases. Even hair and skin."

The smile that explodes on his face nearly blinds me with its brilliance. "No arguments from me."

"I haven't exactly made my parents' dreams come true," I joke, thankful for the ease that seems to still exist between us.

"Know exactly what that's like."

He leans up and shrugs out of the button up, and from beneath the sleeve of his tee shirt I see the pattern of lines that make up the bottom of his tattoo. I clench my fist to keep from reaching out and pushing his sleeve up. I desperately want a closer look, but I know I should ask first.

It's on the tip of my tongue to do just that when Asher knocks the breath out of me with his question.

"Was Adam good to you?"

At first I don't know how to answer. Talking about Adam is one thing, but talking about my relationship with him just seems weird. I search my mind for a way to derail this line of conversation so Asher and I can continue the comfortable back and forth we've been enjoying, but the concern in his next words grabs me by the heart.

"He was such a player for a long time. I worried about you."

He worried about me all that time? Even though we hadn't been in contact with each other, he'd been concerned for me. How can I not answer him? "Yes. Adam was good to me."

And he had been. Adam hadn't been kidding about being tired of the girl-hopping party scene.

Asher breathes a sigh of relief. "I'm glad. He was such a dick to some of the girls he dated. I hated to think about him being that way to you."

"He was growing up," I say, deciding to open up a little about Adam and me. "Part of the reason it worked with us was because it was never really serious."

Asher raises his eyebrows, the silver hoop disappearing under the long sweep of his bangs. Part of me wants to tell him everything, to finally be able to unburden myself with the truth, but how can I do that without sounding callous and insensitive? Especially since I've told absolutely no one.

"Adam and I had fun together. We always had a date to school functions or parties. He never cheated, to my knowledge. I think he was done with that behavior anyway, and that's why he asked me out in the first place. It was comfortable, and we trusted each other.

But we never talked about anything beyond high school."

I can tell I put his mind at ease, but his forehead still creases with concern.

"What is it?" I ask.

"Did the two of you... you know?"

He pins me with his gaze, and my heart stops. Was he seriously asking if Adam and I had had sex? And if so, why?

Suddenly, the possible reasons he might want to know slam into me. Did it make him jealous to think of Adam and me that way?

I want to shout... to ask him if what I suspect is true. But more than anything I want him to know that I've never been with Adam, or anyone else, *that* way.

"No." I shake my head, probably with more force than I need to. "We never... and I've never...."

And yeah, that's probably more information than he wants.

But then a beautiful smile crosses his face, and I'm glad I told him.

Asher shifts slightly on the love seat, the sleeve of his tee shirt riding a bit higher on his upper arm. More of the ink there peeks out at me and I can't stop myself. Without thinking, or even asking, I reach over and push the fabric up and out of the way.

The warmth and softness of his skin seems to surround me, and the feel of it under my fingers sends electricity zinging up my arm. I lift my eyes to his, asking without words if this is okay. His deep brown gaze is hooded with an emotion I can't name, and he nods.

I look back at the tattoo, taking it in for the first time, and my breath all but stops.

"Asher," I whisper. "It's the ship."

On the smooth bronze skin of his bicep is the drawing from his sketchpad... the one he let me see that summer afternoon two years ago. The magnificent ship stands proudly among the waves that toss in the water beneath it, as if defying the rough waters with its strength. Since I saw it that first day, he's added storm clouds and rain, which only enhance the beauty and power of the ship that continues to sail on despite the unfriendly conditions. The waves and clouds wrap around his arm to cover every bit of skin from his elbow to his shoulder.

It is absolutely striking.

But it's the lone figure standing on the ship that catches my eye. Though small, the calm peace in his stance stands in stark contrast to the fury that rages around him.

"It's even more beautiful on your skin." My voice is a mere breath as I stare, transfixed by the image, and trace my finger along the bow of the ship. Somewhere in the back of my mind I realize I probably look ridiculous, but I simply cannot help the way the tattoo has hypnotized me.

"You told me that day you wanted to create a sense

of peace to contrast with the tension." I bring my eyes back to his. "You did."

"It's how I see myself," he says, his voice just a gravelly notch above a whisper. He keeps his arm still while I continue to run my thumb across the ink. "Or at least how I want to be seen. Steadfast in the middle of the chaos."

"That's how I see you." I put the palm of my hand flat against the ship, like I can somehow absorb part of the beauty and serenity directly from him. "Maybe no one else has ever seen it, but I always have. You're a fixed point regardless of what's going on around you."

It's not lost on me that we're skin to skin. I can count on one hand the number of times we've actually touched up until this moment, and nothing prepares me for the intensity feeling his skin against my own inspires.

In this instant, the past two years are erased, as if they never happened.

"Grace." His tone is pleading as he leans toward me.

"Asher." Overwhelming excitement sings through my veins.

"Grace." He whispers my name again, sliding his hand around my neck until he cradles the back of my head in his palm.

He pulls me gently toward him and lowers his head, eyes locked on mine. And then his lips touch mine.

He moves against me, soft and reverent, as his other hand comes up to rest against my cheek. My eyes flutter closed as the beauty of the moment swamps me. Any objection my consciousness might have raised is lost the moment his tongue moves along the seam of my lips in a silent request. He doesn't have to ask twice.

His tongue sweeps inside, sliding against mine and stealing my breath. The sensation of his lip ring moving against my mouth is incredible as it moves fluidly with each press of his lips. My hands, now pressed flat against his chest, fist in his tee shirt, holding tight as if at any moment he'll try to pull away. I've waited so long for this, and nothing is going to take it from me.

It could've been minutes or hours, but when Asher pulls back to look at me, his eyes are heavy and his breathing short. Both hands move to frame my face, thumbs moving softly across my cheeks.

"Should I apologize?" he whispers. The look in his eyes tells me that he'll be devastated if I say yes.

I shake my head, incapable of speech.

I've barely given him an answer before he's kissing me again. This time, he wraps his arms around me and hauls me into his lap. I slide my hands into his dark brown hair and hold on, the way I've wanted to since the first moment we met.

The teenage girl inside me is giddy. I'm making out with Asher Howell. And I love him more than I ever thought possible.

Chapter 19

Asher

I'M KISSING GRACE. Finally.

Every molecule in my body screams with the rightness of it. How had I ever thought I could stay away from her? How could I have put so much distance between us?

I have no answers. All I know is that my arms are locked around her as her mouth fuses to mine, and I never want to let her go.

There are all sorts of reasons I shouldn't be doing this... namely Adam... but I can't stop. I don't want to. Something in me shouts *I saw her first!* Two years of wanting her, loving her, have finally exploded between us. She's in my arms. In my lap. Under my skin. In my heart. She is *everywhere* and *everything.*

Maybe to her it's just a way to forget. A way to stop thinking about losing Adam. But I just don't care. I don't care at all.

All that matters is that we are together in this moment.

I pull back a fraction of an inch, still hugging her close. Her golden green eyes are glassy and gorgeous, hazy with the desire we just stirred up. Strands of her auburn hair have escaped her ponytail and now hang wistfully around her face. She's so beautiful it makes me ache.

She doesn't look upset, which is a relief. I thought I'd gauged her reaction correctly, but I'm glad to know I was right.

She'd wanted to kiss me just as badly as I'd wanted to kiss her.

I refuse to think too much about the ramifications of it.

I run my hands up her back, from her waist to her shoulder blades, pulling her toward me again. Pressing a kiss to one eyelid, then the next, I take a deep breath and speak.

"Mom's gonna text me any minute," I say, already dreading the moment I'll walk out her door. But I know it'll be better to leave now, while things are still dreamy between us.

Grace nods, letting her hands slide out of my hair, over my shoulders, then coming to rest on my chest. My stomach flips over.

No one's ever made me feel like this. Not even close. A simple touch from Grace does so much more than...

I shove that thought way down and slam a lid on it, knowing that after all the stuff I've done the past year to try and forget Grace, I shouldn't even be touching her.

"I should go," I whisper, leaning in to brush another kiss on her lips. "Before she gets antsy."

Grace smiles. "Okay."

"I don't want to, though." I grin back at her.

All this talk about me leaving, and yet she's still on my lap and my arms are still wrapped around her. If I don't go now, I might not ever.

I stand up, taking her with me and placing her feet on the floor. I grab my button-up shirt from the love seat, throw it over my shoulder, and turn back to face her. Our hands find their way to each other, fingers lacing together as we walk toward the door.

I shift close before opening the door, intending to ask if I can see her tomorrow. On the bulletin board by the light switch, I see the picture... the picture I drew her just before I left for Flagstaff two years ago. Had it been there the night before? I think back and realize it wasn't. It must've been covered up by the big picture of Grace and Adam.

Between last night and tonight she'd uncovered my picture. My mind races with what that might mean. I open my mouth, unsure what I'm about to say.

But she speaks before I do.

"We should probably talk about..." She doesn't finish the sentence.

But I know she means Adam.

The guilt bounces around inside me, but I can't

find it in myself to regret what just happened. What I hope very much will happen again. Very soon.

"Later." I reach up and push a stray tendril of hair behind her ear, my hand lingering on the soft skin of her neck. "I know we'll have to, but not right now. I just want to feel *this* right now."

She nods. "Me too."

Leaving her right then is about the hardest thing I've ever done, but I do it, before something ruins what was absolutely the most perfect moment of my life.

Chapter 20

June 18, 2014

Asher

AFTER FINISHING THE last truck unload of the morning, I make my way to the hospital cafeteria for my lunch break, once again reminding myself that I'm thankful for this job. But I seriously can't help how much I dislike it. Especially now that I know what it's like to spend my days doing something I love.

It's only for a few more weeks, though, so I stop complaining and pull my phone from my pocket. I grab a table near the back corner of the cafeteria, which is usually unoccupied.

I'm just about to text Grace when my dad drops into the seat across from me. He looks the same as always – suit, tie, perfectly professional – but I can see the sadness and exhaustion in his eyes. Guilt creeps back into my head when I realize I don't *just* feel sad today. Mixed with the sadness and grief is a happiness that until last night I thought had been lost forever.

"Hey, Dad," I say, laying my phone aside and

grabbing my sandwich from the backpack I'd brought with me.

"Asher." He attempts a smile, but it doesn't reach his eyes. "It's been a few days since we talked, and I wanted to see you. I hope you don't mind."

To his credit, he doesn't even blink when he sees the lip ring. I decided after last night that I was through hiding, so the lip ring stays. He also makes no comment about the ink that's clearly visible on my arms. No way am I wearing a long sleeve shirt while doing manual labor.

"Of course not."

"I wanted to thank you again for agreeing to stay here with your mother for a while," he says. My parents' divorce hadn't been easy, but it had at least been civil, and I know my dad still cares for my mom. "How is she?"

"Hard to tell. She doesn't get out of the house much, if at all, but she gets dressed every day, and she eats regularly. She's talked a bit more the last few days." I pull a bottle of water from my backpack, unscrew the lid, and down half of it. "I figure those are good signs."

Dad nods. "Yes, I think so. Has she made plans to go back to work?"

"Next week. Dr. Young says she can start off just coming in for a couple of hours, then work her way back to full time. He's been really understanding."

"I'm glad." Dad toys with the buttons on the cuff of his sleeve. He seems nervous, and I can tell there's more he wants to say.

"You're not eating?" I ask, hoping a neutral subject will make him comfortable enough to go on. While I wait for him to continue, I start in on my peanut butter and jelly sandwich, the flavors reminding me of my childhood. I probably chose this sandwich unconsciously in order to feel like a kid again.

Maybe that's a natural reaction after losing someone so important.

"I have a lunch meeting in a half an hour," he says. "I was hoping you'd agree to come to my house for dinner tonight."

I look up at him, finishing off my sandwich and reaching for the banana I'd packed. Dad rarely asks me to his house. Most of the time we meet at a restaurant. This must be important.

"Okay," I answer. "What's up?"

He takes a deep breath. "I realize I didn't do a very good job of making you and your brother my top priority after the divorce. I guess I always just thought there would be plenty of time for us to reconnect. I regret that now, obviously. My time with Adam ran out before…"

He squeezes his eyes shut and doesn't continue. I don't need him to finish the sentence. I know what he means. My relationship with my dad has never been strained, but it changed when he and Mom divorced. For half a second I'm angry that it took Adam's death for him to decide to make the extra effort, but I can't stay mad. He lost his son. I lost my brother. We need to be a family now more than ever.

"Dad." I reach across and squeeze his hand. "I'll come to dinner. Will Amelia be there?"

Amelia is my dad's fiancée. I've met her a few times, but I don't know her all that well. Adam always said she was pretty nice, but living in Flagstaff didn't give me the opportunity to get acquainted with her.

And honestly, neither Dad nor I had made much effort to stay in touch since I quit college. He'd been angry with me over my decision, and I'd been frustrated with his inability to respect my choices.

Definitely time to remedy that now.

"She's going to cook dinner and eat with us," Dad says. "But she'll head back to her place afterward. I'd like to spend the evening just you and me. I know we've never done the whole father-son-bonding-time routine, but I feel like we should at least try while you're still in town."

"All right." This means I probably won't get to see Grace tonight, but she'll understand. We hadn't made plans anyway. And I know she'll be glad to know my dad and I are spending time together.

"Will your mother be okay for the evening?" Dad asks.

"I think so." I finish my banana, drain the rest of my water, and collect my trash to throw away on my way out of the cafeteria. "I'll spend some time with her before I head over to your place, and I'll text Grace and see if she can check on her after dinner."

"You sure she'll want to see Grace?" he asks. "It won't be too much of a reminder?"

I shake my head. "She said last night she hoped Grace would come by soon. She even said she thought it would be good to start talking about Adam."

"I agree. Maybe you and I can do some remembering after dinner tonight."

Dad and I say our goodbyes, and with a handshake and a manly pat on the back, he leaves to go to his lunch meeting. I still have a few minutes of my lunch break left, so I grab my phone and text Grace.

> **Me:** You home from work yet?
>
> **Grace:** Just got home a few minutes ago. How's the hospital?
>
> **Me:** One big party, like always. Ha!
>
> **Grace:** Can't be as exciting as changing diapers and wiping noses!
>
> **Me:** I give up. You've got me beat!

Grace responds with multiple smiley faces, and I'm reminded how much I enjoy emoticons when she sends them.

> **Me:** I know we didn't make plans to see each other tonight, but my dad wants me to have dinner with him and his fiancée.
>
> **Grace:** Okay. You should spend time with him while you're here.
>
> **Me:** He wants to hang out, just the two of us, after

Amelia goes home. I don't know what time I'll be back. Probably too late to stop by. I'm sorry :(

Grace: *It's okay. You aren't obligated to me anyway.*

But damn, how I want to be obligated to her.

Me: *I just don't ever want you to think I'm ignoring you. I won't do that. Ever again.*

Grace: *I believe you.*

It astounds me that she can forgive me so easily, especially since I haven't even asked. The realization that I'd made out with her like a crazy man last night, yet hadn't even apologized and asked for her forgiveness, washes over me.

Me: *Grace, I'm so sorry for the past two years. I know I should say this to you in person, and I will, but I want you to know that I hate that I hurt you. Can you forgive me?*

Grace: *Already forgiven.*

Just like that day in the school hallway, after I'd punched Tony Adkins twice in the face, I'm humbled and overwhelmed by the faith she seems to have in me.

Me: *Thank you.*

Grace: *Always.*

I really, really want the word to mean something far greater than I'm sure she has in mind. For now, I'll just be happy that I'm forgiven.

Me: *I have a favor to ask.*

Grace: *Sure. What?*

Me: *Can you check on my mom after dinner? It's the first night she'll be alone for any real length of time. And since I'll be across town instead of next door at your house, I just want to make sure she's okay.*

Grace: *Absolutely. I was thinking about visiting her anyway.*

Me: *You're the best, Grace.*

I'm sure she has no idea exactly how deeply I mean it.

Grace: *Flattery will get you everywhere!*

Well then, I can totally come up with plenty of flattering things to say to her.

Me: *In that case, you're a really great kisser. ;)*

Grace: *Haha! The feeling's mutual.*

My insides twist, and my heart swells. Flirting with Grace via text is perhaps the most fun I've had ever. Except for kissing her last night. Yeah, that definitely ranks highest on the fun scale.

I look at the time and see I have five minutes to get back to the unloading area. With a sigh, I shoot her one last text.

Me: *Love to continue this conversation, but my lunch break is over.*

Grace: *Ok. Don't have too much fun! Talk later.*

Adam's face flashes through my mind as I grab my backpack and put my phone in my pocket. For the first time, I wish I'd talked to him about his relationship with Grace. She says things between them weren't serious, but ten months is a long time to date the same person. Especially in high school. And *especially* for my brother. I don't want to feel guilty for loving Grace, but I wish there was some way to know for certain how Adam would feel about it.

On my way back to work, elation and guilt swim through me. The combination of the two feelings is maddening. Deep down, I know I wouldn't trade kissing Grace for anything in the world, regardless of how guilty I feel. But I do feel guilty. It's like I'm cheating with my brother's girlfriend. I wonder if she feels the same… like being with me is cheating on Adam.

And I wonder if he'd be pissed at us.

Just as I'm about to try and convince myself we aren't cheating and that Adam would be just fine with the two of us being together, I'm bombarded with the reality of my behavior over the past year.

God, I seriously suck so bad.

I'd been so angry about Adam being with Grace that I'd succumbed to every college-age guy stereotype. I hadn't been prepared for the "fangirls" that came with working in a high-end tattoo shop. Combine that with the fact I was lonely and heartbroken and pissed off at the world, and yeah…

I did a bunch of stuff I'm so not proud of.

I tried everything to forget Grace.

Nothing worked.

I should stay away from her, for all sorts of reasons. But I know I'll never be able to.

As I head for the truck that's just arrived and is waiting to be unloaded, I pull my phone out and type one last text.

> **Me:** I'll stop by for a few when I get home from work. Can't just not see you at all today.

I hit send and just accept the fact that my happiness comes standard with a heaping side of guilt.

Chapter 21

Grace

A T TEN MINUTES after five, my phone dings with an incoming text. Without looking, I know it's Asher, and I'm almost ashamed of the giddy smile on my face when I see that I'm right.

Almost.

A: *Be there in 5. OK?*

I respond immediately with a *yes* that's far more enthusiastic than it appears on my cell phone screen.

Looking in the mirror at my red hair, sleek and straight thanks to my flat iron, and the pink tank top with frilly ruffles across the top, heart flips around in excitement and anticipation. It's hard not to acknowledge that I never felt this way about seeing Adam.

Not that I didn't look forward to being with Adam. But it never felt like this. Butterflies never zoomed around in my stomach and excitement never bubbled in my heart when I was expecting Adam at my door. I think I'd convinced myself those feelings weren't real… that they'd just been the imaginings of a silly teenage girl… so that not feeling them would hurt less.

I'll never regret my time with Adam, just like I'll never regret these moments with Asher. I wish with all my heart that Adam could've met a special girl and experienced the same sweet longing I feel for Asher. A pain blooms in my soul with the knowledge that he never will.

The soft knock on my door pulls me from my melancholy. Opening the door, I'm met with the sight of Asher in faded blue jeans and a plain, white tee shirt that's still a bit damp from the sweating he must've done at work.

I step back to let him come in and turn to face him just as he looks down at his chest and notices the line of sweat on the front.

"I probably should've gone home to change first," he says. "I'm kind of gross."

Gross? Absolutely not.

Without warning, he grabs the hem of the shirt and pulls it over his head. Wadding it up in his hand, he uses the drier areas to wipe off his forehead, the back of his neck, followed by his chest.

But the practicality of his actions is completely lost on me as I take in the sight of all that bronze skin. Well-defined muscles criss-cross his abdomen. The ship tattoo shifts as his bicep flexes from his movements.

I swear, my eyes cross and my knees sway. Had two

years really made that much difference? The answer is obvious. Asher is very much a twenty-year-old man and so *not* a teenager anymore.

He looks back at me, the shirt still balled up in his hand, clearly unaware of how he's affecting me.

"How was work?" he asks.

Really? Like I can talk about infants and toddlers right now?

"It was ok. Yours?" I'm proud of myself for putting words together in the face of a shirtless Asher.

"Same. Just work."

I smile, not trusting myself to try to speak. Asher starts to say something, but stops. He narrows his eyes and tilts his head, like he's looking at me for the first time. I wonder if he notices that I went to a little extra effort today.

One corner of his mouth lifts in that grin that's always made my pulse race, and before I know what's happening, he steps closer, snakes an arm around me, and pulls me flush against him.

And proceeds to kiss the daylights out of me.

I'm so lost in the sensation of our mouths melding together that I have no idea how long the kiss goes on. Somehow, my arms find their way around his back and my hands slide upward toward his shoulders. His skin is warm and soft under my touch, and I dig my fingers gently into the muscles beneath them. He groans, pulling me tighter to him, angling his head to take the kiss even deeper.

Just when I think I'll die from the exquisite beauty of this moment, he pulls back, breaking contact with my lips, but keeping me locked in his arms.

"I've got to get cleaned up and head over to Dad's," he says, and I notice his words are breathy and shallow.

I do nothing but nod my head.

"Thanks for checking on Mom later." He presses a kiss on my forehead and releases me to stand on my own.

I manage to stay upright, but barely.

"No problem." My voice is as husky as his.

He shakes the tee shirt loose and puts it back on, and I very nearly weep at losing the vision of his golden torso.

"I'll text you later, okay?"

I nod again.

He leans down and kisses me lightly on the lips before turning and heading out the door.

I watch until he disappears into the back door of his house. Once he's out of sight and earshot, I jump up and down and squeal, as quietly as I possibly can.

It's a totally girly reaction, but I can't help it.

And I don't want to.

Chapter 22

Grace

I SEE STELLA in the kitchen as I step up onto the back patio of Asher's house. She's busy with something on the counter, and for a moment I just watch.

She's intent on whatever it is she's working on, her black hair tied back in a long ponytail, and her shoulders moving up and down. Stella has always enjoyed cooking, and it makes my heart lighter to see her using that love to help her through this difficult time.

I pull my tote bag higher on my shoulder and knock softly on the door, while at the same time I push it open and stick my head in.

"Stella?" She looks up from the mound of dough on the counter. "Is it okay if I come in?"

"Grace." Her voice is not its usual bright tone, but I can hear a bit of a smile in her words as she says my name. "Of course."

I drop my tote into one of the kitchen chairs as she wipes her hands on a dishtowel. The unmistakable scent of baking bread surrounds me, and at once I realize what she's doing.

"I'm so glad you're here," she says, pulling me into a hug. "I've missed you."

"Me too," I say, meaning it from the bottom of my heart.

"I was just kneading the dough for another loaf of bread." She gestures to the kitchen table. "Why don't you have a seat while I get it baking? I've got a loaf that's just about to come out of the oven, and we'll slice it and eat it while it's hot."

"Sounds great." I know we're avoiding the obvious topic of conversation, but for now homemade bread is bringing a bit of a smile to her face, so why not let it continue?

"I haven't made bread in so long," she says, forming the dough into the shape of a loaf and placing it in a rectangular pan. "With Asher out of the house tonight, I decided it was the perfect time to try it again."

"If the smell in here is any indication, I'd say you haven't lost your touch one bit." I pull out a chair and take a seat at the table, eyeing my tote bag in the seat next to me. I say a prayer that Stella will like the gift I brought her, and that it won't make her even sadder.

"There's soft drinks and bottled water in the refrigerator." She opens the oven, reaches in with two oven mitts, and pulls out a perfectly golden brown loaf of bread. Turning it out onto a cooling rack, she goes on. "Or I can put on a pot of coffee if you'd like."

I shake my head. "No need to do that, unless you want coffee. Water is fine with me."

I watch as she slides the next loaf into the oven, then takes two plates from the cabinet and sets them on the table. She comes back with the loaf of bread and a knife, and I hop up to grab the water from the fridge.

"Grab the butter dish if you don't mind," she says. "What's hot homemade bread without a little butter?"

I return to the table with our drinks and the butter, and slide back into my seat. Stella takes her spot across from me, but makes no move to slice the bread. I suppose it needs to cool a few more minutes before she cuts into it. I try to think of something to say that can fill the time, but come up empty. I should've thought about it ahead of time, but once I'd gotten the idea to bring her a gift, that's all I'd thought about. Talking with Stella had never been a chore, and I guess it just never occurred to me it would be difficult to find words to say to her now.

"Grace," she whispers, breaking the silence. She reaches across and takes one of my hands in both of hers. "Please don't feel like you need to stay away because of what's happened."

I nod and swallow past the lump in my throat. There were times during the months I was dating Adam that I wondered if I was more attached to Stella than to him. When Asher left home and cut off contact with me, my interaction with her had been lessened. And I'd missed her. Then when Adam and I started seeing one another, suddenly Stella was a regular part of my life again.

Those thoughts had always made me feel terrible. Now, with Adam gone forever, they make me feel even worse. Adam had been an amazing guy who deserved to be wanted on his own merit, not because his brother didn't want me or because I wanted to maintain a friendship with his mother.

"I'm sad, Grace," she went on. "And I'll be sad for a long time, I'm sure. There's a part of me that will be sad forever. But seeing you doesn't make it worse."

"Okay," I whisper, blinking back tears.

"Asher asked you to check on me, didn't he?" she asked, letting go of my hand to touch the bread and check its temperature.

"He did," I admit. "He told me last night you wanted me to come visit, then when Dave asked him to come over for dinner, he asked me if I'd stop in since it's the first night he won't be around. He worries about you."

"Sweet boy," she says, almost under her breath. "I worry about him, too."

"He says he's staying a few more weeks."

"Until the middle of July." Stella picks up the knife and begins gently slicing into the loaf. "This probably needs a few more minutes to cool, but after smelling it baking for the past forty-five minutes, I don't think I can wait."

I smile at her and do a quick mental calculation.

Mid-July means Asher will be here another four weeks, give or take a few days. After that, it's only another three weeks or so until I leave for cosmetology school.

I watch as she cuts two slices, then slathers them both with butter, which instantly melts and sinks into the fresh bread.

"Dig in," she says, sliding one plate over to me.

If possible, the taste of the bread is even more wonderful than the smell, and for a few moments we're silent while we polish off our slices. The kitchen, with its sage green walls and granite counter tops, feels just as cozy as it did every time I ate here with Stella and Adam, and yet the absence of Adam's presence is practically tangible.

"I have something for you," I say, reaching for my tote bag.

"Oh, Grace," Stella says. "That isn't necessary."

"It's not much." I pull out the box and sit it between us on the table. "I bought a similar one for myself and thought you might like one, too."

The little cardboard box is nothing special. Technically, I assume it's supposed to be used as a way to gift wrap something. The outside is adorned with yellow and pink hearts and words like *love* and *hope*. The top folds down and closes with a tiny piece of velcro.

"It's lovely," she says, looking at the box with a curious expression.

"I bought one to use as a memory box," I explain. "I have all these pictures of Adam, and all the things he gave me. I wanted to put them all somewhere for safe keeping. Some place I could get them out and look at them when I needed to. I started to use an old shoe box, but it just seemed like all those memories deserved something more special than that."

"What a beautiful idea," she says, her voice soft.

"I know you have memories of Adam all over this house," I continue. "And I know the pictures and other things are going to stay where they are. I just thought, maybe if you had a few small things that were special, you might like to put them in here. Maybe put it by your bed or next to the sofa, and whenever you needed to feel close to him, you could open it up."

Stella is silent. She stares at the box, and I see tears forming in her eyes.

"Maybe it's silly," I whisper, "since you have so many things here to remind you of him."

"No," she says quickly. "No. I love it. I love the thought of filling this box with special memories."

"I'm glad." I breathe a sigh of relief. "I know it's just a small thing, but for me it felt like the start of some closure."

"Thank you, Grace." She reaches for my hand again. "I'm so glad you came into our lives two years ago."

"Me too." A tear escapes to roll down my cheek.

"Both my boys were lucky to know you," she says, squeezing my hand. "And I'm happy Asher has you to confide in now."

"We've been friends a long time," I say. Part of me feels like I'm deceiving her with those words, but another part reminds me that until last night, all that had been between Asher and me was friendship. Even though I'd always wanted more.

"And I know he hurt you when he all but disappeared." She releases my hand and reaches for the bread knife. "Thank you for not holding it against him."

I watch as she slices through the bread and prepares another piece for each of us. I'm not quite sure how to proceed with this conversation. There's so much I want to say about Asher and his choices and how he's exactly where he should be, but I know if I come to his defense with too much fervor it will only make her wonder why.

"No one's perfect." It's a cop-out, generic response, but I don't know what else to say.

"It's hard for me to understand his choices," she says. "They're just so different from what I'd always imagined for him. But he seems happy."

"He really is."

"I wonder what choices Adam would've made." Her eyes mist over again, and she seems to focus on some imaginary place. "Would he have stuck with his plan to go into sports medicine, or would he have done something surprising like Asher?"

I smile, but it's a sad smile. I've wondered those things, too.

"I wonder what would've become of the two of

you, with him so far away in Tucson."

Here's my opportunity. I know I need to at least start discussing the notion that Adam and I were never forever material. I'm just not sure how to go about it without sounding callous.

Which is the exact reason I've told no one what happened the day Adam died.

"Stella," I begin, lowering my voice and reminding myself to proceed carefully. "Adam and I were close, but we never discussed anything beyond high school."

She nods, acknowledging my statement.

I go on. "I suspect ours would've ended like a lot of high school relationships."

"Maybe not." Her voice is a whisper.

If she only knew. But I can never tell.

"Well, whatever happened between Adam and me, he would've been a smashing success." I know I've said enough and that it's time to move away from talking about my relationship with Adam. "Whatever he wound up doing, he'd have done it with enthusiasm, like he did everything else."

Stella takes a deep breath and straightens her shoulders. "You're right. And it helps to think of him that way."

As glad as I am that I came to see Stella, our talk has exhausted me. I can tell she feels the same when she reaches up to massage the muscles in the back of her neck.

Baby steps, I think to myself. Walking down

memory lane will have to be done in small doses. At least for a while.

"I should go," I say, pushing back from the table and slipping my tote bag onto my shoulder. "Thank you for the bread. And for the talk."

"I should be thanking you." She stands as well, putting her arms around me. "For the visit and for the box. And for caring about both my boys."

"I'll come by again soon," I promise her.

And then I slip out the back door, my heart both comforted and conflicted by her last words.

Chapter 23

Asher

"THANKS FOR COMING over tonight," Dad says, wrapping an arm around my shoulder as we step out onto the front porch. "I hope we can do this again before you leave."

"Sure, Dad." And I mean it. We'd had a good time together, both over dinner with Amelia and afterward when we watched a baseball game and reminisced about Adam's days on the pitcher's mound.

"I hope you know I meant what I said about reconnecting with you." Dad gives my shoulder a squeeze, then steps back to look at me. "Even once you're back in Flagstaff. I'd like to see where you live. And where you work."

"Yeah?" After all this time, I can't believe Dad actually wants to take part in the life I've made for myself.

"Yes." He takes a deep breath. "Your brother's death has taught me not to waste one moment. I lost him before I could make up for lost time. I won't lose any more with you."

"Okay," I say, my chest expanding with an emotion I can't name. Maybe it's relief, or perhaps even happiness. Whatever it is, I don't argue with it. "I'd like that."

"Your mother will come to the same conclusion eventually," he assures me. "I'll help her along if I can."

With another hug, which is beginning to feel almost natural after two years of distance between us, I slide into the driver's seat of my car. It's almost eleven o'clock. It's too late to see Grace, since I know she works in the morning and is probably getting ready to go to sleep.

I back out of Dad's driveway and head home. Deciding to take a chance, I pull out my phone and dial her number. If I can't see her tonight, maybe I can at least talk to her.

There's a part of me that knows I should stop this... a part of me that knows I absolutely should not do this to Grace. Or to myself. I know she's grieving for Adam, and I realize I'm probably just a distraction. It'll hurt like hell when this all falls apart around me, but the guilt and fear just cannot overcome the sense of happiness and rightness I feel when I'm with her. As much as I love my brother, she should've been mine all along. I know it's my own fault she wasn't, and now, even as much as I want to, I don't know if I'll ever be able to make her truly mine.

Yet knowing this does nothing to stem the massive

flood of love I feel for her. Especially when I think about the fact that she moved the picture of Adam and has my drawing on display in her bedroom.

Sometimes there's a far off look in her eyes, and I know she's holding something back. Part of me wants to know what it is, but a bigger part warns me that I probably won't like it. I'm sure whatever it is has to do with Adam, and I don't know if I can take hearing how much she loved him.

"Hey Asher." She answers on the second ring, and I shove away all the doubts and just focus on her voice.

"You weren't asleep already, were you?" I ask.

"No, not yet," she says.

"I'm on my way home from Dad's, and I just wanted to say goodnight." There was a time I would've laughed like a lunatic at a guy calling a girl just to hear her voice before he hits the sack, but not these days. Because now I totally understand the compulsion.

"I'm glad you did. Your mom and I had a nice visit." Her voice is soft, and I just want to sink in and wrap myself up in it.

"Good." I turn on my left blinker and wait for the light to change. "She's seemed a bit better the last day or so. Like maybe she's coming out of the first wave of numbness."

"I think so," Grace responds. "She was baking bread when I got there. We talked about Adam, and she was sad but able to carry on a conversation. I think it was healthy for both of us."

Hearing Adam's name reminds me of just how complicated this situation is. Not only in terms of whatever relationship I'm going to have with Grace, but also in terms of my mom. I have no idea what she thought of Grace and Adam together. Whether or not she had hopes they'd stay together and eventually get married. If by some miracle I'm able to convince Grace to stay with me, what will Mom think about it? Will she be angry at me and think I've stolen my brother's girlfriend?

Good grief, what a mess. My temples begin to throb, and I decide not to think about it for the time being.

"Thanks for checking on her for me," I say. "Means a lot."

"I was glad to do it. I needed the closure with her." I hear what sounds like rustling sheets and I imagine her climbing into bed in some cute, girly pajamas, her hair messy and her face void of make up. Then I have to mentally smack myself to get my mind back in an appropriate place.

I wish I could take her on a real date. I know it's not possible here in Greyson. People would either look at us weird, because she was Adam's long-term girlfriend, or they'd think we were just out together to console one another. I'm sure everyone would just think we were together for some kind of mutual grieving, but I don't think I could stop myself from looking like the happiest guy in the world to be with her. If people knew how I felt about her, they'd look down on me. Not that I care about that crap, but I don't want Grace to have to deal with it.

But I can't help but think about how nice it would be to spend time with her in a normal way, like two regular people.

An idea pops into my head. Maybe a date in public wouldn't work, but I could come up with something else.

"Do you have plans tomorrow?" I ask. "Like, after dinner time?"

"No," she answers. "Why?"

"I was just thinking it would be nice to do something besides sit in your bedroom." Although, I can't say I mind her bedroom one bit. "Not that your bedroom isn't awesome or anything, but I had an idea for something different. You game?"

"Do I get a hint?" she asks.

Behind our houses runs a line of pine trees, blocking the view of an open field on the other side of the tree line. I'd spent many hours on the far side of those trees, drawing and dreaming. Though I was separated from my house by a mere fifty yards, it might as well have been another world.

Sharing that place with Grace seems like the perfect way to have an almost-date.

"You don't have to dress up," I assure her. "We won't see anybody else. But bring a jacket or hoodie. You know it can get cool after dark."

"Okay. I guess I'll trust you." I can hear the smile in her voice as she teases me with a fake tone of annoyance.

"Meet me in the side yard about nine o'clock?"

"All right," she says, yawning.

"I should let you go," I say, turning onto our street. Approaching my driveway, I can see the lights are off in her bedroom. "Get some sleep."

"I will," she says. "I hope you have a good day at work tomorrow."

"I'll manage somehow."

"Good night, Asher." Her voice is hazy and drowsy, which I suddenly find enormously sexy.

"Good night, beautiful."

The call disconnects, and I wonder if she heard the endearment. I hadn't meant to say it, but it came out anyway. Even if she can't acknowledge it, I hope she heard it. Grace is the most beautiful person I've ever known, inside and out, and she deserves to know it.

Chapter 24

June 19, 2014

Asher

IT'S CRAZY HOW easy Grace and I fall back into old habits. I text her on my lunch break as she's getting off work. The only difference is that she has a car now and drives herself home, so instead of texting me as she walks home, she texts from her bedroom.

Me: *We still on for tonight?*

I smile, thinking about the plans I made for the two of us after dinner.

Grace: *Yep. Still no hints?*

Me: *Nope. Surprise.*

Grace: *Party pooper.*

Me: *Sticks and stones! Seriously though, I'm gonna hang with Mom after work, so I probably won't see you until 9:00 when we meet outside.*

Grace: *All right. Are we hanging out around the house or are we going somewhere? I'm gonna have to tell my parents something. I don't have a curfew* *now that I'm 18, but I should let them know where I'll be.*

Me: *Around the neighborhood and that's I'll I'm saying!*

I figure I'm about to get hit with a string of angry face emoticons, and a smile breaks wide across my face when Grace's text comes through and I see that I'm right.

It's so tempting to stop by and see her as soon as I get home, just for a minute, before going in to spend time with Mom. Part of me wants to so bad, but I know I need to keep my feelings under control and not let their intensity cloud my good judgment. I'm still unsure where Grace's heart stands since she spent the last ten months dating my brother. If I come on too strong it could ruin things before we even have a chance.

And I want this chance more than I want my next breath.

We say our goodbyes, and I head back toward the loading dock. As I'm making my way there, I hear my dad's voice from behind me.

"Asher," he calls. "Got a minute?"

"Sure." I stop, turning back toward him.

"I talked to your mom this morning," he says, coming to a stop right in front of me. "I told her I'm going to come see you in Flagstaff once you go back, and we talked about not letting this distance continue. I think she feels the same, although she may not be able to say it to you just yet."

Wow. Dad's serious about this reconnecting business. It'll be nice not to feel like my family thinks I'm a freak.

"Thanks Dad."

"She mentioned you've been spending time with Grace again." He phrases it as a statement, but I know it's more of a question.

"We were good friends before I left for Flagstaff," I say. "It's nice to have someone I can talk to."

Both of which are true. I just left out the part about the two of us kissing each other senseless.

"I know you were friends." He steps closer. "And I'm glad you can confide in her. But you have to know that I realize your feelings for her were much deeper than friendship two years ago. Maybe they still are. I'm not sure why you pulled away from her once you left, but she spent ten months with Adam. She's grieving for him. You're twenty-years-old and a grown man, but you're still my son, and I don't want you to get hurt if she can't give you what you want from her."

I stand there speechless. I can't believe Dad even paid that much attention to me back then to notice what I felt for Grace. And how in the world am I supposed to respond to what he just said? I can't help but feel grateful he cares, but if I say anything, it'll be like hanging my heart out there for the world to see.

"Dad," I start, but can't continue.

"You don't have to say anything," he says. "Just be

careful. And I'm here if you need me."

"Thanks," I whisper.

With a nod of his head, he turns and walks back the way he came. I head toward the loading dock for the last half of my work day, my mind now occupied with all the what-ifs about my relationship with Grace.

Chapter 25

Grace

MOM AND I are finishing up the dishes after dinner when I decide it's time to tell her I have plans with Asher. Dad's already immersed in a baseball game on TV, and with Brian still at Stanford, it's just mom and me in the kitchen.

"Asher's been over to talk a couple of nights this week," I say, loading the last of the dirty plates into the dishwasher.

"Really?" Mom asks. "You haven't said anything."

Which, in mom-speak, meant *it must mean something if you've kept it a secret.* No one can say Paula Ballard didn't have the standard mom instincts.

"He's sticking around for a few weeks to be with Stella," I explain. "I think he just needs someone else to talk to about everything."

Which is true enough, just not the entire story.

"Makes sense," Mom says. "I assume he's still living and working in Flagstaff."

I nod, wondering just what she thinks about Asher

working as a tattoo artist. It's not something I've ever discussed with her. Once Asher dropped out of my life, it was just too painful to talk about him.

"And are you seeing him tonight?" she asks. Her tone is questioning, and I can tell she's trying to determine if there's more to all this than what I'm saying.

At some point, I'll probably confide in Mom. Of everyone in my life – Brian and Dad, Stella, and all my friends – I think Mom is the most likely to understand my feelings for Asher. But I'm just not ready to share it with her yet. It's too new, and I just want to keep it all to myself for a while.

"I think we're going to hang out outside," I say.

"Okay," she replies, pushing the buttons to start the dishwasher. As it quietly begins to whir away, she turns back to face me. "Just let me know if the two of you decide to go somewhere else."

Maybe moms have a sixth sense about things and can tell when their daughters aren't going to divulge anything else, because just like that, Mom lets it drop.

I assure her I will, then make my way to my bedroom to get ready.

I turn on some music then open my closet. I spend a considerable amount of time staring, trying to come up with the perfect outfit. Silly, I know, but I want to look nice enough that Asher notices. But I also figure I should be practical. Even in June, it gets cool in the mountains of northern Arizona once the sun goes down.

I settle on a pair faded blue jeans, soft and well worn, but free of any holes that might let in the chilly air. I pull on a bright green boho-style top with light brown paisleys down the front and grab a loose fitting twill jacket the same shade as the paisleys.

Tossing the jacket onto the seat, I move to the mirror to work on my hair. I take a few minutes to touch it up with the straightening iron, taming the ends that had begun to frizz as the day wore on. Once I'm satisfied with it, I pull it away from my face and brush it all to the left. I fasten it into a low side ponytail that falls over my left shoulder. For half a second, I consider searching for something more girly than a plain hair band, but decide that would be going overboard since I rarely wear hair bows.

I grab the jacket and step out the door at exactly nine o'clock, just as Asher is stepping off the patio behind his house.

The logo for Resolution Ink, the tattoo shop where he works, spreads across the front of his black, long sleeve tee. I know it's the shop logo because I googled it. Many times. If anyone else knew how often I'd done that I might be ashamed, but for so long it had been the only way I could feel close to him.

The sleeves of the shirt cover his tattoos, but the silver hoops in both his facial piercings glint in the light from the back door.

Khaki cargo pants and a pair of black, lace-up

leather boots make him the perfect balance between super-hip twenty-year-old and menacing college drop-out.

And yeah… I like it. A lot.

"Hey you," he says, coming to a stop right in front of me.

"Hi." My voice is almost squeaky, and I hope there's no drool running down my chin.

"Ready?" he asks with a grin.

"Not sure," I tease. "Since I have no idea what we're doing."

"Don't worry," he laughs, slinging an arm around my shoulders and turning me toward the line of trees behind our houses. The warmth of his touch seeps into my skin. "Trust me."

The blanket spread out in front of us catches my eye, as well as the small cooler off to the side. Something sweet and lovely spills out of my heart and courses through me?

"A picnic?" I whisper the words to myself.

"Just a small one," he says, leaning his body into mine. "Just dessert. Hope you saved room."

I smile up at him, not trusting myself to speak. I'm too bowled over that Asher planned a late-night picnic for the two of us. I want to grab hold of the romance of it, wrap myself up in it, and never leave.

Chapter 26

Asher

G RACE AND I settle onto the blanket, our backs to the line of trees. Above us the darkening sky is beginning to fill with stars, which is the precise reason I brought her here.

But while I wait for it to get darker and more stars to take their place above, I pop open the cooler and begin unpacking.

Her eyes widen in surprise when I hand her the little cardboard box with the red emblem on top.

"You remembered?" she asks, a huge grin spreading across her face as she opens the lid.

"Of course," I say. "Dark chocolate truffles. Your favorite."

No way had I forgotten how much she liked the sweet confections from the candy store down the street from the high school.

She picks one up and takes a bite, closing her eyes and sighing with the most content look on her face. It's like… the sexiest thing I've ever seen.

After a long moment of savoring the chocolate, she lifts the remaining half of the truffle, offering it to me. I can't even describe the look in her eyes. It's more than friendship, more than want. Whatever it is runs much deeper than either of those things.

I could break the intensity. Reach up and take the chocolate from her with a laugh. Pop it in my mouth and make some kind of lighthearted remark, but the expression on her face stops me. The silence between us is so thick, so loud, there's no way can I ignore it.

Her bright green eyes sparkle even in the dim moonlight, and I never take my gaze from hers. I slide my hand from her elbow to her wrist, easily encircling the soft skin there. With a gentle pull, I bring her hand close enough that I can close my lips around the candy. Even though I'd known it was about to happen, my system is still electrified when my mouth makes contact with her fingers. Shocks, of the very best kind, barrel through me, and I have to fight the urge to moan at the pleasure of it.

I don't let go of her wrist, even after the chocolate's gone. Instead, I lean forward and press my mouth to hers, a soft brush of lips; just enough to make certain the sweetness of the moment is acknowledged.

"I brought more than truffles," I say, pulling back from her enough to look into her eyes.

She smiles, her eyelids lowered in curious flirtation. "Then don't keep me in suspense."

Lifting the lid on the cooler, I reach in and grab the

giant iced mocha with a dash of cinnamon and whipped cream topping.

"Is that…?" her voice trails off.

"Absolutely. Another one of your favorites."

She takes a long sip of the cold coffee, and the look of contentment on her face makes me feel like a million bucks.

"Asher," she says, pulling the straw away from her lips. "You remembered both these things?" She stops and shakes her head, like she still can't believe it.

For half a second I wonder if my brother ever even knew these things about her, much less remembered them. But then I silently reprimand myself for automatically thinking the worst of Adam and for bringing him in to a moment that's just about Grace and me.

"I remember everything, Grace." My eyes find hers again, and I pray she recognizes the sincerity in my expression. "I know you probably think I forgot about you, but I never did. And I'm so sorry that I hurt you."

She sighs like she's contemplating something important. I wait for her next words like they're essential to my existence. Which, I suppose, they are.

"I hope when you're ready you'll tell me what happened and why you stopped talking to me. I know you were going through a lot, trying to figure out what you were going to do with the rest of your life, and your parents' disapproval made things so much worse. But I hope you know, at least now, that I'm the one person who never would've judged your choice to leave college. Even back then, I was the one who didn't think you'd made the biggest mistake of your life."

"I know that now," I respond, placing a kiss on her forehead. "And I knew it then, too. I just got lost for a while."

She nods, but says nothing. Instead, she just fits her head onto my shoulder, nuzzling into my neck, and I'm consumed all over again by the happiness and love overflowing in my heart.

I slip my arm around her waist and hold her tight against me. For long moments we sit together that way, reveling in the silent comfort we have between us.

When I decide it's dark enough to see the stars, I move away from her slightly, straightening the wrinkles in the blanket.

"Time for your astronomy lesson," I say with a wink, which causes her to giggle.

I *so* love that sound.

"It's summer break," she argues in a fake voice. "I'm on a break from school."

"You'll like this class," I promise her, remembering how she always enjoyed the Navajo stories I shared with her. "Lay back and I'll start teaching."

"Yes, Mr. Howell," she teases, and once again I'm struck with how much I love the playful side of her. "Is this one of your grandfather's Navajo stories?"

"It is. And I think you'll like it."

"I remember a few weeks ago, right around the

time of the funeral, when the Navajo flags were lowered in honor after the last original codetalker died," she says. "I thought about the colors on the flag and what you told me."

It makes me smile that she remembered, even in the midst of all the grief and chaos surrounding Adam's death.

We lay back and position ourselves flat on our backs, facing the sky now bright with stars, and I begin to talk.

"When I was a very young boy, my grandfather told me the story of the Great Bear, which is the constellation Ursa Major. I can remember sitting next to him, staring up at the sky, and feeling a sense of amazement that out of all the billions of stars up there, a few could be connected to make something new. That's when I began to think artistically, when I first felt the desire to create. Being able to see how the dots connected to make a greater picture lit something inside me. Started the fire that drove me to become an artist. Because I wanted to create something beautiful and imaginative and new."

"Then the world owes your grandfather a great debt," she whispers. "Because the world would be a much less beautiful place without your creations."

In that instant, I almost roll over and tell her I love her. It's physically painful to hold the words in, but I know it's much too soon. I'm afraid if I spill everything to her I'll send her screaming in the opposite direction.

So I take a deep breath and continue.

"Do you see the Big Dipper?" I ask, pointing over to our left.

She takes a moment to find it, then nods.

"If you come this way from the dipper part, you can see the stars that make up the rest of the body of the bear."

She turns toward me, close enough that our bodies touch, and follows my finger as I trace the shape of the constellation.

"You have to imagine the lines connecting the stars in order to see the shape."

"I see it."

"Below the body are the legs." I point and trace those as she nestles even closer. "The Navajo legend says that Ursa Major, otherwise known as the Great Bear, came from the tale about the Changing Bear Maiden. The story says that a young girl decides to marry a bear and take him for her husband, although her family disapproves."

"I think I kind of agree with her family," Grace replies.

"Yeah, me too." I laugh with her. "Sometimes the legends are pretty far out there. But anyway, her younger sister tells their father. He kills the bear, and then the girl changes into a bear in order to get back at her family. When the younger sister and the seven brothers run away from the sister, she turns back into her human form and chases them, eventually killing six of the seven brothers."

"Morose, but interesting," she says.

"Right," I agree. "Then all of the brothers flew up into the sky and became Ursa Major, the Great Bear."

Grace lies back on the blanket, looking up at the stars. Not knowing what she's thinking, I reach my hand out and find hers, holding it tentatively, and we lay there next to each other. It's crazy how nervous I feel about holding her hand, especially since we've had our mouths plastered together more than once recently, but somehow holding hands seems even more intimate than the kisses. I slide my hand on top of hers, feeling her fingers grasp onto mine, and my heart soars.

I pick up our joined hands, raising them just enough so I can see them. The sight of our fingers woven together is almost more than I can stand. I can't believe after all this time we are in this place together.

Grace breaks the silence with whispered words.

"Is this weird for you?" she asks.

How do I answer that? Rather than trying to formulate a perfect response, I decide to be as honest as I can.

"A little." I pull our hands up so I can press a kiss to hers. "But I just don't care. Is it weird for you?"

She turns her head and smiles at me. I smile back because there's no way I can do otherwise.

"A little," she admits. "But it's also just really good and feels really right."

She turns back to look at the sky, but leaves our

hands clasped together and scoots close enough to me that our legs and shoulders are pressed against each other.

And in the quiet of the night, as we look up to the stars, I'm positive there is no other woman in the world for me.

Now I just have to figure out how to tell her.

Chapter 27

June 26, 2014

Asher

FOR THE NEXT week, Grace and I continue the same pattern. Except for the night I had dinner with my dad again, we hang out at her house or out back beyond the trees after dinner. She even came over to eat with Mom and me one night. We kept it light and didn't even sit next to each other at the table.

Our times alone are still the most precious moments I've ever spent. Just being near her fills me with something vital, but being able to touch her, being able to kiss her just because I want to, it's like I've been given every piece of my deepest dream.

Almost.

We still haven't talked about Adam and how her relationship with him – and his death – could affect us. Though I've wanted to a million times, I haven't told her that I love her, that I've loved her since the day I punched Tony Adkins right in front of her. And I still have no idea what her true feelings are where I'm concerned. Am I just a way to move on from her boyfriend's death? Is she surprised by what's developed between us? Or has she had feelings for me all along, the way I have for her?

I admit it. I've been reluctant to bring Adam up in conversation. I'm a chicken shit. I'm afraid of what she'll say if I start that conversation. Afraid the beautiful picture I've painted of the two of us in my mind will shred to pieces.

So, it's no surprise when I shove all the complications out of my mind as I'm driving home from work.

I'm completely stoked about tomorrow because I'm headed to Flagstaff for the day. It's been planned since I decided to hang around here in Greyson for a while, but once things heated up with Grace, I'd stopped counting the days until I'd be heading back there for a day.

I grab the phone from where it lays on the passenger seat of my car and dial Dad's number. He arranged the day off for me when he got me my old job back, but I just want to remind him.

"Dave Howell," he says when he picks up the phone. I don't know why he doesn't just look at the caller I.D. and see whether or not it's a business call. He doesn't have to be all formal with me.

"It's Asher."

"Hello, son."

"Listen, I just wanted to remind you about my day off tomorrow." I come to a stop at the light in front of the candy store and consider turning in to get Grace another box of truffles. But the thought of her triggers another idea, so I keep the car pointed toward home.

"Yes, it's on my calendar," he replies. "And I double checked with your supervisor and he's aware."

"Thanks. I've got to give Eric my half of the rent." The apartment the two of us share is pretty small and sparse, typical bachelor pad, but it's home and I love it. "Plus, I have a couple of appointments."

Being the newbie at Resolution Ink, I still don't get a lot of specific requests for appointments. I mainly handle the walk-in traffic, which is cool. I'm building my reputation, my clientele, and hopefully some of those folks will request me when they come in to get more work done.

The two appointments tomorrow were scheduled before Adam died. Bing offered to move them to other artists, but I didn't want to do that. If I'd been requested, I was going to do the work. My hands itch to feel the buzz of the tattoo gun, and though I'm not resentful at all to be here with Mom, I can't wait for the day I'll be back doing what I love.

"Be safe on the drive," Dad says.

"I think I'll see if Grace wants to come with me." I'm testing the waters, seeing how he'll react. I know he's got his suspicions about me and Grace, but something tells me he won't have as big an issue with it as Mom might. "It'll be a nice break for her to get out of town for a bit."

The thought of having Grace all to myself for an entire day and evening makes me smile. I can show her what my life is like, let her see me in my element. I'll take her to Bean Brew, the coffee shop where I worked for a while and still like to hang out. She could come with me to Resolution and see where I work.

"Well, if she goes with you, be even more careful." I know he means more than just driving safe, but he doesn't elaborate, for which I'm grateful.

We say our goodbyes and hang up as I'm pulling into the driveway. I know Grace is home. We texted during my lunch break. But I notice her mom's car is there as well.

So, I take a deep breath and head to their front door.

Chapter 28

Grace

I'M RUMMAGING THROUGH the refrigerator looking for a snack when the doorbell rings. We rarely have visitors who ring the bell, and the sound kind of startles me.

Mom looks up from the table where she's sorting the bills and says, "I'll get it."

Figuring it's some kind of salesperson, I continue my search through the fridge. I see nothing of interest, so I shut the door and decide on an apple just as I hear Mom's voice.

"Asher, this is a surprise."

Asher? At the front door?

I manage to stop myself from sprinting into the living room to see what this is all about and wait until I'm calm enough to walk out of the kitchen like a normal, sane person. The apple in my hand forgotten, I casually make my way to the front of the house.

Asher stands just inside the front door wearing the standard jeans and tee shirt work attire. Mom's asking him something about how he and Stella are doing, and I wonder what she thinks of the lip ring he kept hidden until after the funeral. For a moment, I stand just outside the room, watching and listening.

"We're doing okay," Asher says. "I guess no one is ever prepared to deal with something like this, but there've been moments in the last week or so when Mom seems to be rebounding. At least a little."

"I'm glad to hear that," Mom replies.

I step into the room and Asher sees me. All kinds of questions run through my mind. Why didn't you text me? Why didn't you come to my bedroom door? What could you possibly want to talk to my mom about?

"Grace visiting a couple times has been good for her," he says, nodding his head in my direction and alerting Mom to my presence.

"Hi Asher." I move closer to them, trying to gauge what's going on.

"I wanted to ask you something." He turns toward me, and with Mom behind him and unable to see his face, he smiles and winks.

"Okay." His expression tells me he has some kind of plan.

"I have to go to Flagstaff tomorrow," he begins, turning back so he can see both Mom and me. "I need to pay my roommate my half of the rent and take care of a few other things. I was wondering if you might want to come with me. I thought it might be good for you to get out of town for a day."

My pulse spikes. A whole day alone with Asher, with no one around who's aware of the situation. The depth with which I want this is startling.

"I know you have work and you might not be able to take off, so if you can't go I understand. I just wanted to make the offer."

And instead of just asking me himself, he'd come over and asked in front of my mom. Another girl might be irritated, but I see it for what it is. His attempt to make things less awkward with my parents and prevent me from having to do all the explaining.

I look at Mom and she doesn't seem disagreeable. I know she wouldn't try to stop me, but it's nice to know she isn't going to put up a fight.

"I think I can get the day off," I say. "I can call and ask, then text you."

Asher nods at me, then looks at my mom. "I figure we'll grab dinner once I'm done with my errands, then head back here after that. Is that okay?"

"If Grace wants to go and can get the time off from work, it's fine with me." Kudos to Mom for her choice of phrasing, letting me know that the decision is up to me. "Maybe she can show you where my sister and her husband live."

"Sure, Mom." I cut her off before she can go any further. I still haven't talked to Asher about my plans, other than to say I'm going to cosmetology school, and I don't want her to blurt it out. This trip to Flagstaff will be the perfect opportunity to tell him. "I'll do that."

"All right then," Asher says, looking at me once more. "I'll talk to you later, and we can make plans."

"Sounds good." And it did. I want to make plans with Asher for lots of things, but a trip to Flagstaff is a good place to start.

He slips out the door, and I stand there thinking that after just a week, it seems strange for him to leave my house without kissing me. A smile starts to form on my face, just thinking how much has changed between us.

Then I look at Mom, and she's eyeing me like she knows exactly what I'm thinking.

"You seem very anxious to go with him," she says.

I shrug. "It'll be fun."

"Yes." She makes the *mom* face that says she knows I'm being intentionally vague. "Asher is a very interesting young man."

Understatement of the year.

I bite into my apple and say nothing.

"I assume you've noticed that lip ring?" she asks.

I nod. I've noticed it. And felt it against my own lips.

"I thought he'd be covered in more tattoos," she goes on. "I only saw the one on his arm that stuck out below his sleeve."

"He has one on the other wrist," I say. "And he told me he has a large one on his upper back."

"Still though, you see people with tattoos all the

way down both arms. I guess that's what I was expecting."

"I'm sure he plans to get more eventually. It's not like you walk into a tattoo shop and walk back out an hour later completely covered. It takes time."

"I suppose." For a moment I think she's going to drop it, but no such luck. "You know your dad and I think the world of Stella, and we've always thought highly of Asher, too."

I heard the *but* coming a mile away.

"But it just seems like he's taken a very unconventional path."

"So?" Just one word, but I say it with all kinds of indignation.

"Well, it seemed harmless enough when the two of you became friends in high school, but Brian's always had concerns."

Seriously? She's throwing Brian's *concerns* in my face?

"Mom, I don't know if you realize this, but Brian was a jerk in high school. He thought anyone who looked different, dressed different, or hung out with different people had to be up to something dangerous or criminal. I'll grant that Brian's grown up a lot since then, but back in high school he was not the best judge of character. Especially Asher's."

Mom sighs. "But tattooing?"

"He's not running a prostitution ring or selling drugs, Mom," I say, exasperated. "He has a full time job that he fully supports himself with. And it's not like he's forcing tattoos on people. They come in because they want them. He's providing a service some people want."

"I just find it strange," she says, wrinkling her nose.

"Mom, you're a classy lady." I move to stand directly in front of her, and in the gentlest voice possible, I continue. "Don't be judgmental. It's not attractive."

She's taken aback by my words. I've never spoken to her like that, but I can't help but think it's important for people in her generation to not be so quick to make assumptions about people like Asher.

She nods. "I'll trust your judgment then."

I hug her, then grab my phone to arrange for my day off.

Chapter 29

Grace

"I'VE THOUGHT ABOUT getting a tattoo some day," I say to Asher later that night as we lay on the blanket out back, staring up at the star-filled sky.

"Seriously?" He sounds surprised, like he never thought anyone from his life here in Greyson would even consider it.

We've planned our day in Flagstaff tomorrow. It's an hour and half drive, so we're leaving in time to get there for lunch. Asher wants to take me to the coffee shop where he worked for a while. After that, he has a couple of appointments at Resolution Ink. I'm more than a little stoked to see him in his element.

"Yeah," I reply. "I've even looked at some potential drawings online." I wonder if it would totally freak him out if I ask him to tattoo me. The thought had crossed my mind more than a few times since he started his apprenticeship.

"When did you start thinking about a tattoo?" he asks, rolling on his side to face me.

"About the time you quit school," I admit, reaching down to zip my hoodie against the cool night air.

"You don't need to get a tattoo just because that's what I do for a living." I can hear the concern in his voice.

"It's not that," I say, but then backtrack a bit. I roll over and lean up on one elbow so that I'm facing him. "Well, not entirely. Before you started tattooing, I'd never thought much about them. I didn't think they were bad or anything. It was just not something that had ever crossed my mind. But once you started apprenticing, it made me wonder about the reasons people got tattoos. I started looking at them online, just out of curiosity, and I was kind of amazed, not just at the artistry, but at the symbolism and meaning behind them. Most people don't put something permanent on their bodies just because they think it's pretty. They choose something meaningful to them. I think that's pretty cool."

I hope my explanation put his mind at ease. Because if and when I finally ask him to tattoo me, I don't want him having any reservations.

He blinks. Once. Twice. As if trying to decide what to say. I'm about to start worrying that I've said something wrong, but then he speaks.

"I can't believe you looked into tattoo art just because of me," he whispers.

"I figured it was important to you," I say. "So I wanted to know more."

"My family didn't even do that. At least not that I know of. They've never even seen where I work."

I reach up, placing my palm against his cheek. "I'm so sorry they haven't been supportive. I think maybe Adam wanted to be more interested than he let on, but he was afraid to go against your mom and dad."

Asher nods. "That was always my thought, too. But Dad is trying to make up for it. He's going to a lot of effort to reconnect with me, as he puts it. He says he wants to come to Flagstaff once I'm back there for good, to see where I live and where I work."

"I'm glad. They should be proud of you. I am."

He leans forward, just enough to place his lips on mine. His kiss is soft, his lips slow and gentle. I know it won't be long before we have to go inside, so as not to raise suspicions about what we're doing out here together, but for the moment, I savor the feel and the taste of his lips against my own.

"Thank you," he whispers, pulling back to look in my eyes. "For believing in me."

"I always have, Asher," I whisper back. "And I always will."

Chapter 30

June 27, 2014

Asher

W E'RE COMING INTO Flagstaff on I-40 West when
Grace tells me her aunt and uncle live in one of
the neighborhoods close to Coconino High School. It
seems important to her to show me their house. Not
that I'm not interested, but it just seems odd. But hey,
Grace wants to show me, so since we've got plenty of
time to knock around and grab lunch before my
appointments, we take a quick detour to their neighborhood.

"Turn right at the next street, and their house is the
fourth one on the left," she tells me.

"Nice neighborhood," I say, turning on my blinker.
"Do they have kids?"

"One," she answers. "My cousin, Jennifer. She's
four years older than Brian. She got married last
Christmas and lives in Kingman now."

I slow the car as I approach the house. It's the typical bungalow style that's pretty common in this area. It

sits back a bit from the street, and the long driveway separates the house from a detached garage with the same style roof and windows.

"Do you all visit them here often?" I don't even try to kid myself about the reason I'm asking. I want to know if Grace might be in town from time to time once I'm back in Flagstaff to stay.

"Occasionally," she answers. "They come to Greyson more than we come here since Mom and Aunt Becca grew up there."

Trying not to sound to bummed, I say, "Yeah, that makes sense."

"The garage has an apartment above it," she says, her voice soft, as if she's nervous. "Other than the tiny bathroom, it's basically just one big room. They renovated it so Jennifer could live there while she went to NAU. I thought it was so cool that she got her own apartment."

"And it was probably way cheaper than a dorm or an apartment close to campus." I bring the car to a stop in front of the house and put it into park. "Do you want to go in and say hi?"

She shakes her head. "I'm sure they're both at work. I just wanted to show you where I'll be living when I start cosmetology school."

It takes a half a second for my mind to catch up, but when it does my heart slams against my chest with a force that's almost violent.

She's coming here?

She's coming here!

I'm almost afraid to respond, like maybe I heard her wrong and this amazing bubble will burst.

"You're coming to cosmetology school in Flagstaff?" I can't even find it in me to be ashamed at how shaky my voice sounds as I ask.

She nods, a small smile spreading across her face.

"Why didn't you tell me before?" Although it's not like it matters why she's just now revealing it. The fact is she's moving to Flagstaff. And I'm ecstatic.

"I don't know." She shrugs one shoulder. "I was afraid maybe you'd think it was weird."

"No way," I say, before bursting out in laughter. "I'm so freaking happy right now I could scream. Like, a totally non-masculine scream."

"Really?" she asks, her smile widening. "You're happy I'm coming here?"

I reach across to slide my palm against her cheek, pulling her gently toward me. Leaning so close our noses almost touch, I bury my other hand in her gorgeous red hair.

"Grace," I whisper. "How could I not be happy that you'll be so close to me?"

I feel her exhale, and the way the tension leaves her body is visible in the small space of my car's front seat. I don't know why she worried. In the back of my mind, I know she made these plans months ago, before Adam died and before the two of us reconnected. Logically, I know my being here had nothing to do with her decision to come to Flagstaff, but in this moment, I just don't care. She will be here, in the same city as me, where no one has any preconceived notions about what she and I should or shouldn't be to one another because of my brother.

Because there's no way I can keep from it, I seal my lips to hers. I don't take it further because that's not the kind of kiss this moment calls for. Instead, we linger in a gentle brush of lips that says everything I'm too afraid to say out loud to her.

After a long moment, I pull back and say, "How about some lunch?"

She nods, the enthusiasm in her smile absolutely brilliant.

I head toward downtown, and my heart feels lighter than it has in a very long time.

Chapter 31

Grace

U GLY MUG IS a crazy cool coffee shop. Located a block or so off Butler Avenue and close to the NAU campus, the mugs they serve coffee in aren't actually ugly. They're just varied. And that's putting it mildly.

A series of shelves behind the cash register contain mugs of every shape, size, and color combination known to man. It's a total eye-catcher. And the rest of the place doesn't disappoint. The exposed brick on the interior walls is probably part of the original structure. The rustic look of the brick contrasts nicely with the bright chrome light fixtures and mismatched tables and chairs.

It's like every ultra-hip young adult hangout I've ever imagined.

"Were you like a master barista when you worked here?" I ask, bumping Asher with my shoulder as we stand at the counter, looking over the menu.

"Hardly," he says. "Although I did learn a few

tricks while I was here. I mainly bussed tables and ran food to the customers."

Just then a twenty-something guy with blond hair and gauged ears comes out from the kitchen.

"Asher Howell," he calls. "You back in town?"

"Just for the day," Asher answers. "Got a couple of appointments this afternoon."

"I heard about your brother, man," the guy says, shaking Asher's hand and pulling him in for one of those side hugs that guys are known for. "That sucks. Everybody here's been thinking about you."

"Thanks." Asher nods. "I appreciate it."

The guy looks at me, back to Asher, then at me again and says with a wink, "Are you gonna introduce me? She's a looker."

"Shut up, Gabe," Asher snarls, pretending to be irritated. He slides an arm around me and goes on. "But you're right. She is gorgeous. This is Grace Ballard. Grace, this is Gabe Jenkins. We got hired here at the same time. Gabe's worked his way up to manager."

"All without sleeping with the boss," Gabe deadpans.

"He's a little irreverent," Asher informs me.

I like Gabe immediately.

"It's nice to meet you, Gabe." I reach out to shake his hand and notice the star tattoo on his forearm.

"Nice to meet you as well," Gabe responds and nods toward his ink. "And yeah, that's his work."

"I thought it might be."

"So this is *the* Grace, huh?" Gabe asks Asher.

Asher waits a beat before responding, and in that second all sorts of thoughts run through my mind. Does this guy know I dated Adam? Or has Asher talked about me with his friends here?

"Yeah," Asher answers. "The Grace from next door."

His answer is kind of ambiguous, but he doesn't mention Adam, so I'm going to go with the notion that Gabe doesn't know that I dated Asher's brother my entire senior year of high school.

"Ready to order?" Asher asks.

We step to the counter and place our orders. Asher orders black coffee with a shot of espresso and a ham and provolone panini. I decide on the vegetable frittata topped with chipotle sour cream, served with sourdough toast, and a macadamia nut white mocha to go along with it.

Gabe rings us up, and Asher pays, refusing to let me chip in. The receipt prints and Gabe steps up to the window into the kitchen.

"The panini and frittata are for our man Howell," Gabe yells. "So nobody spit in it!"

Chapter 32

Asher

GABE MAKES SURE I get my favorite mug – the one covered in graffiti art. I figure it's also no accident that Grace has one covered in hearts of all different colors. Gabe's pretty perceptive.

"Oh my gosh," Grace says after a bite of her frittata. "This is so good."

"Yeah." I smile across the table. "The food here's as good as the coffee."

We dig into our food, and I can't help but notice that though several of my former coworkers wave from behind the counter, no one comes over to speak. I imagine that's also Gabe's doing. He's making sure Grace and I have some privacy. Even though he has no idea how complex our relationship is, he's effectively given us our first real date.

Grace finishes her lunch and slides her plate to the side. She reaches into her bag and pulls out a piece of paper. As I'm downing the last of my coffee, she places the paper on the table in front of me.

"What do you think?" she asks.

On the paper is a picture of a tree branch. It's simple, just a straight branch with two small pieces forking off from the main part, along with four small leaves, as if the tree is just beginning to bud.

"I looked for a long time before I found one that looked like I wanted," she says. "And this one's still not perfect, but I thought maybe you could modify it some."

And then it hits me. It's the tattoo she wants. I sit there kind of dumbfounded. When she talked about it last night, I thought getting a tattoo was just an idea she'd flirted with. It never occurred to me that she'd be this serious.

"I like the symbolism," she says, pointing to the small leaves on the branch. "New life, new beginnings. It's how I feel about this time in my life. Like, I'm finally moving out of Brian's shadow and becoming me."

I still haven't said anything. Too many things running through my head. Grace wants ink? Holy cow! The thought is so freaking sexy. Would she want me to do it? Probably. Could I even hold my hand steady enough? I'd have to, because when she's serious about it, it's got to be me. There's no way I can let Bing, Shane, or anyone else put their hands on her.

"You've really thought a lot about this," I finally say. This isn't some trendy piece of ink that exists just so the person can say they have a tattoo.

"I have."

"You want to get this today?" I ask, my heart racing. Imagining marking her skin has me all kinds of torn up. In a good way.

"Yes," she says. "Well, only if you have time."

"I have time." My words are quick, because no way do I want her questioning whether or not I'll do this for her. But then another thought creeps in. "What will your parents say?"

Grace is of age, but I still wonder what their reactions would be.

"I don't know." She shrugs her shoulders. "I know that I don't want them to know, at least not yet. Not because I want to be dishonest with them, but because I want it to be about me, you know? This is something I want for myself. I've been what everyone expected for a long time. Or at least I've tried to be. They expected me to be like Brian, and it took a long time for them to come to terms with the fact that I'm not a brainiac like him. And I know they've never been disappointed in me, but it's hard for them to understand that I don't have the same kind of ambitions he does. So, this is my way of breaking free of those expectations. Because I've always wanted to be daring and creative. I want to make a statement about myself. And I don't want to have to explain it or justify it to anyone."

The smell of a freshly brewing pot of coffee hits my senses and I grab both our mugs. "How about we talk about specifics over a refill?"

"Okay," she says. "Just plain coffee with cream this time."

It only takes a minute before I return with our filled mugs of coffee, but it's long enough that I've gotten a handle on the shock and euphoria of Grace wanting a tattoo. Maybe now I can discuss things with her without grinning like a crazy fool.

"Just to be clear," I begin, taking a sip of my coffee. "You want me to do this? Because if you'd rather have one of the others, that's okay." Well, not really, but I'll grit my teeth through it if it's what she wants.

"Of course I want you to do it." She seems surprised that I'd even ask her that. "Who else?"

"I just didn't want you to feel like it had to be me," I explain. "Some people are uncomfortable having someone they know personally do their work."

"Well, I can't imagine being comfortable with anyone but you."

Relief swims through me.

"Next question." I stop and watch her take a drink, then drag my thoughts away from the sight of her lips on the edge of the mug. "Where do you want this tattoo?"

"That's where I need your advice," she says, sitting her mug to the side and leaning across the table on her elbows. "I want it somewhere that I can cover it up pretty easily, but I don't want it somewhere that I can't see it. So, not on my back or anything like that."

"A lot of girls have their work done on their sides,"

I explain. "It's actually a really attractive place, very feminine, but if you wear a two piece bathing suit it'll show."

And just like that, images of Grace in a bikini filter into my mind. I take a deep breath and calm myself.

"Another option is just below the waist line, either off to one side or in the center below the navel." I force myself not to think about that part of her body. "You'd still have to be careful choosing a swim suit if you didn't want the ink to show, but it would be concealed by your everyday clothing."

"I like that idea," she says. "Maybe on the right side."

"I think that's the best place, too," I agree. "Your design will work nice there, especially once we size it proportionally."

"I've never been sure about color." She turns the design sideways on the table and points to the leaves. "Sometimes I think I'd like the leaves green and the branch brown, but then I also like the idea of regular black ink."

"Have you ever thought about white ink?" I ask. I don't know why I didn't think of it before. "It's *there*, but not as easy to see without looking close. It's not so *in your face*. It would be like our little secret."

And damn, if I didn't like the idea of the two of us having our own secrets.

"Sounds interesting," she says.

"White ink can be a little persnickety. It can discol-

or in the sunlight, but with where you're putting it won't get a ton of sun anyway. I can show you some pictures at the shop and you can see what you think."

"Then let's go." She hops up from her seat and offers me her hand.

Of course, I take it and follow her out the door.

Chapter 33

Grace

RESOLUTION INK SITS between a used bookstore and clothing boutique. Just a short drive from Ugly Mug, it's still close enough to campus that it's easy for college kids to find.

Asher swings his car into a lot behind the building that I assume is for employees. The other vehicles in the lot consist of a Harley Davidson motorcycle, a bright red old Ford truck, and a vintage Volkswagen van painted yellow. Asher's ten-year-old Mazda R-X, that he's had since high school, seems rather tame in comparison.

"Just a heads up," he says, putting the car in park and turning toward me. "Everyone here is pretty tatted up, and there are a few more piercings than what I have, too."

"I'm not going to gasp in shock, Asher." Although it's sweet of him to forewarn me.

"I know you won't, but it can be kind of over-whelming to take it all in at once." He pulls the keys from the ignition. "And Shane is even more improper than Gabe, even though he means nothing by it."

"Don't worry," I say, opening my door. "I can hold my own."

He meets me at the back of the car and pulls me to him for a kiss. Quick, but scorching, my knees are wobbling by the time we pull apart.

"You can hold my own, too," he says with a wink, then grabs my hand and heads inside.

We use the front entrance to Resolution instead of the employee entrance in the back. Asher says it's so I can get the full effect, but I figure he doesn't want me to walk by the tattoo stations and get freaked out by an up close look at the process.

The lobby is amazing. The hardwood floors are stained a dark, mahogany color, and the walls are painted a deep, burgundy red. Black trim along the floor and ceiling, as well as around the various door facings, completes a trendy, modern interior.

Hand in hand, we walk right up to a counter consisting of a clear case full of what I assume are lip rings and eyebrow rings, and probably a lot of other rings that I'd rather not think about. Behind the counter is a young twenty-something girl with jet-black hair that hangs in gorgeous waves around her shoulders. Her nose is pierced and when she looks up at us and smiles, I see she also has a silver stud just below her bottom lip.

"Hey Asher," she says. "Good to have you back for the afternoon."

"Thanks." He drapes an arm around my shoulder. "Grace, this is Rachelle Taya. She keeps this place running. Rachelle, this is Grace Ballard."

"Happy to meet you, Grace." Rachelle stands and extends her hand. "Asher's told us about you. All good things."

"Nice to meet you, Rachelle." Again, I wonder how much these people know about me and Adam.

"I'm going to show her around a bit before my first appointment," Asher says. "After that is it all right if she hangs out here with you while I finish up with my clients?"

"Of course. We'll be BFFs by the time you're done!"

From the lobby area, Asher leads me down a short hallway. Each of the four tattoo rooms has a large window that allows those in the lobby a glimpse of the work going on inside. Blinds on each window can be pulled down for privacy if a tattoo requires a client to remove clothing.

The first room we stop by is Bing's. As the owner of the shop, he has the room closest to the lobby. Asher pokes his head in to speak to his boss.

"Good to see you, Asher." Bing looks up from the man's bicep he's currently working on. "How are things?"

"One day at a time," Asher answers. "But we're all doing okay, I guess. This is Grace."

"Hello, Grace." Bing nods toward me. "I'd shake

your hand, but…"

"No worries. Nice to meet you, Bing."

Unlike Asher's hair, with long, dark bangs and the shaggy length on his neck, Bing's hair is trimmed into a buzz cut. Both arms are covered in full sleeve tattoos, mostly black ink with a few spots of color. I guess him to be in his early to mid-thirties.

Asher and Bing talk business for a moment. It's so interesting to see Asher here, in the place where he found his path. He's so proud of everything here. I never went along with his parents' disappointment when he came to work here, but now I'm even more sure.

This is the exact place he should be.

The next room is Shane's, and it's there I see what Asher meant with the warning about piercings. In addition to multiple piercings on his left eyebrow, Shane also has a barbell looking piece piercing the bridge of his nose. Some might find him menacing looking, but when he looks up from where he's arranging his station and grins, the bright blue of his eyes makes him look boyishly cute. His baby blond hair is short around the neck and ears, but long enough on top to be spiked in every conceivable direction.

"Hey man!" He walks over fist bumps Asher, then pulls him in for a hug that completely contradicts his appearance. "Are you doing okay? I've been worried about you."

"I'm making it, bro," Asher responds. "Shane, this

is Grace. Grace, meet Shane Dawson."

We shake hands and exchange the normal pleasantries. He's polite and cheerful, and I have no idea what Asher meant about him being *improper.*

"Dude, you should've been here yesterday," Shane says. "Dex did a Jacob's Ladder on this guy's dick, and he screamed like a little baby the entire time."

Okay. Apparently he has no filter. Not that I'm offended or anything. I'm actually pretty amused.

"Shane." Asher tilts his head toward me. "Manners."

"Oh hell." Shane turns toward me. "Apologies, Grace."

"It's okay," I say, still laughing. "I'm sure you guys aren't used to having to watch your language."

"Dex isn't here today," Asher explains. "He's the piercing guru, but he's only part-time."

"Caleb's out this week, too," Shane says. "On vacation in San Diego."

"I should get my station set up." Asher threads his fingers through mine. "Grace is going to hang with Rachelle while I'm working, then she's got a small piece I'm going to do for her."

"You sure you want him touching you, sugar?" Shane asks, wiggling his pierced eyebrow. "Because if not, I'll be happy to."

"Shut up, Shane," Asher barks.

I can't help but laugh.

Such an unconventional crew. I really, really like

them.

I watch as Asher readies his room, sanitizing every-thing and setting supplies onto the counter. It's all very clinical and methodical, kind of like when the dentist gets out all the tools necessary to clean your teeth. But still, I'm fascinated while watching him work. He's so happy here. His spirit is light.

He glances at the clock above the door, then back at his station. He nods, satisfied that everything is ready.

"Let me get you some pictures to look at," he says. "You can look through them while you hang with Rachelle."

I take the drawing from my bag and hand it to him. "I want you to put your own touches on this. Make it unique. I want it to be your design."

He nods, a smile spreading across his face. Without warning, he presses his mouth against mine, hard and fast. "I'll do something nice for you. Promise."

When we return to the lobby, Rachelle has pulled one of the comfy, overstuffed chairs from the waiting area behind the counter. She's also apparently raided the snack room because several cans of soda, a package of chocolate chip cookies, and a bag of chips are spread out on her desk area.

"I wasn't sure what you liked to snack on, so I got a bit of everything," Rachelle says.

"I'm not picky," I say. "But this is totally unneces-sary."

"Don't argue when she gets an idea," Asher says.

"Can it, Asher," Rachelle scolds. "I deal with you boys all the time. Don't judge me for being excited that we have a girl in the mix now!"

Asher just laughs, and I'm just really touched at her easy acceptance.

I settle into the chair, and Asher hands me a small photo album. "These are white ink pieces that we've done here. I did the large quote on the girl's back and the small flower on the ankle. The others are mostly Bing's work."

As soon as I open the album, I know that he's right about the white ink. It's exactly what I want. Dainty and feminine. You really have to look to see the details. I like that... that you have to make an effort to see beyond the obvious. It's kind of – I don't know – poetic. A metaphor about looking beneath the surface of a person to find out who they really are.

Before I know it, Rachelle and I have killed half a bag of potato chips and Asher's first appointment is over. I can't see the tattoo, since his bicep is covered in protective black plastic, but the man seems very pleased and compliments Asher as he steps up to the counter. Rachelle collects the payment and hands him a sheet with aftercare instructions, along with a small tube of ointment.

The bell above the door rings, and in walks a blonde with a skirt that barely constitutes clothing. I look down at my pink peasant skirt that comes almost to my ankles and suddenly feel inadequate. I thought I was being a bit edgy by pairing the skirt with a cream colored spaghetti strap tank, but one look at the boobs spilling out of Amazon woman's v-neck tee, and I realize my efforts were futile. Add to that, the blonde's about a hundred feet tall with legs half that length, and yeah... she's every girl's nightmare.

"Asher!" she squeals, and her voice is as grating as her appearance. "It's been forever!" She saunters up next to him and threads her arm through his.

I want to vomit.

Asher looks panicked, his eyes darting from the blonde to Rachelle.

Rachelle double-checks the computer and nods, I assume confirming that this chick is Asher's next appointment.

"Why don't you go on back," he says. "I'll be right there."

She pouts a little, but does as he says. Once she's out of earshot, Asher approaches the counter.

"I didn't recognize the name," Rachelle says, her voice apologetic. "She made the appointment under Elizabeth instead of Lizzie."

"I totally spaced on it, too," Asher replies. "She just wants the infinity sign on her ankle right? Did I at least remember that correctly?"

Rachelle nods and clicks a couple of places, then the printer buzzes to life. She grabs the paper and hands it over to Asher. "I'm sure you already looked at this, but here it is again just in case."

"This won't take long," he mutters, turning to head down the hall. "Thank God."

I look at Rachelle for some sort of explanation. She shrugs her shoulders, rolling her chair over to where I sit. "Tattoo shops tend to accumulate fans. Especially reputable shops like this one. Sometimes fans are a good thing because they spread the word about our business and help build our reputation. Other fans are not so great. Lizzie is one of our more annoying ones."

"Oh," I say, because I have no other response.

"No worries, Grace." Rachelle pats my arm and hands me a cookie. "I've seen the way all the guys in this place look at her. And I've seen the way Asher looks at *you*. Don't give that trollop another thought."

She's right. Clearly, Asher is not thrilled to see Lizzie. Anything but, actually. And he's never been the type who goes for over-exposed girls who reek of desperation. Asher is better than that, and I, of all people, know it.

So I pull my mind from the girl in his tattoo chair and focus on the fact that I'll be sitting in that chair myself shortly.

Tremors of excitement flutter through me, and I can't help the giggle that escapes.

I'm getting a tattoo today.

Chapter 34

Asher

I'VE NEVER BEEN so glad for a tat to be over. I can't believe I overlooked the fact that my second appointment of the day was with Lizzie. Of course, she did manage to conceal her identity by using her actual first name when she made the appointment.

Maybe she's not as dumb as she comes across.

But I'm still dumb as shit for ever associating with her. Waves of guilt roll through me as I walk her up to the counter so she can pay and get out of here. Thank goodness she only wanted that small piece done on her ankle, which didn't take long and didn't require me to get up close and personal with her *parts*.

But Lord help me if she says one more word about nipple piercings while we're out in the lobby. While I worked on her ankle, she'd tried her best to "show me" why she thought she was the perfect candidate for nipple rings. I told her if she wanted her ink done right she was going to have to be quiet and let me work, and that if she was serious about any sort of piercing, she needed to talk to Dex.

Let Dex have his turn being the object of her obsession.

Lizzie walks too close to me as we near the counter. I can feel Grace's eyes on me, but I can't make myself look at her. Somehow I know that if I meet Grace's gaze, it'll make Lizzie seem important, and that's something I definitely don't want. So instead, I just ignore Lizzie's overtures and keep my eyes focused on the counter.

Plus, I'm just ashamed of myself. I did a lot of stupid things in my attempt to forget about Grace, and I've never regretted them more than I do at this moment.

"Rachelle will get you squared away," I say. "I'm going to get started on my next appointment."

Lizzie starts to say something, but Rachelle launches into a detailed list of aftercare instructions, forcing Lizzie's attention to the paper on the counter. Thank goodness for Rachelle. I totally owe her for bailing me out.

"Grace, you ready?" I ask.

"Absolutely." She pops up out of her seat and walks toward me. She seems completely unfazed by Lizzie and her obvious agenda. Her smile is the same – bright and full of joy. Relief that I can't describe descends on me.

I reach out my hand, intending to motion for her to walk ahead of me, but instead she grabs my hand and twines our fingers together. My heart expands almost painfully. Neither of us looks back to see if Lizzie has seen our joined hands, because she doesn't matter. Grace isn't trying to make a statement to her. She's making a statement *about us.*

We get back to the room, and Grace hops up in the chair like she's done it a hundred times. I don't know what she's feeling inside, but outside she's calm and cool.

And I'm all kinds of nervous. Part of me can't believe she's putting this much trust in me, but I'm so honored that she is. I'm determined to do a good job for her because this is the most important tattoo I've ever done.

It's almost like I'm marking her as mine. I know that's not it, but I can't help but think this will somehow link us together in some kind of cosmic way.

"You nervous?" I ask, needing words to fill the silent spaces and ease my nerves.

"Not really," she answers. "I mean, I'm not a fan of needle sticks, but I'm not afraid of it. And I trust you, so that makes it easy."

My heart slams against my rib cage. Good grief, I'm completely undone by this girl.

I pick up the design I've created for her and offer it, hoping she likes what I've done. I stand next to her as she studies it, looking down at the drawing and attempting to see it through her eyes.

It's the same basic idea, but I added a few more offshoots from the main branch, several more tiny, budding leaves, and I curved the branch so that once it's on her skin, it will curve just to the inside of her pelvic bone and flow with the natural shape of her body. Despite my best intentions, everything in me reacts to the thought of touching the skin on that part of her body.

And yeah… I don't need to think about her body in *that* way right now.

"I love it," she whispers. She points to the curved area and continues. "I love this curve and the bit of shadow you created."

"The curve will go this way." I demonstrate on my own body where the design will be placed. "Kind of work with the natural shape. The top part of the branch might show above the waist of a bikini bottom, but not much. And with the white ink, it won't be too noticeable."

"It's perfect." She smiles up at me. "I can't wait."

I'm humbled. There's no other word for it. Grace has always had such faith in me, and she still does, even though for nearly two years I've done nothing to deserve it.

"All right," I say, trying to get a grip on my emotions. "If you're satisfied with it, I'll go make the transfer, and then we'll get started."

"I'll be waiting," she says with a grin.

Within minutes, I'm back in the room, transfer in hand. I lay it gently on the counter and walk over to the chair.

"I'm just going to lean the chair so you're lying flat, okay?"

She nods and leans her head back against the head-rest.

I maneuver the chair so the back is flat, then drop the arm rests to a comfortable level for her. I slide my rolling chair to the side and pick up the transfer.

"Okay," I begin, forcing myself to be professional, which is crazy difficult because this isn't some random client. This is Grace. "I need you to roll up your shirt and roll down the top of your skirt so I can see where I'm going to be working. But don't worry. You don't have to expose anything, well, *personal.*"

Like a champ, Grace grabs the hem of her tank top and folds it up. I try not to guess how close she gets to her breasts. That's just… not appropriate for the situation. But, seriously, I'm a guy and I'm crazy about her, so my mind goes there anyway.

I look away, pretending to busy myself with the supplies on my counter as she does the same with the waistband of her skirt.

"Ready," she says, just as I'm snapping on my black gloves.

I take a deep breath and put my game face on. I put what I need on the moveable cart, then roll it over to my seat. I don't look at her face as I plop down into my chair. I'm afraid if I do, she'll see exactly how affected I am by this bit of her exposed skin.

"First I'm going to wipe the skin down to sanitize

it," I say, gently swabbing the area with the prep cloth. "The next stuff you'll feel is gel. This is what allows the transfer stencil to adhere to your skin."

Grace is silent and still, and as I press the transfer paper onto her gelled skin, I decide to risk a glance at her, just to make sure she's okay. Her eyes are closed as if she's concentrating.

"You doing all right?" I ask, worried that maybe this is just a little too weird for her.

"I'm fine," she whispers. "Just trying to be calm."

I gently peel the transfer paper back, revealing the design on her skin. It lays perfectly on the contours of her body, and in white ink it's going to be beautiful.

"See what you think." I help her up onto her elbows so she can take a look at the placement. "It stays to the left of this bone," I say, gently touching the point of the bone on the right side of her abdomen. "But it curves along beside it."

"Wow," she breathes. "I can't wait to see the finished product."

"We're good to go then?" I ask. "Because if you're having second thoughts, it's okay."

She shakes her head. "No way. I'm doing this."

"Grace," I begin, thinking about the unpleasant aspects that come next. Touching her skin is like heaven, but knowing what the tattoo needle feels like, I'm not relishing the thoughts of hurting her with it. "There's nothing I can do to make this not hurt. I wish I could. It's not that terrible, but it does sting."

"Asher, you're so sweet to worry about me." She presses a soft kiss to my cheek, then lays back down. "But I'm tougher than I look."

I know that's true.

So I sit down and get to work.

After a moment, I feel myself slip into the zone where nothing else exists but me and the image I'm creating. I smile to myself as the design begins to come together on her skin, even though with each strike of the needle I cringe inside, knowing it's hurting her. Once the outlining is complete, I breathe a sigh of relief.

"The worst is over," I say to her. "Outlining is the toughest part. The shading won't sting near as bad."

"Okay," she says, her eyes closed and her breathing even. "I'm doing fine."

"I know you are," I say, turning back to the tattoo.

"How much will I owe you for this?" she asks.

"Not a thing." The truth is, she'll never owe me a thing. "This one's on the house."

"Asher, you can't do that," she argues.

"Oh yes I can." Damned if I'll let her pay me for the privilege of doing her first tattoo.

"At least let me pay for the supplies," she says. "Even if you won't let me pay you for your time."

"Grace, it's non-negotiable." I pause what I'm doing and look up at her. "I'm honored you wanted me to do this for you. It's my gift. Please just accept it."

She presses her lips together and closes her eyes. I

wonder for a second if I've pissed her off.

"In that case, thank you. It means a great deal to me."

Satisfied that she understands how important this is to me, I return to the business at hand.

When it's done, I'm more proud of this ink than any other large, intricate piece I've ever done. Because it's on her. And because she trusted me to do it. And yeah, because every time she looks at it she'll think of me.

"We're done, Grace," I say, wiping the area down one last time. "But when you look at it, it'll look kind of purple. That's just the stencil ink. It'll fade away over the next few days."

I help her out of the chair and walk her over to the full-length mirror on the back of the door. She holds her tank top up as she looks, and I watch as her eyes fill with tears.

"It looks red and puffy now," I say, praying she's not disappointed. "That's just from the needle. It'll go away in the next day or so. And once the stencil fades, you'll be left with just the white ink."

"It's beautiful." Her voice is soft and I notice a tear spill down one cheek. "So much better than I ever imagined."

"Good." I swallow hard, overcome with emotion. "I'm so glad you're happy with it."

"I love it," she whispers, still staring at it in the mirror. A second later her eyes find mine in our reflections, and she says, "Thank you."

I can't not kiss her then. There's just no way I can keep from it. So I don't even try. I turn her to face me and frame her face in my hands. Lowering my lips to hers, I say a silent prayer that what we feel for each other right now will stay with us forever.

Her hands are trapped between us as she holds on to her shirt, and I'm careful not to brush up against the newly tattooed skin. As I move my mouth over hers, I'm astounded all over again that this remarkable young woman wants me.

But for how long? The nagging question creeps into my thoughts, and I shove it away, banishing it from this moment. We've avoided talking about Adam and all the potential implications his death – and his relationship with Grace – for this long. A while longer won't hurt.

Right now she's mine. We've just shared something completely different than she and Adam ever shared – or ever would've shared.

Surely that means something. I know it does to me.

Chapter 35

Grace

ONCE WE LEAVE Resolution, we grab an early dinner at a Mexican restaurant. I'm not terribly hungry after all the snacking Rachelle and I did, but it's difficult to resist tableside guacamole and the sizzling steak fajitas that we split.

"How's it feel?" Asher asks for like the twentieth time, nodding toward the site of my new tattoo.

"It's fine," I say, smiling at him from across the table. It's covered in a dry lock pad, which Asher said protects it while also allowing the skin to breath. "Stop worrying."

"Can't help it." He grins as he pops another chip in his mouth. "You can take the cover off it when we get back tonight. Just be sure to use the ointment Rachelle gave you."

"I'll take good care of it. I promise. And if I have any questions, I'll just text Rachelle," I say with a giggle.

He flashes his eyes at mine, then shakes his head

and laughs.

"Last stop for the day is my apartment," he says. "I just need to give Eric my rent money, then we'll head back to Greyson."

The waiter returns with our check and a box for our leftovers. Again, Asher pays the entire bill and won't even let me take care of the tip. I've felt like a princess the whole day, which I realize may have been his plan all along. I think about Brian's preconceived notions about Asher in high school and Mom's uneasiness about him the other day. There's so much more to him than anyone realizes, and it makes me a little angry that so many have misjudged him just because he looks a bit different and because he's taken a untraditional path.

As we leave the restaurant, I look off to the left toward the mountains. I've been to Flagstaff plenty of times, but the scenery never fails to take my breath.

"I love this city," I say, leaning into Asher as he wraps his arm around my waist. "It always amazes me how you just wind up the interstate, higher and higher, and then all of a sudden a city's just nestled there in the middle of the pines."

"Yeah." We round the passenger side of the car, and he opens my door. "The landscape never gets old."

Asher slides in the driver's side and cranks the car, easing out of the parking lot and into traffic.

"So, my roommate, Eric, is a typical college guy," he says. "Likes to party. Doesn't take life too seriously."

"Isn't that most college guys?" I ask, wondering where he's heading with this line of conversation.

"I guess to some degree, most guys go through that phase. It's just not my scene anymore."

"Do you and Eric not get along or something?" It would really suck to have a roommate he didn't like.

"We get along fine," Asher answers. "We're friends, but I don't want to live there long-term. I don't think we'd stay friends if I did."

"Makes sense," I say, thinking about the fact that even though he's technically college-age, he's totally different in terms of maturity and responsibility. "I guess you look at things differently because you've already started your career and you work full-time."

"We just have different priorities," he says. "When I texted him to let him know I was coming by to drop off my rent money, he told me that his sister and her boyfriend are here for the weekend. Apparently they're both starting at NAU this fall and came up to look for jobs. I have no idea what to expect when we get there, so be prepared for anything."

"Have you thought about getting your own place?" I ask.

Asher nods. "Shane and Caleb rent a sweet condo. The other guy that lives with them is graduating in December and moving back to Phoenix. I'm moving in with them once he leaves."

"That sounds dangerous." I nudge him in the shoulder. "Three tattoo artists in one condo."

Asher laughs. "The three of us are actually pretty sedate in comparison to what most people thing tattooists are like. Shane sewed his wild oats in high school and pretty much prefers the Xbox to a loud party any day."

"How old is Shane?" I ask. "At first I thought he was older than you, but when he smiled he looked almost the same age."

"He's twenty-one. I don't know his entire story, but he dropped out of school at sixteen, got into some trouble in New Mexico. Drugs and stuff, I guess. He had a cousin who worked as a tattooist in Albuquerque. He managed to get Shane an apprenticeship in the shop where he worked, then apparently threatened his life if he screwed it up."

"How long has he been at Resolution?"

"A couple of years," he says. "He finished his apprenticeship when he was nineteen, then worked for a few months at the shop where he apprenticed. But I think the crowd he used to run with in Albuquerque became too much of a temptation, so he took the proactive approach and moved away."

"I really like him," I admit. "Even with no filter. He seems kind."

"Yeah, he is." Asher smiles, cutting his eyes toward me. "I'm glad you see that in him. He's paid his dues and learned his lessons."

"What about Caleb?"

"Caleb's from Kentucky," Asher says. "Came out

here on vacation one summer and discovered the prettiest girls in the world are in Arizona."

"Yeah, right," I say with a giggle.

"Seriously." Asher laughs along with me. The sun is beginning its descent, casting shadows in the interior of the car. "He said he just wanted a change when he got out of high school, and he remembered all the pretty girls from when he and his family came to the Grand Canyon on vacation."

"That's hysterical! Who moves across the country just because they saw good-looking women in a city?"

"Apparently, Caleb does." He turns on his left signal and we make our way toward an apartment complex at the end of the street. "He never had any intention of going to college. He just moved out here and got a job with a crew that painted the interior of rental properties. After a few months, word got out that he could draw and paint, and people started hiring him to paint murals in their kids' rooms. Tattooing had always been in the back of his mind, kind of like me. Bing took him on as an apprentice a couple of years before I came along."

"So he's older than you?"

"Twenty-four."

He pulls into a space at the apartment building, bringing the car to a stop under one of the lights in the parking lot.

"This shouldn't take long," he says. "The apartment's a total bachelor pad. No decorations. Thrift store furniture. So don't look too hard at anything."

"Quit worrying." I open my door and step out, leaning on the roof to look at him across the top of the car. "I'm not going to decide I don't like you if your apartment is plain or messy."

"Just consider yourself warned."

Chapter 36

Asher

GRACE AND I climb the outside steps up to the second level. It feels a bit weird to be knocking on the door of my own apartment, but since Eric has company, I decide to be considerate.

When Eric opens the door, I'm pleasantly surprised. It's Friday night, and he and his sister and her boyfriend have two large pizzas on the table and a movie playing on the television. Beer is noticeably absent. It's almost weird to see Eric with a can of soda when a pizza is present, but he's always been protective of his sister, so I guess he's doing the typical big brother thing.

"You guys eat yet?" Eric asks. "We've got plenty of pizza."

"Thanks, but we grabbed dinner on the way here." We step inside, and I push the door closed behind me. "This is Grace Ballard, by the way."

"Hey Grace." Eric shakes her hand in a surprisingly good show of manners. "Eric Sanchez."

"Nice to meet you," Grace says.

"Hey, this is my sister, Natalia, and her boyfriend, Chase."

The two of them look up from the movie to wave and say hi.

"They have any luck with the job search?" I ask, pulling my wallet from my pocket and handing Eric the rent money.

"Put in a bunch of applications," he says. "Headed out to look again tomorrow."

"We've got to head back to Greyson." I reach for Grace's hand. "But I need to grab a thing or two from my room."

"Sure, man." Eric leans closer and lowers his voice. "I wasn't about to let the two of them sleep together in your bed. I told Chase no way was he screwing my sister in my apartment. He's taking the top bunk in my room and she's using the pull-out couch."

And yeah… more information than I really wanted. At least my bed was undefiled.

Grace and I make our way down the short hall, covered in the same tan carpet as the tiny living room area. Flipping the light switch, I look at my room and wonder what she thinks.

The double bed is just a mattress and box springs on a frame, with no headboard. There's just enough room on the far side of the bed for a small dresser and bookshelf, and just enough room at the foot to open the closet door.

"It's not much." I turn to Grace and shrug. "But I've always been kind of proud of it because it's my place and I did this on my own."

She slides her arms around my waist and leans into my chest. Her embrace is warm and sweet as I press a kiss to the top of her head.

"It's a great place," she says. "I imagine most people are proud of their first apartment."

Releasing her reluctantly, I open the closet door and find a couple of pullover hoodies that'll come in handy on the nights we stargaze. From the bookshelf, I find my spare phone charger and look back at Grace.

"Ready to head back?"

"I guess," she sighs. "This day has been so amazing. I kind of hate to see it end."

"Me too." I smile at her across the room. "We'll do it again. Often, once you're living here."

We say our goodbyes and head out to the parking lot. Like Grace, I hate to see this day end. Being back in Flagstaff, with her by my side, feels amazing. Pretty soon, she'll be living here, too, but I can't help but think that once we're back in Greyson the weight of Adam's death will press in on us again.

I put my key in the ignition, trying unsuccessfully to push away the dread I feel about returning to Greyson. But then I turn the key.

Nothing. The engine doesn't turn over. There's just a soft clicking noise.

I try again. Same thing.

I look at the clock. Almost ten o'clock. Unless Eric knows of an all night auto parts store, it looks like Grace and I are stuck in Flagstaff for the night.

I should be frustrated. I'm not.

✧   ✧   ✧

"IT'S DEFINITELY THE starter," Eric says, stepping out of my car and closing the door behind him.

"I figured it was," I reply, glad that Eric had worked summers in his uncle's mechanic shop.

"I can put it in for you, no problem. But it'll be tomorrow morning before we can get the part."

Beside me, Grace shifts her weight. Spending the night in Flagstaff had not been on our agenda, and I hope she's not upset.

"Looks like we're going to have to stay the night," I whisper, wrapping my arm around her shoulder. She slipped on a sweater earlier, and though I miss the sight of her bare shoulders, the material is soft under my fingers.

"Looks like," she replies. "Lucky the starter went out here at your apartment instead of somewhere else."

She's taking this like it's no big deal. I hope maybe she's a little bit happy that our time here has been extended.

"It'll be a full house," Eric says. "But we've got the room. I'll head in and let Natalia and Chase know."

I give Eric a moment to get back inside the apartment, then turn to Grace.

"I'm sorry," I say. "I know this is weird."

"No big deal," she says, shrugging her shoulders. "Neither one of us has to work tomorrow, so we'll just get some sleep, get your car fixed, and head back in the morning."

"Are your parents going to go ballistic?" I ask. Despite the fact I've never felt it necessary to defend myself or justify my choices, I still want her parents to at least be comfortable that she and I are close, even if I'm not their first choice.

"What can they say?" she asks, a gleam of mischief in her eyes. "You didn't intentionally sabotage your starter so you could lock me up and defile me with your wickedness, did you?"

"When did you become a comedian?" I ask, laughter punctuating each word.

"I think you bring it out in me." She elbows me in the ribs, then turns to face me. "I should call my mom."

"I'll do it," I say.

She raises her eyebrows. "Seriously?"

"Yeah. I want your parents to know I'm an honorable guy."

"Okay then." She stands on her tiptoes and presses her lips to mine. "Be honorable."

Chapter 37

Grace

I PULL MY sweater closer around my shoulders, listening to Asher's end of the conversation with my mom. I'm mentally calculating my choices for sleepwear – considering all I have are the clothes I'm wearing – when Asher's voice catches my attention.

"I know it's not necessarily the most appropriate situation, Mrs. Ballard, but I can't get the part for my car until tomorrow morning." The steadiness in his voice is in direct contrast with the look of panic on his face. "My roommate's sister is here for the weekend, so I'm sure we can give Grace and her a room to themselves."

He's quiet for a moment, and I can't help but wonder what Mom is saying. We're standing just outside the apartment door, and from the living room I hear laughter, along with the loud volume of the television.

"Thank you so much for understanding," Asher says. "And again, I'm really sorry."

I can't stop the grin that forms on my face. I've

seen Asher display lots of emotions, from furious at Tony Adkins to kind and gentle with Stella and with me, but this one is new. Nervous and uncomfortable.

It's kind of cute.

"Of course," he says to my mom. Then he holds the phone out to me and whispers, "She wants to talk to you."

I take a deep breath and bring the phone to my ear. I'm sure Mom has some words of wisdom for me, I just hope they don't involve any sort of preconceived notion about Asher.

"Hi Mom."

"Grace," she begins. "Asher informed me what's happened."

Asher points to the apartment door and mouths *be right back*. I watch as he steps inside. The curtain in the front window moves to the side, and Asher waves from the other side. My heart warms, realizing he's keeping an eye on me.

"Yeah. We were just getting ready to head back to Greyson and his car wouldn't start."

"He also asked if we would be upset if the two of you stayed at his apartment tonight."

"I know," I say. "I heard. And it only makes sense, since that's where we are."

"I have a couple of things to say, and I promise not to nag," she says.

"Okay." I try not to groan. "I'm listening."

"First, it's late, but I know Aunt Becca wouldn't

think twice about coming to pick you up if you're uncomfortable staying there." She pauses for a second. "Are you uncomfortable?"

"No. Not at all."

"All right. Second thing." I hear her sigh heavily. She must be gearing up for her big point. "You're technically an adult. So is Asher. But at the same time, you're not necessarily full-blown adults. I know you know what I mean. I trust you. I trust your judgment. But I'm also aware that there's more between you and Asher than helping each other through the loss you've both suffered. There's always been more between you."

"Mom –" I try to interrupt, but she just keeps going.

"I just want you to be careful," she says. "Be sensible. Protect your heart, okay?"

I can't fault her for that piece of advice. She isn't being judgmental of Asher. She's just being my mom. Which is pretty cool.

"Okay," I whisper. "I will."

"Let me know when you're on your way tomorrow."

Asher pushes the door open and sticks his head out. I nod, letting him know it's fine for him to come back outside.

"Will do, Mom."

I disconnect the call and hand Asher his phone once he reaches me.

"We have an issue," he says, dropping his phone

into the pocket of his jeans. He runs a hand through his hair, clearly worried about something.

"What is it?" I can't imagine what could have him upset. Sure, his car is messed up, but we aren't stranded on the side of the highway, and he has a plan to get the car up and running first thing in the morning.

"I told Eric we should let you and Natalia have the bunk beds," he begins. "He could take my room, and Chase could have the couch. I volunteered to just crash on the floor."

"Sounds reasonable."

"That's what I thought." He leans back against the door. "But he doesn't get the fact that I'm trying to do the right thing. He just went on and on about how they still have another movie to watch, and how he's got some project he's working on using the computer in his room."

It dawns on me. "That leaves your room, right?"

Asher sighs and his shoulders slump. "It just doesn't occur to him that you and I might not want to share a bed."

"Most people would make the same assumption." And despite the fact that he and I aren't sleeping together, a part of my heart is happy that we look enough like a couple that Eric thought so.

"Not that I haven't thought about it. I mean, you know." His face turns red and he pushes off the door, walking to the railing at the top of the steps. "Shit."

"Asher, I get it," I say, hoping to ease his mind.

"I have those feelings for you." He doesn't turn around. "How could I not? But there's no expectation. Tonight or ever. And absolutely no pressure."

"Okay," I say, because it is. He's torn up over something that's not bothering me at all. "So we sleep in your room."

He turns around, hands in the pockets of his faded jeans. His head is dropped, eyes fixed on the red Chucks on his feet.

"Just like that?" he asks, lifting his eyes to mine.

"This," I say, moving my hand between the two of us, "is new and different from anything either of us has experienced before. But I know you. And I'm not weirded out by staying in the same room with you. You didn't even have to tell me that you'd never pressure me. I've always known that."

He steps toward me and wraps his arms around me, banishing the cool night air and surrounding me with his warmth. Hugging him close, I sink into him, barely holding in the desire to tell him how much I love him.

"Okay, then." He presses a kiss to the top of my head, and my heart leaps. "Let's go."

Chapter 38

Grace

I CAN TELL Asher is awake.

We'd talked for a while before settling down to try to sleep. Nothing significant had come up, and it felt good to just talk about normal, every day stuff. He'd given me a pair of his gym shorts to sleep in. They're way too big, but with the drawstring, they work fine.

Asher had changed into a pair of shorts as well. My pulse picks up as I remember the moment he took his shirt off. I'd seen him shirtless once before, but only for a moment, and only from the front. This time, his back had been to me when he pulled the shirt over his head, and I'd seen the swirls of color representing the Navajo Nation spreading across his back, from shoulder to shoulder.

I'd been speechless.

I have no idea how long we've been laying here. I'm under the covers, while Asher is on top of them. Even with no parent around to walk in and jump to the wrong conclusion, he's still trying to make it clear that nothing inappropriate is happening.

His chivalry makes me smile.

I can still hear the TV, and the lights from the parking lot seep between the curtains to prevent the room from falling into total darkness.

Asher is still, but in the slight illumination, I can see the movement of his eyes blinking.

"You awake?" I whisper.

"Yeah. Sorry." He turns his head toward me. "Did I wake you up?"

"No. I dozed off for a while, but I woke up a little bit ago." I shift from my back to my side, facing him. "Sometimes it's hard to sleep in a strange place. What's your excuse?"

"Just thinking about things." A beam of light from the window falls across his face, but I can't make out his expression. "Can't seem to turn my mind off."

"Want to talk about it?" A spike of fear pricks my heart. There are so many things that could be bothering him. Not the least of which is the fact that we've still yet to talk about Adam and my relationship with him. Maybe now is the right moment to tell him the truth, while we're lying close, cloaked in the soft darkness of his bedroom.

I'm just about to open my mouth and spit out the words I've been holding inside since Adam died, when Asher speaks.

"I worry about Mom," he says. "Worry how she'll

be once I come back here for good."

A lump forms in my throat. He's such a good son.

"I think she'll be all right," I reply. "Or at least as all right as she can be. She's strong."

"Yeah." I see him nod slightly. "I'm not a parent, but I just don't know how you come back from something like this."

"I guess you just do." I want to scoot right up next to him and wrap my arms around his chest, but I stay where I am. "She still has you, so she'll go on for you. I'll go hang out with her until I move here. And I'm sure my mom will check on her after that."

"Dad says he's going to make sure she comes and visits me here. He wants her to let up on me about the job situation." He rolls to his side and props his head on his elbow. "I'm going to see if I can get her to go down to Sedona for a few days and visit her parents. A change of scenery will do her good."

"Getting out of town for a bit sounds like a good idea."

Abruptly, he flops back onto his back and throws his arm across his eyes. "I don't mean to be insensitive. I worry about Mom so much, and I just forget that you lost him, too."

I can't deny that sometimes I forget that I'd lost Adam. It's not because I don't miss him. It's because I lost a friend and a buddy, not the love of my life like everyone believes.

"We all lost him," I whisper. "I think more often

you forget about yourself. You bury your own feelings and worry about everyone else. But you lost your brother, Asher. That's huge."

He lets out a breath and just nods. His arm still covers his eyes, and his chest trembles. He was so stoic at the funeral, and thinking back, I'm not sure he's cried at all over his brother.

Without speaking, I move until I'm pressed against his side. Laying my head on his shoulder, I slide my arm across his chest and hold him tight. He takes his arm away from his face and wraps it around me. For a long moment we hold each other, while he cries silently for the brother he lost.

"I know you feel like you have to hold all this inside so you can be strong for your mom, but you don't ever have to do that with me."

I feel him take a deep breath and let it out in a big sigh. His lips press against my forehead and stay there for several seconds. "Thank you."

Tell him now! I'm mentally shouting at myself to tell him the truth about Adam. The thought is almost excruciating because I know it'll bring up all sorts of emotions that are messy and will totally screw up this really lovely atmosphere we've created. But I know I have to do it.

Just then, a roar of laughter erupts from the living room. It seems Eric, Natalia, and Chase are still going strong on their movie marathon. With the moment lightened, I'm saved from having to make my confession.

"Sounds like they're having fun," I say, reluctantly pulling away from Asher and back to my own pillow.

He lets out a chuckle. "Yeah. Eric's not the most sensitive roommate. At least I don't have to work first thing in the morning."

At the mention of his job, the blonde Amazon woman named Lizzie flashes through my mind. I know Rachelle told me about her, but something still bugs me. And the fact that she's still bugging me is rather irritating. Several times I'd almost asked Asher about her, but talked myself out of it.

That it now seems easier to talk about Lizzie than about Adam is a pretty sorry statement. But I ask him anyway.

"That girl, Lizzie." My voice is barely audible, but I know Asher hears me because he turns to face me again. "Did you date her?"

"Why do you ask that?" It doesn't escape me that he's avoiding the question.

"It was obvious that you knew each other," I say. "I just wondered."

He moves closer, enough that I can see his brown eyes even though the room is shadowy. He takes a deep breath and holds it, closing his eyelids for a few seconds before answering.

"I didn't exactly *date* her."

Chapter 39

Asher

"OH." GRACE'S VOICE is nothing but air as she processes what I've just said.

I know I should've told her a long time ago, or better yet just left her alone, but I wanted so badly for my past mistakes to not matter.

But I know they do.

Opening my eyes to look at her, I see the moment she understands, and it breaks my heart. She presses her lips together and closes her eyes, and I feel worse than garbage because I know there's more I have to tell. "When I started apprenticing at Resolution, I wasn't prepared for the celebrity that came with it." More than anything I want to reach out and touch her, but I don't think she'd welcome it right now. "I mean, I was just learning to tattoo, but apparently there are these *groupies* that tattooists pick up, and… yeah. Lizzie wasn't the only one."

The admission tastes like acid on my tongue.

"I'm not judging you," she says, opening her eyes to

look at me. I'm a tiny bit encouraged by the fact that she's looking at me again.

"I want you to understand, at least a little." As if there's any excuse that could make my behavior less awful. I take a chance and reach for her hand. When she doesn't pull away, I thread my fingers through hers. "Mom and Dad were so pissed at me. I felt like I was all alone. I was acting out, trying to forget. It was stupid, and I know that now."

"You aren't the first," she whispers, squeezing my hand. The warmth of the gesture floods through me and I feel like weeping with gratitude.

"Doesn't make me hate it any less. I wish I could take it all back. Those girls, they meant nothing. And I don't say that to try and somehow make it better that I was with them like that. I know that makes it worse. I know I took something that should be meaningful and special and made it worthless."

"Yeah, you did," she says, and I'm actually glad that she's not letting me off the hook. "Did you bring them here?"

"No." I spit the word out as quickly as I can. I don't want her thinking for a second that she's sleeping in a bed I shared with someone else. "This is going to sound awful, but those girls didn't require a lot of effort. I went to parties. Most of the time there was plenty of private room for... *that*. Sometimes I went to the girl's place, if she had one. I didn't want them here. Even in the worst of it, I knew that if I let them into *my* space, it would be that much harder to stop."

"But you did stop, right?" Even in the shadows of the room, I can see how important my answer is. She wants to know I made the decision to stop being such a douche. That I didn't just put it on hold because my brother died.

At least in this, I can give her exactly what she wants.

"Yes. I got to the point I just couldn't stomach it anymore." I bring my hand to her face and push a strand of hair behind her ear, lingering on the soft skin of her neck. "I could barely stand myself anymore, so I knew I had to make a change."

"What prompted it?"

"Do you remember when I came home for Adam's birthday in February?"

She nods. "I saw you, but we didn't talk or anything."

"I avoided you because I was so ashamed of myself." I take a deep breath and decide to give her the whole truth. "When I saw you across the driveway, I just knew I couldn't do it anymore. I couldn't fill my time with meaningless girls and meaningless sex just because I missed you."

"You missed me?" Her eyes go wide with surprise.

I nod because I don't think I can say anything at the moment.

"I never went away." She lifts her hand to where mine still rests on her neck and circles her fingers around my wrist. "You did."

"I was so confused," I say, knowing it's no excuse for the way I abandoned her. "Not about you, but about life in general. Not knowing what I wanted to do with my life weighed on me, and then when I finally made a decision I was sure about, my parents nearly blew a gasket."

"I wish you'd talked to me then," she says. "I would've supported you."

"I wanted to make something of myself. I wanted to be a success, so I could come back home and prove to everybody that they were wrong about me. But nothing I did seemed to be enough."

She's silent. Her hand still on my wrist, thumb stroking softly on the underside. I close my eyes and whisper my next words.

"And I was so damn jealous of Adam." When she doesn't seem shocked by my words, I go on. "I feel awful for even saying that now, but it's the truth."

I look at her then and find her looking back at me with a small smile on her face. Hope swims in my heart.

"I was jealous of Lizzie today," she says.

"Seriously?" I can't believe she'd ever feel jealous of a woman like Lizzie.

She shrugs her shoulder and nods. "She's like a walking Barbie doll. And she certainly had all the necessary parts on display."

"Grace," I whisper, sliding my hand into the hair at

the base of her neck and pulling her face closer to mine. "You are beautiful and sexy and everything a woman should be. You are so much more because you know what real beauty is. And I don't take for granted how lucky I am to be with you, for however long you'll have me."

I know I should address what this is between us. I know we need to at least try to define it in order for it to be real. But that will mean talking more about Adam and about Grace's relationship with him. Which means bringing up the guilt I know we both feel.

Maybe I'm a terrible and selfish brother, but I just don't want to kill the mood that's between us right now. So I push it to the back of my mind.

"I'm not mad at you," she says, her breath warm on my face as she speaks softly. "You made mistakes, but they don't define you. Do I hate that you cheapened yourself and gave parts of yourself to girls who'll never truly appreciate it? Hell yes. But one stupid period of time in your life doesn't ruin things forever."

"After everything," I say, swallowing hard. "Ignoring you for all that time. And now this. You just forgive me so easily. How do you do that?"

"Remember the day we first met?"

From the living room I hear the TV shut off and the tell tale squeak of the sofa bed being pulled out. Eric and the others must finally be winding down for the night.

"The day I hit Tony Adkins?" I ask, lowering my

voice even more as I hear movement in the hallway.

"You stuck up for Kyle," she says. "You defended someone who couldn't defend himself, and you didn't complain about getting punished for it. *That's* who you really are. I've always known it."

And she's the girl who's believed in me since that day, even when I didn't deserve it. Happiness sings in my veins, and I don't think it's possible to love her any more than I do in this moment.

"Can I just hold you while we sleep?" I ask, rewarded by the huge smile that spreads across her face.

I roll onto my back, pulling her against my side. She nestles her head into the crook of my shoulder and I wrap both arms around her, content in a way I never imagined.

Chapter 40

July 2, 2014

Grace

W E'VE BEEN HOME from Flagstaff for three days.
On the drive home, we'd agreed we should skip a night or two of hanging out and give our parents a chance to get used to our relationship.

And that's exactly how we'd referred to it. Our *relationship*. We didn't label it as a romance or a friendship. I'm not sure whether to be bothered by the ambiguity or grateful for it.

Our texts have been sparse since our return. In a way I'm not surprised. I could feel the tension in Asher the further east we drove on our way home to Greyson. I hated it, even though I understood it.

Our day in Flagstaff had been magical. Almost as if it had been carved out of time just for us. But now that we're home, there's a distance that can only be explained by the intensity of what we experienced on our trip.

And the issue we've avoided addressing since this

entire *relationship* began. Adam.

Now it's Tuesday, and with every opportunity I get to take a break from the kids in my daycare class, I'm sneaking a look at my tattoo just to remind myself that my time with Asher had been real.

About halfway through my morning, I decide to text him, just to see what sort of response I get. He hasn't ignored me since we returned from Flagstaff, but he's been slow to respond and not very talkative.

Me: *You were right. The tat itches.*

He rarely texts until his lunch break, so I'm surprised when my phone buzzes immediately with a response.

Asher: *Told ya!*

I try not to be disappointed with his two-word text and decide to be glad that at least he'd responded quickly.

Instead of texting him back, I put my phone back in my pocket and head to the break room to grab a bottle of water. I always work up a sweat playing outside with the kids, but today I feel warmer than usual.

I grab my water from the refrigerator and plop down in a chair at the small table. The cool water hits my throat, and at first I'm relieved, but then I try to swallow. My throat feels about a hundred times smaller than normal as I force the water down. With my hands,

I touch the sides of my neck and at once feel the swollen nodes. Checking my forehead the way my mom always used to, I can tell I have a fever.

Great.

Sandy, my boss, walks in, takes one look at me, and knows.

"Grace, honey," she says. "You're sick."

"Yeah. I'm figuring that out." I attempt another drink of water because the liquid feels good on my throat, but regret it when I realize all over again how difficult swallowing is when my tonsils are the size of baseballs.

"I think you need to see a doctor." She does the standard forehead check and confirms that I have a fever. "This came on fast. You were fine when you got here this morning."

I nod, reaching for my cell phone. Quickly, I look up Dr. Parker's number and dial. It only takes a minute for the nurse to tell me to come right on over and they'll work me in. Next, I call my mom. She and Dad are out of town for the day at some sort of conference. Naturally, she goes into overprotective mode and offers to come home. I talk her out of it and promise to call her once I leave Dr. Parker's office.

With an apology to Sandy for cutting out two hours early on my shift, I head out to my car and make my way to the doctor's office.

✧   ✧   ✧

"IT'S STREP THROAT, Mom."

I pull into the driveway, glancing toward Asher's house for a brief second, and grab my purse and prescription.

"Do you need me to come home early?" she asks. "It's not a problem. Your father can ride home with one of the tax attorneys."

"Mom, no. I'm eighteen-years-old. I can handle it." Stepping into the house, I lock the door behind me and head to the kitchen. "I'm just going to take my medicine and go to bed."

"Promise you'll call if you get worse?" she asks.

"I promise," I tell her, although all I can imagine doing for the next five hours or so is sleeping. I find the biggest glass I can and fill it with water from the dispenser on the refrigerator. "I'm sure I'll make it just fine."

With another offer to come home if I need her, Mom and I hang up. I down the first dose of my antibiotic and some ibuprofen and make myself drink half the glass of water, despite my screaming sore throat. Filling my glass back up, I pull my phone from my purse and head for my bedroom.

I situate the water and my phone on the nightstand. I strip down to nothing but my panties and slip on the oversized tee shirt and boxers that I slept in the night before. As I slide between the covers, it occurs to me that Asher's car was in his driveway when I came home. Apparently, he's off today, and I wonder why he didn't say anything. My heart clamors for me to let him know I'm home sick, but my pride says no. If I'm feeling a little bitchy about his distance, I figure a raging case of strep throat entitles me to it.

So I leave my phone on the nightstand untouched, and fall asleep almost instantly.

✧ ✧ ✧

I'M VAGUELY AWARE of someone coming into my room. I don't know how long I've been sleeping, but I figure it's Mom, home from the conference, so I don't open my eyes as a hand checks my forehead. I can tell my skin is still burning with fever, and yet I feel cold beneath the covers.

The hand smooths my hair off my forehead and tucks a few strands of hair behind my ear. When the touch against my skin ends, I assume Mom has left the room and burrow further beneath the covers, hoping to sink back into sleep.

I'm laying on my side, facing my closet door, and suddenly I feel the mattress dip behind me as someone else lays down in the bed with me. I tell myself to roll over and see what's going on, but my body doesn't comply.

"Hey," Asher whispers, and my heart soars despite how lousy I feel.

"What are you doing here?" I ask. I know it probably sounds ungrateful, but I don't have it in me to worry about it.

"Your mom called," he says. "Asked if Mom or I could come check on you. She told me where the spare key was."

So apparently me being sick warrants his attention more so than me just being me. Immediately, I reprimand myself for the thought. So he's been distant for a day or two. In the grand scheme of things, it's a very, very small thing. If he needs a few days to process what's happening between us, I shouldn't be ugly about it.

He's here to take care of me, and it speaks volumes about how he feels. If he's only in it for the good times, he'd have left checking on me to Stella and not risked a case of strep throat.

"I'm contagious, Asher." My voice isn't much more than scratchy breath. "You should stay away."

"I'll just stay back here," he says, cuddling up behind me.

"I don't want you to get sick."

"Then don't breathe on me." I feel him chuckle as he spoons against me. "Quit arguing. I know it hurts to talk."

It's no use trying to convince him to stay away, so I release a big, heavy sigh to let him know I give up. Besides, if I'm honest, I don't want him to go. I feel too lousy and he feels too good.

"I can feel you shivering," he whispers. "You know this feels good." He wraps his arm around me, the mountain of covers providing a germ-barrier between us. He pulls me close, letting the warmth from his body seep into me. I might feel as physically lousy as I ever have, but my heart feels cherished and cared for. I want to believe he feels that way about me, because that's how I feel for him.

He squeezes me gently and kisses my hair, and happiness courses through me despite how sick I am. Sleep comes quickly with him next to me, and I drift blissfully into it, wrapped in the comfort of his arms.

Chapter 41

Asher

I'M LAYING IN a bed with Grace for the second time in five days.

True, she's sick this time and I wish she wasn't, but I'm still happy to be close to her this way.

In just a few minutes her breathing evens out and her body stills, and I can tell she's fallen back to sleep. I stay where I am, my body spooned against hers, hoping that even in her sleep she'll be warmed and comforted by my presence.

I've missed her since we got back from Flagstaff. That twenty-four hour period gave me a taste of what it could be like to have her all to myself, to make her a part of my life, to be with her and not have the cloud of Adam's death hanging over us.

Though we'd agreed to hold off on hanging out together at night – just to keep our parents from nosing around too much – I've put some distance between us that has nothing to do with our agreement. Being back in Greyson, with the reality of Adam's absence smacking me in the face, I've been forced to realize that no matter where we go, his death will always be a factor in our relationship. Even once we're in Flagstaff together, where no one will look at us funny if we're a couple, the fact that Grace dated my brother is not going away.

So I did the chicken shit thing and backed away from her. Only a little, but I know she's noticed. When her mom called this afternoon and told me she was sick, I couldn't get over here fast enough. And now that I'm here, all I want to do is take care of her.

When she's well, the two of us are going to sit down and have a long talk about Adam. It'll probably be the most awkward and uncomfortable experience of my life… talking with the girl I love about her romantic relationship with the brother I loved and lost. But I want Grace enough to deal with the hard stuff.

Beneath my arm I feel Grace sigh and relax even more. Reaching up to touch her forehead, I feel the cool sweat that indicates her fever has broken. Strep throat is pretty unforgiving, and this probably won't be her last fever, but I'm glad she's gotten a bit of relief for the time being.

I move away from her, sliding across the mattress as gently as I can. She's undisturbed as I make my way over to the love seat where I dropped my backpack when I came in. Her parents won't be back until after dinnertime, so I brought my laptop and sketchpad. I told Bing to start scheduling appointments for me starting the third week of July, so hopefully I've got some messages in my email and some designs to start working on.

Mrs. Ballard told me what time Grace took her medicine, so I set an alarm on my phone so I'll know to wake her up and give her another dose of ibuprofen. Maybe it'll be enough to keep her comfortable.

I grab my laptop and settle onto the love seat, sitting at an angle where I can keep an eye on Grace. The thought crosses my mind that taking care of her feels as natural as breathing, and I hope this will be the first of many times I watch over her.

IT'S ALMOST SIX o'clock when I hear Grace's parents arrive. Fortunately, I'd thought ahead enough to call Mrs. Ballard and let her know I'd be hanging out here until they got home. Even with her sick and conked out in the bed, being discovered in her bedroom would probably not go over very well.

While she slept, I've been working on a new sketch for her. Seeing the one on her bulletin board, and remembering why I chose the Navajo basket, inspired me to do something new for her. Something that will hopefully symbolize this new phase of our relationship.

I'm just packing up my pencils and sketchpad when her mom quietly opens the door.

"Hi Asher," she says, her voice soft as she steps into the room.

"Mrs. Ballard." I stand, pulling one strap of my backpack onto my shoulder. "She's slept pretty much the whole time."

"Thanks for keeping an eye on her." She walks closer, meeting me at the door that opens to the side yard. "Dean and I felt so much better knowing she wasn't alone."

"No problem." I want to tell her Grace will never have to be alone, not if I can help it, but I figure I should keep that bit of information to myself. "Her fever broke not long after I got here. I woke her up to take another dose of ibuprofen a couple of hours ago. I think it's kept the fever down."

"I know how much you've always cared for her," she says, lowering her voice like she's afraid Grace will hear her.

"Yes ma'am. I have," I say. "And I still do."

"I believe that. So all I'll ask is that you be careful and be very sure before the two of you make any big decisions."

"Of course." I nod my head and swallow hard, more nervous than I've ever felt in my life.

"Well, then. Thank you again for looking after her."

"Can you let her know I was here?" I ask, reaching for the doorknob. "I don't know if she'll remember or not. And when she's feeling up to it, I'd love it if she'd call and tell me how she's doing."

"I'll tell her you were here, but I doubt she'll need

any prodding from me to give you a call."

With a smile, I slip out the door and head back home. I'm both worried about Grace and somewhat reassured by my conversation with her mom. Mrs. Ballard didn't seem to object to our relationship. And having made the decision to finally sit down and get all the Adam issues out on the table, I feel hopeful in a way I hadn't expected to.

Grace and I will be fine.

Chapter 42

July 3, 2014

Asher

IT'S THURSDAY AND Grace is still off work.

She's probably not contagious anymore – I know this because I asked one of the nurses at the hospital – but just to keep the kids at the daycare safe, she's not going back until Monday. Tomorrow is July Fourth, so the daycare is closed then anyway.

We've been texting a lot since she got sick, but I haven't seen her since the day I stayed with her while her parents were out of town. I haven't wanted to push things with her parents, especially since her mom seemed pretty accepting when we talked the other day. But two days with no Grace is too long.

I'm dying to see her again. To hold her again.

So, instead of texting her from the hospital cafeteria on my lunch break, I decide to surprise her at home. Her folks are at work, and so is my mom, so I know I can spend a few minutes with her alone without anyone being the wiser. Not that I'm trying to hide anything. I just don't want all the questions that will undoubtedly come if one of the parental units catches me rushing home on my lunch hour just to spend a minute or two with Grace.

I turn onto our street, finishing the last bite of my turkey sandwich, and see Grace's car backing out of her driveway.

I eye my phone lying on the passenger seat. I should pick it up and call her, ask her where she's going. She's probably just running an errand or going out to pick up some lunch. She mentioned last night that she was tired of chicken soup and orange juice.

But as she takes a left out of our neighborhood instead of a right that will take her toward town, I leave my phone where it lays and decide to follow her. As I drain the last of the liquid in my can of soda, there's a little voice in my head that says I'm bordering on stalker status and invading her privacy. But I love this girl. I just want to see her for a minute before I have to go back to work. What's so wrong with that? If she sees me in her rearview mirror, I'll just tell her the truth. I wanted to surprise her on my lunch hour.

She doesn't see me, though, and I keep several car lengths behind her. She seems intent on her destination, and though I can't see her eyes because of the sunglasses she's wearing, she doesn't do more than glance in her rearview mirror as she navigates her way to the west side of Greyson. With every moment that passes, the dread inside me increases.

When she takes the last left turn onto Prairie View Street, my stomach sinks to the soles of my feet and my lunch threatens to go the opposite direction. I know where she's going.

Greyson Memorial Cemetery.

The inside of my car suddenly seems far too small, suffering from a deplorable lack of oxygen. Somehow, I find the wherewithal to press the brake and hang back as she pulls into the parking lot. From the street, I watch as she climbs out of the car holding a box of tissues and something else I can't identify. Once she's far enough away from the lot, I swing in and back into a corner spot. I'm far enough away so as not to be too obvious, but angled so I can see her profile.

She sinks down onto the ground next to Adam's grave, and her shoulders immediately begin to shake. A haze clouds my vision and sweat breaks out across my forehead. It takes me a moment to realize what I'm feeling.

Jealousy.

I'm choking on jealousy, watching the girl I love cry over my brother. All this time I've told myself my love for her was enough to overcome the fact that she spent ten months as my brother's girlfriend. I've held on to what she said about her relationship with Adam not being serious. I've reminded myself over and over that she took down Adam's picture so the drawing I did for her would be visible. I made myself believe that those things meant I ranked higher than Adam.

Apparently not. Even if she loves me more than she loved him, the fact that he's gone makes it impossible to overcome his place in her heart.

Hatred bubbles up inside me, hot and ugly. Hatred for Adam. Hatred for myself. Misery and self-loathing overwhelm me until I can hardly breathe. I have to physically fight the urge to get out of the car and rush over to Grace. What I'd say if I did, I have no idea. I peel my hand from the steering wheel, where it's clenched tight enough my knuckles have turned white, and move the gearshift to drive. I pull out of the parking lot and point my car back toward the hospital.

The sky opens up, rain pelting against my windshield. Fitting, I think to myself, as resentment burns in my gut the entire way back to work.

I don't text her at all the rest of the day.

Chapter 43

Grace

THE RELIEF I feel after spilling my guts at Adam's grave is almost tangible. Logically, I know he's not here, but saying everything out loud is cathartic in a way I hadn't imagined.

On the outskirts of the town, Greyson Memorial Cemetery isn't creepy at all. It's well landscaped and maintained, and far enough away from the regular business activity that it's really quite peaceful. The entire time I've been here I've only heard one other vehicle.

I look at the picture of Adam and me I've laid beside his headstone. It's the one I removed so Asher's drawing would be visible. It seems somehow fitting to bring it here and acknowledge the happy times.

"We were happy that night, weren't we?" My voice is soft even though no one is around to hear me. I take a deep breath, calming from the tears that started the moment I got here. "There were good times, Adam, and I'll never regret them."

I think back to the last conversation the two of us shared. The one I've told no one about. If I'd known it was the last time I'd speak to him, I would've said so many things. I would've told him how much he'd meant to me, how much he'd helped me. And I would've told him how much I'd always loved his brother. He'd deserved to know that.

So, I'll tell him now.

"I believe that somehow you can hear me," I begin, tracing the letters of his name on the stone. "That you're looking down and watching all of us try to move on with life now that you're gone. I wonder if you're confused by what you're seeing or if you'd suspected it all along."

My eyes travel to the picture again, and a tear escapes to roll down my cheek as I look at Adam's brilliant smile. He'd been so full of life and had brought so much joyful energy wherever he went.

"So, today I want to tell you the truth, the way I never did when we were together." I pull a tissue from the box and wipe my eyes, then move a little closer. I know it's silly, but I just want to feel like he's sitting right next to me.

"I started falling in love with Asher the day he hit Tony Adkins and stuck up for Kyle Martin. Part of me thinks surely you knew how I felt, but just in case, I want to finally be honest."

Behind me I hear a car pull out of the parking lot, but I don't turn around to look. People come here for their own reasons, and I'm sure whoever it is doesn't want me intruding. The sky is overcast, and the air is still. It suits my mood. Contemplative and melancholy.

"I never stopped loving Asher. When he left for college and then dropped out of my life, I was heartbroken. I felt like a part of my heart was dying. The summer before our senior year started, when Asher came home for a week and totally ignored me, then left to go back to Flagstaff without even looking at me, I was devastated. When you asked me to go with you to that back to school party, I probably should've said no. I should've told you then that I loved your brother. But I didn't."

A drop of rain lands on my hand, and another on my shoulder. I know my time here is limited, so I quickly go on.

"I don't want you to think I just used you as a distraction," I say. "It never felt that way to me. You were fun, and I enjoyed spending time with you. I loved that you never pressured me for any huge commitment. That you never asked me for things I couldn't give you, physically or emotionally. I loved that you seemed to be happy to just have fun together without all the labels of being in love or committed long-term."

As the rain picks up, I stand up and pull my hood up over my head.

"I never told anyone about the day you died and what we talked about." I take a deep breath and close my eyes, remembering the conversation we had a mere two hours before he died. "It just seemed so cold to tell people what happened. I was afraid people would think I was an unfeeling bitch. So I just never said anything. I didn't think it would matter, but now it does. Some day, very soon, I'm going to have to tell Asher. I hope he'll believe me and understand why I've kept it a secret. And I hope you'll understand."

I take a few steps toward the parking lot then turn back. For a moment, I consider picking up the picture, but I know I have smaller copy in the memory box I put together. Somehow, it feels right to leave this one here with him. I know it won't survive the rain, but Adam's life is more than a picture. It's a thousand memories that will never fade away.

"It's never been a competition between you and Asher. Even if you were still here, it wouldn't have been. I was crazy about you Adam, but I love Asher. I always have. I pray that somehow you can give us your blessing, because he's my future. He has been since the very beginning."

Chapter 44

July 4, 2014

Asher

I'M COMPLETELY *not* in the holiday spirit. Holidays are just one more day that I'm reminded of the difficulty that comes with having divorced parents. Naturally, both Mom and Dad want to spend the day with me. Dad's having some of his friends over, and he and Amelia are cooking out by the pool. Grace's parents invited Mom and me to their barbecue as well.

And of course, both my parents insist I spend the day with the *other* one. There's no way to win in that situation. So I split the difference. Dinner with Dad and Amelia, which was impeccably proper and distinguished, and now back home for dessert and the city's fireworks show. There's a better view from our house anyway.

And yeah... the situation with Grace is also killing my Independence Day vibe. She texted me yesterday after the incident at the cemetery, but I haven't responded. I feel like shit for ignoring even one text, like I'm breaking my promise to never ignore her again, but I don't trust myself not to say something that will hurt us both in the long run. I got another message from her this morning, asking if I'd be around for the festivities. I gave her a short, no-nonsense reply that I'd be at Dad's for dinner, but would be back for the fireworks.

She hasn't tried to text me since.

Now, as I make my way down the street toward home, I'm all kinds of torn up and confused about seeing her again. Part of me is angry with her, and I know that's unfair. She can't help it that she misses Adam, especially not when I practically pushed the two of them together when I pulled my stupid disappearing act. A huge part of me is jealous, which makes me feel completely hopeless because the person I'm jealous of is dead and I can do nothing to relieve this awful envy.

But the bigger part of me just wants to prove to Grace that she belongs with me. That she's mine and I'm hers. I don't know what words I can say to make her believe that, so I decide to rely on actions.

I pull into the driveway and notice two things. First, the party has apparently moved to the patio behind our house. Probably because of the table and comfy chairs, and the extra bit of view the patio's elevation allows. Second, Grace is slipping inside her bedroom door. Alone.

And just like that I have a plan.

I put the car in park and hop out, closing my door

as quietly as possible so nobody notices I've arrived home. No one on the patio pays attention to me as I make my way across the side yard to Grace's door.

I push the door open, just enough to call out to her, but not so much that I'll embarrass her if she's changing clothes.

"Grace?"

"Asher?" I hate the uncertainty in her voice, like she's not sure if it's good or bad that I'm here.

"Can I come in?" Please say yes. Please.

"Of course."

I step in and close the door behind me. Grace is pulling a long sleeve tee shirt on over her tank top, and just the glimpse her bare shoulders has my skin heating.

She smooths the tee shirt over her abdomen, adjusting the hem to come down over the top of her jeans, and then looks back up at me. "What's up?"

"How long have you been on antibiotics?" I ask.

She looks at me funny, but answers anyway. "Four days."

"How long since your last fever?" I know she wonders where I'm going with these questions, but I'll show her soon enough.

"It's been since Wednesday afternoon," she says. "Why are you asking all this?"

"And how are you? How's your throat feel?"

She narrows her eyes. "Not perfect, but a lot better."

I nod and walk toward her, purpose filling each

stride. When we're toe to toe, I snake my arms around her waist and pull her to me, lifting her until I can cover her mouth with mine.

I feel her resist for about half a second, probably worrying she's going to give me the crud she's been suffering from, but then the kiss takes off and she softens under my lips. I seriously could not care less about potential germ spreading at this moment.

Backing toward the love seat, I do my best to keep the kiss going, but she's intent on pulling back. Reluctantly, I let her, but I promise myself it's only for a second.

"What if I'm still contagious?" she asks. It's all she manages to get out before I kiss her again, this time sliding my tongue between her lips. She doesn't deny me, and I'm so grateful I could cry. My legs bump the love seat and I drop onto the cushions, bringing her with me so she's straddling my lap.

I never want to move from this spot. Ever.

After a long moment of exploring the warmth of her mouth, I break apart a millimeter, keeping my lips against hers, and reply, "It's been long enough. Twenty-four hours on antibiotics and a day or so without a fever. I asked one of the nurses at the hospital."

"Why?" she asks, continuing to rain kisses against my mouth, toying gently with the hoop in my lower lip. I smile at her responsiveness, at the sweetness of her mouth against my skin, and think maybe I've successfully proven my point.

"Because I was desperate to kiss you again." The honesty tumbles out of my mouth just as I dive back into kissing her like she's water and I'm dying of thirst.

Which is actually a pretty good comparison.

She buries her hands in my hair, and I groan from the pleasure of it. As long as I live, I'll never get tired of her hands on me. Her tongue sweeps across mine again, hard and fast, before she backs off once more.

"What if the nurse is wrong and you get sick?"

I trail kisses along her jaw until I reach her ear. I brush my lips against the tender spot below her earlobe and whisper, "I don't care. I can't be without you anymore."

If I was going to catch strep from her, I'd probably already be sick, since she was surely contagious while we were in Flagstaff.

She grabs my face with both her palms, lifting my lips to hers again. It occurs to me that we haven't been together like this since we returned on Saturday, and by the desperate way we cling together, it's fairly obvious we're starved for each other.

I know the words I just said are true. I can't be without her. When I came into her room tonight, my intent was to prove to her she belonged with me. I don't know if I accomplished my goal, but I did prove something to myself.

I belong to her. Now. Always.

Grace buries her face in the crook of my neck and I

wrap my arms around her, holding her against me as our breathing slows.

"I've missed you, Asher." The warmth of her breath against my neck spreads throughout my body.

"I've missed you, too," I answer. "So much."

"Can we just stay like this and not go back out?" she asks with a giggle. "There's plenty of fireworks right here."

"That would be nice," I say, laughing along with her, because I couldn't agree more. "But they'll just come looking for us. We better head out there."

She nods, sliding off my lap and offering her hand to me. I grasp her hand as I get to my feet, pulling it to my lips and pressing a kiss to the center of her palm. She laces our fingers together, and we step out the door. Neither of us makes a move to let go.

I cut my eyes toward her just as she looks up at me, raising my eyebrows in a silent question. With a smile, she shrugs her shoulders and lifts our joined hands to place her lips on the back of mine.

And together we walk hand in hand toward our families on the back patio of my house. Let them think what they want about the two of us. We've just made a declaration.

Chapter 45

July 18, 2014

Grace

AT EIGHT O'CLOCK on Friday night, I'm packing boxes in my room, preparing for my move to Flagstaff. Even though I've still got about a month, I'm so anxious for the next phase of my life to start that I've already started boxing up winter clothes, shoes, and other stuff I won't need for the next few weeks.

My mom is glad that for once I'm not procrastinating. I figure she's got to realize it's more about my enthusiasm than about getting a head start.

I smile to myself as I toss several pairs of fuzzy socks into a box.

They land softly on top of two pairs of tennis shoes and a number of fleece pajama bottoms. Without warning, my imagination conjures an image of Asher and me, cuddled on the tiny couch of my Flagstaff apartment, me wearing fuzzy pajamas and socks, the two of us watching a movie as the snow falls outside.

I guess not everyone would find the image especially romantic, but I think it may very well be the best fantasy I've ever had.

Asher and I have seen each other every night since July fourth; even on the nights he's eaten dinner at his Dad's. We still haven't talked about Adam, but I've begun to think maybe we don't need to. Since the night of the fireworks, when we arrived on his patio holding hands, making it clear that we were *more*, I've felt like everything is out in the open.

But even as the thought crosses my mind, I know Asher needs the truth from me regardless.

He's headed back to Flagstaff this Sunday. He starts back at Resolution full time on Monday. I know he's looking forward to getting back to work, and I'm happy for him. But being apart for days at a time? Yeah, it's going to really suck.

I've already mapped out two trips to Flagstaff before I move. One to look for a part-time job and another to move a few things into my apartment. Asher's also figured out a couple of times he can make it to Greyson, so we'll see each other at least a few days in the next month. But regardless, the next few weeks loom ahead of us like a big black cloud. In about an hour, we're meeting out back behind the trees again. It's my turn to bring the snack, so I made extra marshmallow-y rice crispy squares. I happen to know they're one of Asher's favorites. He's bringing a thermos of hot chocolate.

My stomach flips every time I think about being

alone with him. Not because making out with his him is amazing – although it really, really is – but because when we're alone, nothing else seems to exist. And nothing else seems to matter except the reality of our feelings for each other.

And that's when I know. Tonight's the night. When we're together under the stars, surrounded by the feelings we share, I'm going to tell him the truth about Adam and about the last time I saw him. Even if no one else in the world ever knows, Asher and I will, and that's all that matters.

Then I'm going to tell him that I love him. How I always have. How he's the one I've always wanted. The one I'll want forever.

A tiny thread of fear prickles my heart as I imagine coming clean about Adam. There's nothing there to be ashamed of, but the fact that I've kept it to myself for so long makes me worry. I take a deep breath and tell myself to chill out. What Asher and I have is real and strong, and I can't imagine anything can come between us now.

I seal the box up with packing tape, then grab a black marker and label what's inside. Glancing at my phone, I see I have about ten minutes to get ready, so I shove the box to the far wall with all the others I've already packed and move to the mirror above my dresser.

My auburn hair is loose around my shoulders, hanging in the slight waves it naturally has if I forego the straightening iron. I run a brush through it, just to make sure it's smooth and tangle free. Satisfied with my hair, I eye the plate of marshmallow treats covered in plastic wrap sitting on my dresser. Staying out of them has been a challenge, but I've managed.

I grab the jacket I tossed onto my bed. I'm just about to slip my arms in when I hear a soft knock at my door. Knowing it can't be anyone but Asher, I hurry to answer.

"Hey Grace," he says with a smile.

Not that I'm ever not aware of how gorgeous he is, but it strikes me all over again in this moment.

Dark brown hair, random and messy in the most appealing way. Bangs slanting across his forehead, partially obscuring the eyebrow where the silver hoop glints. Full lips set against bronze skin, another silver ring twinkling from the lower one. Knowing how that hoop feels against my own lips causes my body to heat.

His signature faded, frayed jeans, along with another vintage tee shirt – this one bearing the name of a diner here in Greyson that closed long ago – along with the ever-present red high top Chucks make him look downright drool worthy.

"Hi Asher," I whisper, a bit overcome by the beauty of the man standing in front of me.

In one hand he holds the thermos of hot chocolate. His other arm clutches what looks like two hooded sweatshirts, which is odd.

"Is it supposed to be cooler than usual tonight?" I

ask, pointing toward the hoodies.

He shakes his head, holding the black sweatshirt out to me.

"I thought you might like to wear this one," he says. "And maybe keep it once I head back to Flagstaff."

I drop the jacket I'm holding to the floor and immediately reach for the one he's offering me. I hold it up, smiling when I see the words Resolution Ink and the shop's official logo blazing across the front.

"I would love that." My voice wavers with emotion, because in my heart I know this is more than him just trying to keep me warm.

I pull the sweatshirt over my head and slide my arms in until my hands emerge from the sleeves. It's way too big, the waistband falling well below my butt, but I couldn't care less. Grabbing the neckline, I pull it up to my nose and inhale. A sense of comfort and rightness floods through me.

"It even smells like you." I close my eyes and breath his scent in once more.

"I wore it around the house for a while after I took a shower."

He looks almost embarrassed by the admission, but that one small gesture touches my heart more than anything ever has.

I throw my arms around him, nuzzling my face into his neck. His arms come around me, holding me tight as he kisses my forehead.

"Thank you, Asher. I'll wear it every day."

He squeezes me tighter and I feel the smile form on his lips as they continue to rest against my skin.

"Ready?" he asks, releasing me from his embrace.

I nod and turn back to grab our dessert.

He throws an arm around my shoulder as we step out the door. Stopping in the soft glow of the moonlight, he bends down and kisses me. It's a gentle kiss, just the warmth of his lips pressed against mine, but I feel it all the way to the soles of my feet.

"You look good in my shirt," he whispers.

I giggle and lean into him as we make our way behind the pine trees to our own private little world.

✦　✦　✦

WE'RE LYING ON our blanket, me snuggled into Asher's side, his left arm holding me close. He's starting on his third marshmallow square and still insisting he's going to eat the entire plate. I make a mental note to fix him a big batch to take with him when he leaves for Flagstaff on Sunday.

My stomach sinks just a bit as I imagine watching him drive off, but I remind myself it won't be the same as before. This time I won't watch him leave from my bedroom window with a heart full of sadness and longing. This time I'll stand beside him, give him a hug and a kiss, maybe wipe a few tears, and wave with a smile as he heads back to the city and the job he loves.

The city where I'll be joining him in a few short

weeks.

I know once we're there together, everything will be perfect.

But first, I have to talk to him about Adam. Even though I'm nervous, I know we've avoided it long enough.

Just as I'm about to open my mouth, my phone buzzes with an incoming text. Asher's beeps a second later, and he looks down at me with curiosity.

"Weird," I say, sitting up and reaching for my phone. Asher does the same.

I see the text has come from Jordan Green, Adam's best friend, and my friend Sydney's on-again off-again boyfriend. The first line of the text is all I can see, but the words *"Before we all head off to college..."* don't give me any idea what it's about. I haven't spoken to Jordan since the day of the funeral, and I wonder what he wants.

I swipe to unlock the screen, then open the text and read it.

> **Jordan:** *Before we all head off to college, I thought we should get together and have our own memorial for Adam. Tomorrow night at my house. Nine o'clock. Hope you can make it.*

"Is yours from Jordan?" Asher asks.

"Yeah." I lift my eyes to his. "You got it, too?"

Asher sighs and nods his head. "I don't want to spend my last night in Greyson with anybody but you, but I don't see how we can gracefully bow out of this."

I agree with him on both points. I've mourned Adam in my own way, and will continue to do so. So has Asher. But Jordan's idea of a memorial given by Adam's friends is actually really sweet. Especially since all of us are about to go in different directions.

"We should definitely go. It's nice that Jordan wants to do this."

"You and I can hang out back here after we come home," Asher says. "It'll be later than usual, but I can just sleep in the next morning. I don't have any certain time I have to leave for Flagstaff."

The wind shifts, bringing a bit of chill with it. I pull the hood of Asher's sweatshirt up over my head, taking a second to appreciate the scent of him that lingers on the fabric.

"Do you think anyone will notice if we leave at the same time?" I ask. "Not that it matters. I just figure it'll be easier to avoid their questions."

"We'll just drive over there separately." He scoots closer and pulls me to him, sharing the warmth of his body with me. "I'll leave first and come get our stuff set up out here. You can head out a little later and meet me."

"Sounds like a plan." I lean into him, laying my head on his shoulder.

Maybe tomorrow night will be a better time to initiate the conversation about Adam. It seems more appropriate to talk about him and finally tell Asher the truth after we've spent time remembering him with his friends.

Making the decision to wait until tomorrow night is easy, because honestly, I'm glad to put it off.

Another day won't matter.

Chapter 46

July 19, 2014

Asher

I'M NOT SURE why I'm so freaking nervous about going to Jordan's. It's not like I even know the guy very well. He was Adam's buddy, and the fact that he wants to gather my brother's friends together one last time before they all scatter is really kind of cool. I'm glad he included me.

But something in me is completely unsettled.

It's those unnamed feelings of tension that are foremost in my mind when I get dressed. I go for the pair of jeans with the most rips, despite the fact that northern Arizona nights are cool, even in the summer. Next, I grab a black Resolution Ink tee shirt that's just a tad too tight. I take a look in the mirror, noting the way the sleeves are just short enough that a good chunk of my ship tattoo shows. My arm muscles are also obvious, which is a plus.

The black lace-up boots come next, and I'm satisfied I look a little bit like a badass, like people have always assumed I am. The eyebrow and lip rings only add to the look. Maybe there's a bit of badassness in me, but only when it's necessary. But if the kids at Jordan's get together want to give me a wide berth because they think tattooists have a short fuse and a hair trigger, I'm not going to argue.

I grab a jacket to throw in my car, just in case. I pick up my keys and phone, dropping them in my pocket, and head out into the living room.

Mom's sitting on the couch, flipping through a magazine while some cooking show plays on the TV.

"Hey Mom." I sit down next to her, noticing that the magazine has pictures of fancy cakes and cookies. "As much as you've been baking lately, I keep expecting you to open up a bakery."

She laughs. It's a nice sound. One I haven't heard much of lately. "One of the other hygienists in the office is having a birthday party for her daughter. She asked me about baking the cake and cookies."

"That's awesome, Mom," I say. "You're a great cook."

"She seems to think I could do cakes and such on the side and make a bit of money." Mom closes the magazine and looks at me. "What do you think?"

"I think if you enjoy it, it's a great idea." And the timing couldn't be more perfect. "What have you got to lose?"

"Exactly!" she says. "And it'll be nice to have something new to focus on, besides just work. Especially since you'll be back in Flagstaff."

I pick up her hand, sandwiching in between both of mine. "I'm going to miss you, Mom. You know that, right?"

"I know." She smiles and pats my cheek with her free hand. "And you'll be missing Grace quite a bit, too, I'm sure."

I just nod at her. I'm not sure how to respond because I have no idea how Mom feels about this thing with me and Grace. Luckily, Mom saves me by going on.

"Thinking about baking as a side business has made me reconsider a lot about you."

I have no idea how baking is related to me, but I don't argue. I'm sure the look on my face shows my confusion, but Mom just goes right on.

"A year ago, I'd have never imagined I'd be considering baking cakes and cookies for other people and getting paid for it." She chuckles beneath her breath. "Just goes to show you how life takes unexpected turns, and sometimes you wind up doing something you never imagined."

I'm still not clear on what this has to do with me, but I don't interrupt her.

"I didn't give you room to let life surprise you," she says. "When something new came along that wasn't exactly what you had planned for your life, I automatically discounted it as foolishness. I never thought of it as one of life's unexpected turns."

"Mom, it's okay," I say, squeezing her hand tighter in mine. "I always knew you wanted the best for me."

"I did want what was best for you. I still do. But I was wrong to just assume I knew better than you what would make you happy. And I'm sorry I haven't supported your new career."

She takes both her hands and places them on my cheeks, like she used to when I was a little boy and she was about to say something really mushy to me.

"I want you to know how proud I am of you for going after your dreams. For making a life for yourself. For being true to yourself."

Her words mean everything to me. I never doubted her love. Never once thought she'd abandon me if I needed her. But hearing her say she's proud of me... it fills a place in my soul that had been longing for her approval.

"Thank you, Mom," I whisper, leaning forward to wrap my arms around her. "So much."

She takes a deep breath. "You're welcome, son. I love you."

"Love you, Mom."

I release her and sit back on the couch, fishing my keys out of my pocket.

"You're heading to Jordan's, right?" she asks.

"Yeah, for a while."

"Please tell him and the others that it means a great deal to know they want to honor Adam this way."

"Will do," I say, standing up from the couch.

As I head out to my car, there's a lightness in my heart that's a direct result of the conversation with Mom. I hadn't realized how much I needed her approval and support. I can't wait to tell Grace.

And yet, as I settle in behind the wheel, I can't shake the feeling of unease that's plagued me all day. Something about this get together at Jordan's isn't sitting well, and I have no idea why.

I back out of the driveway, thinking all I have to do is get through an hour or so, and then I can politely excuse myself and leave.

That moment can't get here soon enough.

Chapter 47

Asher

JORDAN'S BACKYARD IS full of people. At least ten chairs sit around a glowing fire pit, and just as many people are standing up, milling around and talking. I see Grace across the yard, talking with Sydney. I shoot her a small smile.

Jordan appears at my side and slaps me on the back, offering me a can of soda.

"Thanks man." I pop the top of the soda and take a long drink. "It's very nice of you to do this. My mom wanted me to tell you how much she appreciates it."

"No problem," he says, leading me over to a group of guys standing near the cooler. "We've just been talking about Adam's best moments."

"Like junior year, when he started the food fight in the cafeteria." This came from Harvey, a guy Adam had played baseball with. "I've never seen Bledsoe so mad!"

I remembered Adam telling me about the food fight. I'd done my brotherly duty and shamed him for it, but inside, the thought of Adam slinging mashed potatoes across the lunchroom had me seriously cracking up.

"I didn't envy the trouble he got himself into sometimes," I say. "But there were times I wished I could have just a little bit of his impulsiveness."

Jordan laughs out loud. "I bet, Asher. We were all kind of in awe of how ballsy he was."

"Remember when he got caught making out with that French exchange student, Marcelle, in the girls locker room?" Garret Parker pipes up. "Every guy in school had been dying to get with her, and Adam beat us all to it!"

The guys all howl with laughter, and I give a small laugh because it seems weird not to. But truthfully, this is one aspect of my brother's personality I'd never loved, much less been envious of. He didn't treat girls very nicely, at least until Grace. If nothing else, I'm glad he put that behavior behind him before he died.

"Yeah, he was always one step ahead of us with the girls," Jordan says. "Until Grace hooked him."

At the mention of her name, my pulse ratchets up several notches. I should've known this would happen. Should've been prepared to hear people reminisce about my brother and Grace as a couple. Even though I believe Grace about things not being serious between them, and even though I know deep down what she and I share is deeper than anything that came before, I can't help the small spark of jealousy that flickers inside me when I think of my brother with her.

Especially in a situation like this one where I can't lay claim to her or acknowledge publicly that I love her more than my own life.

Rather than saying anything, I just nod, despite the feelings of jealousy. What Jordan said is true. Adam was a first class player until Grace taught him to be kind and decent.

As Garrett and Harvey and the rest of the guys start going on about Adam's prowess with girls, Jordan throws his arm around my shoulders and leads me away from the group. Looking around the yard, the girls situated around the fire pit continue their conversations, and Grace and Sydney have stationed themselves with a group of kids near the back door of the house. When she sees me looking, one corner of her mouth raises and I fight the desire to wink.

"I just wanted to take a minute to tell you how much Adam admired you," Jordan says, coming to a stop at the edge of the yard closest to the driveway. "He was always talking about you going off to Flagstaff, going off on your own path."

Funny. He never said as much to me. I'd always suspected he was pretty stoked by the idea of his big brother being a tattoo artist, but to my knowledge he'd never stood up for me with Mom and Dad or anyone else for that matter. It's nice to know that, at least with his friends, he had my back.

All at once, the sadness of my brother's absence hits me. It happens so unexpectedly, yet so often, that I can't anticipate it.

"Thanks." I take a long swig of my soda, hoping to calm my galloping emotions. "I appreciate you telling me. You were a good friend to him."

"Yeah, we looked out for each other." Jordan takes a step back and turns to face me, arms crossed across his chest. "Which is why I've got to ask you, what the hell's going on with you and Grace?"

I feel like I've been kicked in the gut. Every muscle in my body clenches and I have to fight to keep my face from giving everything away.

"What are you talking about?" I ask, amazed that I'm able to keep my voice calm. I notice Grace has moved away from Sydney and is heading this direction. I pray someone stops to talk to her before she gets all the way over here.

But, no. Just as she gets within earshot, Jordan continues.

"Sydney and I drove by on July fourth," he says. "We thought maybe we could convince her to come watch the fireworks with us. Sydney was worried Grace was depressed since we hadn't really heard a word from her since Adam's funeral."

I see the shock on Grace's face, her eyes wide and her hand clamped over her mouth.

"Imagine our surprise," Jordan goes on, "when we saw you and Grace leaving her bedroom together, holding hands."

I search my mind for some explanation and decide

on the truth. Or at least part of it. "My mom and her parents were over on our patio to watch the fireworks. I'd just gotten home from my Dad's and I saw her go into her room. I just went over to say hi and walk back over with her."

I left out the part about how the two of us attacked each other with our lips.

"Yeah, that doesn't explain the hand holding or the way she kissed your hand." The look on Jordan's face is so smug I want to punch it right off.

"Just looking out for her, man," I say, hating the words. "She's my friend. She was Adam's girl. We've had a lot of grief to share."

None of that is false, and yet I can taste the lie as it rolls out of my mouth.

Jordan is not convinced. "That's what I wanted to believe, but I just couldn't get the picture of the two of you out of my mind. Sydney tried to convince me I was making something out of nothing, and we ended up having a big fight about it. She hasn't spoken to me in a week. So, I decided I had to be sure."

I'd had about enough of Jordan's superior attitude. Regardless of what he thinks about me and my choices, I'm not some disobedient child who needs to be taken to task. And even if I am, Jordan Green is not the one to do it.

"I think you need to watch what you say, Green." I step toward him, crushing my soda can in one hand and flinging it away.

"But I'm not finished with my story," he says. I'm just about to tell him that he *is* finished, when he barrels on. "I drove back over to your house last night. Parked down the street and walked up, so you wouldn't see my car. And guess what I saw? You and Grace, leaving her bedroom together again, only this time you kissed her on the mouth."

I hear Grace's quick intake of breath. "You spied on us?" she asks, horrified.

Jordan snickers when he realizes she's behind him, but keeps his eyes glued to me.

"So I'm going to ask you again." He squares his shoulders and looks at me, even though I've got a good five inches on him. "Are you moving in on Adam's girlfriend?"

I swallow hard, telling myself to just get in my car and leave. I'm about to dig my keys from my pocket when Jordan turns around to Grace.

"I never pegged you for a slut, Grace, but seriously? Two brothers?"

And then I know I'm not leaving. Not by a long shot.

When Jordan turns around to face me again, I draw my fist back and knock the shit out of him.

Chapter 48

Grace

I CAN'T BELIEVE that Jordan spied on us. Can't believe he thinks he has any right to butt into our business. Can't believe the truth about Asher and me has come out this way.

In the same instant that I'm upset about it, I'm also relieved. So what if he knows? I love Asher and I want the whole world to know.

But part of me sees it from Jordan's perspective. He lost his best friend, and now he's discovered his best friend's brother and girlfriend are an item. I know that's got to be a tough one, but that doesn't excuse his sneaky, devious methods.

I'm just about to intervene, to try and diffuse the situation, when he turns to me and says, "I never pegged you for a slut, Grace, but seriously? Two brothers?"

And that's when Asher loses it.

His fist plows into Jordan's face, and I have to jump back to get out of the way of Jordan's flying body. Jordan gets his balance back and charges at Asher. He doesn't get very far, though, because Asher throws another punch, this one knocking Jordan on his back.

By this time, everyone has gathered around and is shouting at the two of them to stop.

Asher drops to his knees, straddling Jordan's torso.

"Say what you want about me," he says, landing another punch to Jordan's jaw.

"But you keep your mouth shut about Grace." He punctuates that command with one last hit.

Jordan spits blood out and looks up at Asher, but he doesn't fight back. "Get out of here, asshole."

Without a word, or even a glance in my direction, Asher stands up and walks to his car. Sydney's arm is around me, though I have no idea when that happened, and she whispers, "Just let him go. Let him cool off."

But I can't. I can't let him go home and stew on what happened. The two of us created this problem together. We need to deal with it together.

"I have to go Sydney," I say. "I can't stay here with Jordan. Not after the things he said. And I have to talk to Asher."

By the time I get to my car, Asher is long gone. I break several speed limits and run several stop signs on my way home, but it's all for nothing.

Because when I get there, Asher's car is not in the driveway.

✧   ✧   ✧

IT'S AFTER MIDNIGHT when Asher's car pulls into the driveway. I know because I've been watching the clock for the last two hours, waiting for him to come home. I started to go out looking for him – maybe at his dad's house or the cemetery – but in the end, I knew the best thing do was wait for him here.

I'm out my bedroom door before Asher even has his car door open. Wrapped in his sweatshirt, with tear streaks still on my face, I stand in front of the car and just look at him.

He hesitates, like maybe he's considering cranking the car and taking off again, but he doesn't. After a long moment of staring at me, he climbs out of the car. He says nothing. Just walks right up to me, hands shoved in his pockets.

"I'm not going to apologize for beating the shit out of that asshole," he says, his voice a whisper but no less intense. "Not after what he said about you."

"I'm not asking you to apologize," I reply.

"Then what, Grace?" Annoyance laces his words, and I take a deep breath, not knowing what to say next.

"Are you angry with me?" I ask.

Asher's countenance deflates. His shoulders droop and his head falls forward. His stance goes from *don't mess with me* to *completely defeated* in a half a second.

"No."

"Where've you been?" I take a tentative step toward him, but he doesn't react.

"Just driving."

"It wasn't your fault, Asher," I say. "Any of it. Jordan seeing us on July fourth was just a coincidence. And that he spied on us last night is just creepy."

"But don't you see, Grace," he says. "If we continue down this path, that's what you'll have to deal with. Disapproval. Everyone we know here in Greyson will think you're a terrible person for being with me."

"I don't care what other people think." Vehemence pours out of me with those words. "We're both leaving here for Flagstaff anyway. So why should we care?"

"But I do care." He pins me with his gaze. "I care what people say about you. What they think about you. And inside, I can't help but think about Adam's disapproval. Is he looking down at me with hurt in his heart?"

Oh God. Dread races through me. This is what I've been afraid of. That guilt will make Asher walk away from me, sacrificing his own happiness, and mine too, for his brother.

He sighs, heavy and full of sorrow, and says, "I don't know if I can continue to ignore the fact that I've betrayed my brother."

I cover my face with my hands, my heart splintering into pieces.

"I don't blame you," he says, circling both my wrists with his hands. Gently he pulls them from my face so he can look at me. He's so beautiful I could weep. "I should've never pursued you. I gave up my chance with you a long time ago, when I let my pride and my fear keep me away from you. And after everything I did, all the mistakes I made trying to forget about you, I should've never touched you again."

"Stop, Asher." I choke the words out, tears spilling from my eyes once again and rolling unbidden down my cheeks.

"No, it's true. I became something horrible and my brother became the gentleman, the one who treated you right. I shouldn't get to have you now that he's gone. Not when I didn't deserve you while he was still here."

"Would it make any difference if I told you I broke up with Adam before he died." The words are surprisingly easy to say considering I've been holding them inside for almost two months.

"What?" His eyes narrow and his hands tighten on my wrists.

"The day he died," I say. "I broke up with him. He pretended to be torn up about it, but the truth is I know he was relieved. I knew he was going to Tucson and no way was he not going to play the field when he got there. And honestly, I wasn't that upset by the idea. He didn't have the heart to break up with me, so I ended things. Two hours later, he was dead."

Asher takes a step back, letting go of my hands to scrub his own hands down his face.

"Why didn't you say anything?" he asks.

"What was I supposed to say when my phone started blowing up with calls and texts, everybody telling me how sorry they were about my boyfriend? *Oh, I'm sad and everything, but it's okay because I broke up with him just before he died.* How would that have sounded?"

Asher just stares.

"The truth is, I was really sad. I was devastated by Adam's death. But not for the reasons everyone thought. At school, everybody thought of us as the golden couple, like they expected us to stay together through college and then get married. But that was never Adam and me. I was sad because a great guy was gone. I was sad because someone I cared about would never get to realize his dreams. I wasn't sad because my soul mate was dead."

He shakes his head and laughs, but there's no humor in it. "I think that just makes it worse, Grace. He got dumped, then he died, and now I'm making moves on his girl."

"I didn't dump him," I whisper, pleading with him to understand. "It wasn't like that. It might as well have been mutual."

"I just can't do this anymore," he says. "At least not for a while. Maybe not ever. The guilt, it's just too much."

He turns to walk away, taking my entire world with him. But I won't let him have the last word. If he's going to end things with me this way, he's going to do it knowing the whole truth.

"Just so you know, Asher," I begin. He stops walking but doesn't turn around. "This thing between you and me wasn't just some casual thing for me. It was never just about burying my grief over Adam. Never just a distraction. You were not a rebound."

"What do you mean?" he asks, still keeping his back to me.

"I've loved you since you stuck up for Kyle Martin and knocked the crap out of Tony Adkins. Since that first moment I've loved you and there has never been another guy in my heart. Never. It's always been you, Asher."

I'm shaking with the honesty of my admission, my face cold as the chilly night air assaults my wet cheeks. Asher is motionless for several moments, and I worry he'll simply walk away and out of my life without acknowledging what I just said.

He turns around, his dark brown eyes zooming in on mine, the intensity palpable despite the darkness of the night and the distance between us.

"Then why Adam?" he asks.

I throw my arms up in the air, barely resisting the enormous desire to shove him in the chest and scream in his face. How can one guy be so clueless?

"Because I thought you didn't want me!" I say, walking toward him and shoving my finger in his chest. "I wasn't stupid. I knew you were completely out of my league. But somehow I convinced myself you could want me as much as I wanted you. Then you left and never came back, and I was forced to accept that you didn't want me. So... why Adam? Because he PAID

ATTENTION TO ME! He was nice. It was fun and comfortable to be with him. It was nice to have someone to walk the halls with at school."

Asher just looks at me, stone faced, eyes empty and void of emotion.

"He paid attention to me," I say, lowering my voice. "And I liked it. Because except for those two months two summers ago, when you and I got to know each other, no boy had every paid attention to me before."

I see the muscle in his jaw clench, as if he's biting back whatever words he's thinking. For half a second I think he's going to kiss me, but then he takes a trembling breath and a tear rolls down one cheek.

He takes a step back, then turns and walks into his house.

And I collapse into tears there in his driveway.

HE'S GONE THE next morning when I wake up.

Chapter 49

August 1, 2014

Grace

WORST TWO WEEKS of my life.

I miss Asher so much I ache with it. Each morning I wake up and feel even more miserable that I did the previous day. My heart is cracked wide open and I swear there's a physical pain in my chest that will not go away.

What's worse is I'm still packing to move to Flagstaff. In fact, I'm just about finished. All the enthusiasm I had for getting ready to go… yeah, it's long gone.

Because two weeks ago Asher crushed my biggest reason for moving.

My phone rings. I stare at it like it's a foreign concept. Phone calls and texts have been few and far between since Asher hightailed it out of town and out of my life.

Picking the phone up from my dresser, I see it's Sydney calling. I can't imagine what she wants. Not after her stupid ass boyfriend ruined everything.

I answer anyway.

"Hello Sydney." My tone is flat, on purpose.

"Grace." Immediately she sounds repentant. "I'm so sorry about Jordan. I've wanted to call you so many times, but I was just so embarrassed."

"I don't know why you're embarrassed. You didn't do it." That, at least, is true.

"But I knew Jordan had it in his head something was happening with you and Asher. After we saw you guys on July fourth, he just wouldn't let it go." She stops, and I hear her take a deep breath. "I should've called you then, but I just kept thinking he'd let it drop."

"Obviously he didn't."

"I know, and I feel terrible. A week or so before the get together at his house, we had this huge fight. He was talking crazy, like he was going to get revenge on Asher for messing with Adam's girl. I told him he had to give it up. It wasn't his business anyway. But he wouldn't listen to me. I hadn't spoken to him for several days when I got the text about getting all of Adam's friends together."

"And you didn't find it the least bit suspicious?" I asked. "That he'd been up in arms about Asher and then suddenly he's throwing a memorial for Adam?"

"I should have." Her voice lowers. "But I didn't. I convinced myself he was trying to move on."

"Did you know Jordan came back to our neighborhood and spied on Asher and me the night before his get together?"

"Not until I heard him say it to Asher that night."

"That's a pretty disturbing thing, Sydney." I plop down on my bed, falling back onto the pillows to stare at the ceiling. "He stalked around in the dark so he could watch us."

"I'm finished with him, Grace," she says. "He was always a shitty boyfriend. I don't know why I kept going to back to him. But this last episode was it for me. I'm done. I don't think he even cares. After two years, I don't mean enough to him for him to give a damn when I end it."

"You always deserved better than him." I say this because it's true. Not because I'm letting her off the hook for not warning Asher and me about Jordan's behavior.

"Is it true?" she whispers. "You and Asher? Are you together?"

When my feelings for Asher first began, Sydney knew. As my only true girlfriend, she'd been my sounding board. She shouldn't be surprised.

"Not anymore," I answer. "Not since that night."

"Oh no! Was it because of Jordan?"

I sigh, heavy and deep, because the truth is Jordan only accelerated what was probably inevitable. "Not exactly. He didn't help matters. There were things Asher and I needed to talk about, things I needed to say. I'd been putting it off, waiting for the right time. Jordan forced my hand because he stirred up every guilty feeling Asher had about being with me."

"Do you love him, Grace?" When I don't answer, she continues. "I know you did our sophomore year. Is it still the same?"

I feel the lump in my throat and the tears gathering in my eyes. My chest shakes with the effort not to cry.

"It's so much more, Sydney," I breathe. "So much more."

"Is there any hope?" she asks.

"I don't know." It's the most honest answer I can give.

"Why don't you come to Phoenix with me?" she suggests. "You could get into cosmetology school there."

I point out the obvious. "And where would I live that's practically rent free? I can't live in the dorm with you."

"Surely we could find you some place affordable."

"Sydney, I can't. Living in Aunt Becca's apartment means my parents can afford to pay my tuition." After a second, I give her the rest of the story. "And I need to be in Flagstaff. Just in case."

"Well, keep it in mind. Just in case," she says. "I really am sorry, Grace. And I hope things with Asher work out. It's obvious how much you love him."

"Thanks Syd. I'll keep in touch."

We say our goodbyes, and I stay where I am, sprawled across my bed. A large part of me wants to crawl under the covers, pull them over my head, and just hide. But I refuse to wallow. I've waited for this time of my life for years. To be able to spread my wings and make my place in the world. Long ago, I made peace with the truth that I'd never be my brother, and I'm okay with it. I have my own dreams, and while my mark on the world might be smaller than Brian's, it will be *my* mark.

Even still, the misery of Asher's absence sits on my chest like a boulder.

For the second time in twenty minutes, my phone rings. Picking it up to look at the screen, my breath catches when I see Stella's name. I haven't spoken to her since Asher left, which is just as well, since I have no idea what to say to her.

But I can't ignore her call. Regardless of my status with Asher, I love Stella.

"Hello?" I answer.

"Grace, it's Stella." Her voice holds a hint of sadness and confusion. "I wondered if you might come by for a visit tonight."

"Well, I guess so." Nervous energy pours through me. It's not that I don't want to see Stella. It's just I have no idea how to explain what happened. And what if she's mad at me? If Asher told her the truth about my break-up with Adam, she might well be ticked off at me.

"I know you're leaving soon, and I wanted to be sure we had a chance to talk before you go. I'm home all evening, and I've got a loaf of bread about to come out of the oven."

"Okay." She can't be too angry if she's offering me homemade bread. "I'll be over in a few minutes."

Standing, I take stock of my appearance in the mirror. In Asher's sweatshirt, which is really oversized on me, no make-up, a ratty ponytail, and frown lines the size of tree branches, I look pathetic.

Removing the sweatshirt is difficult, since I've worn it every night since Asher left, but I can't go over to Stella's in it. So, I lay it gently on my pillow, then pull my hair out of the elastic band that holds it and run a brush through the locks. Satisfied it looks less like a bird nest, I pull it back into the band and create a messy bun. I can't make myself do a full make-up job, so I settle for a bit of powder on my face to at least make an attempt to hide the sadness.

I grab a jacket from my closet and slip it on. As I head to the light switch to kill the overhead, I notice Asher's drawing. It's the only thing left on the bulletin board. I know I'll take it with me to Flagstaff, but I haven't been able to take it down and pack it just yet. I feel like I need to look at it multiple times every day, just to remind myself that I didn't imagine everything.

On a whim, I remove it and carefully roll it, sliding it into the small tote bag I carry back and forth to work. If Stella has questions about Asher and me, or about how my relationship with Adam figures in, maybe the drawing will reassure her that my relationship with Asher began a long time ago.

Chapter 50

Grace

"**C**OME IN, GRACE." Stella pulls me into a hug as soon as she opens the patio door. I'm profoundly relieved she's not wary of me. "I've got a hot piece of bread already buttered for you."

"I'm so glad you called," I say, hanging my tote bag on the back of my chair. "I've wanted to talk to you, I just wasn't sure if you'd want that."

"I hope I haven't made you feel unwelcome by not calling." She sits down across from me. "I just wanted to give you a bit of space."

I give her a small smile and say, "You never make me feel unwelcome."

"Then let's enjoy the bread first," she replies, "and then we'll talk about what's going on."

Over two slices of bread each, we talk about everything from my apartment in Flagstaff to Brian working as an intern for some super important techie business this summer.

Stella finishes the last of her coffee and clears our

dishes. Returning to the table, she asks the question I know she's been waiting to ask.

"Tell me what happened with Asher." Her voice is soft, not at all demanding.

"What did he tell you?" Before I launch into my side of the story, I want to know what Asher said to his mother when he left.

"Nothing." She shrugs her shoulders. "When he left to go to Jordan's everything was fine. We had a lovely talk. The next thing I know, I wake up to him banging around in his room, packing everything like he was on some kind of deadline. When I asked him what was wrong, he said he had to leave. I pointed out it was the middle of the night, but it made no difference. He took his things, gave me a hug, and left."

My heart constricts at her words. Jordan's immense stupidity and my withholding important information has caused Stella pain and confusion. She doesn't deserve any more heartache heaped on her.

"I'm so sorry," I whisper. "Have you spoken to him since?"

"A few times," she answers. "But only general conversations. I can tell the subject is not open for discussion."

"Stella, I hate that this has caused tension between the two of you."

She waves her hand. "Don't worry about that. Our relationship has been tense before. When it comes down to it, I'm his mother and he's my son, and everything between us will be fine. But I would like to understand a little. Did something happen at Jordan's?"

I take a deep breath, dread forming in the pit of my stomach. Talking to Stella about what happened that night is near the bottom of my list of things I want to do, but she deserves to know the truth.

"Jordan lured us over to his house to confront Asher about his relationship with me. He'd seen us together on the fourth of July, then came back over the night before his party. He watched us from across the street and saw Asher kiss me."

I worry that it will be uncomfortable for Stella to hear about Asher kissing me, but she doesn't even blink.

"So the memorial for Adam was all a ruse?" she asks, clearly hurt by Jordan's dishonesty.

"For Jordan, yes. For everyone else, it was real." In this, at least, I could give her comfort. "People were talking about Adam, sharing memories. It was only Jordan who had ulterior motives."

Stella sighs and nods her head. "I'm glad to know that some hearts were in the right place."

"Jordan said awful things to Asher," I say. "He wanted to provoke him, but Asher didn't take the bait. He stayed pretty calm, at least on the outside. Then Jordan said something about me, and that's when Asher hit him."

"What did he say?" she asks.

"It was really ugly, Stella."

"I raised two boys," she says. "I've heard ugly talk before."

"He said, 'I never pegged you for a slut, Grace, but seriously? Two brothers.' A split second later, Asher plowed his fist into Jordan's face."

"Good for Asher."

My eyes widen in surprise. I cannot believe she just said that.

She notices my expression and says, "Not that I condone violence, but that boy had it coming. Asher is an honorable young man, and I'm glad he defended you."

I smile. Regardless of what happens between Asher and me, he is indeed an honorable guy, and his defense of my character that night will remain one of the most potent memories of my life.

"That may explain why he wanted to leave so suddenly, but why did he leave without speaking to you? And I'm assuming the two of you haven't talked since, so what does Jordan's behavior have to do with it?"

I lean my elbows on the table and drop my head slightly. "It shouldn't surprise you that being together, even though our feelings are very genuine, caused Asher and me a fair amount of guilt. We'd avoided talking about Adam and the guilt we felt, which wasn't smart. I think eventually we would've gotten it all out in the open and been fine, but Jordan kind of forced our hands."

Stella says nothing, just reaches across the table to

take my hand in hers.

"Asher didn't come home until after midnight, and when he did, he told me he couldn't deal with the knowledge that he'd betrayed his brother."

"Oh Grace," Stella whispers. "I'm so sorry."

"There's more." I take a deep breath. "I told him I'd broken up with Adam the day he died."

"What?" I can see she's shocked.

"Adam didn't have the heart to end things, but I knew he wanted to," I say, making a point to look directly into her eyes, despite how uncomfortable it is. I want her to know I'm being honest. "I knew when he got to Tucson he'd want to meet other girls and play the field. I think he was afraid I'd be upset about it, but I wasn't. Not at all. The whole time we were together, we both knew what we had was a 'senior year romance' and nothing more. So, I asked him to come over that morning. When I first told him I thought it would be better if we ended things then, he pretended like he was wounded, but it was just an act. He was relieved. It was basically a mutual decision. I just initiated the conversation."

"You never said anything?" she asks. "Never told anyone?"

"How could I, Stella? Two hours after that conversation, Adam was dead." I see her flinch, feeling the same stab of pain I do at the memory. "No one knew the two of us had ended things. People started calling and texting, telling me how sorry they were, asking if I was going to be ok. What could I say?"

Stella nods, perhaps seeing a small bit of my point.

"Besides, I *was* sad and heartbroken," I say. "Sad because Adam was a wonderful guy who was taken from us way too early. But everyone thought I'd lost the one great love of my life, and there was just no way I could tell them anything different without sounding like a terrible person. And anyway, it didn't matter. Adam deserved to be grieved and honored, and if I'd said anything about what happened, it would've taken away from that."

"You were in an impossible position." Stella reaches for my hand again. "I understand why you kept quiet, and I appreciate that you didn't want to cause more upheaval for all of us. But why did you wait to tell Asher?"

I sigh, my shoulders drooping. "At first for the same reasons. But then, once things with Asher became more than friendship, I was afraid he'd think I was making it up just to let us both of the hook."

"You don't honestly think he'd believe you lied, do you?"

"Looking back, no. I don't think that," I admit. "But at the time, I was just scared and confused. Then the longer I went without telling him, the bigger the secret became, and I just got more and more afraid."

"I've never wanted to interfere with my boys' personal lives," Stella says. "So I didn't ask any questions when you and Adam began to date. But I couldn't help but wonder, because I knew Asher had feelings for you."

My breath catches. "You knew?"

"Of course, honey. Everyone knew. Even Adam, which is what made his sudden interest in you so curious."

"Asher had been gone for almost a year by then." I close my eyes, the memories of the first year without him washing over me. "He'd disappeared from my life, and I had no choice but to believe he wasn't interested anymore. Adam came to the same conclusion, I guess."

"You and Adam genuinely cared for one another," she says. "I could see that."

I nod. "I'll never regret the time I had with him."

"But your heart has always been Asher's." It's not a question, but rather a statement she makes with conviction.

Reaching for my tote bag, I decide to show her the drawing. I've loved it since the moment he gave it to me, especially the way I became a part of the basket that represents his heritage.

"Asher gave this to me the night before he left for Flagstaff two years ago." I slide the paper across the table. "The past two years, I've held on to it because it reminds me I didn't just imagine what was between us. I guess now it'll have to do the same thing again."

Stella unrolls the paper, and I watch her expression change as the picture is revealed. I imagine I looked much the same when I unrolled it the night Asher gave it to me. The image of my face is the last part of the drawing to be revealed, and her face softens with a smile as she looks.

"Grace, this is beautiful," she whispers, her hand trailing along the edge of the paper.

Her eyes shift to the basket, and I hear her quick intake of breath. It almost sounds as if she's shocked.

I launch into an explanation. "He told me he wanted to show how friendship could unite people from different backgrounds."

Tears gather in her eyes, then spill over. I'm not sure what to say. The drawing has always moved me, but seeing Asher's mom react so strongly is perplexing.

"I didn't want to upset you by showing it to you," I whisper. "I just hoped to reassure you that what's between Asher and me began a long time ago. Before Adam."

Stella laughs. Like, a full blown belly laugh. And now I'm *really* unsure what to do.

"Oh, I've known since we moved into this house," she says, once she manages to get her breath and speak. "But if I hadn't, this drawing proves it."

I'm still too stunned by her reaction to the picture to speak.

"Grace, sweetheart." She slides the picture back to me. "You must not give up on Asher. Go to Flagstaff and make him see reason."

"I don't know if I can." The admission hurts in a place deep down in my soul.

Stella nods to the drawing. "After seeing that, I know you can."

I don't know what it is about the picture that makes her so sure, but I decide to hold on to her certainty.

As I stand to leave, she comes around the table to hug me again, and I welcome her affection.

"Thank you, Stella," I say, returning her embrace. "For the bread, the talk… for everything."

"Remember what I said." She steps back to look in my eyes. "Don't give up on him. You make him happy. He needs you to remind him that it's okay to embrace that."

I swallow hard. I have no idea if I can do it, but I know I want to.

"I'll try." The promise is surprisingly easy to make.

Heading back to my house, I feel a sense of peace that I didn't have before. I have no idea how I'll convince Asher to see reason, but knowing Stella wants me to and believes I can gives me hope.

Chapter 51

Asher

"WHY DON'T YOU just call her?" Rachelle asks for the hundredth time this week. "You're miserable, and you're making everyone else miserable."

I count to ten, then count backwards to zero, before speaking to her. My latest client just left the shop, and apparently Rachelle didn't like my reaction to her compliment of the ink I'd just done.

I don't know why a snarl and a muttered *whatever* isn't acceptable.

"Drop it, Rachelle," I snap. "You have no idea about anything."

"Of course I don't!" She pops up from her seat behind the counter, all five foot, one inch of her barely seeing over the top. "Because you haven't told me anything!"

"Then why can't you take the hint?" I ask, my voice hissing as I head down the hall. "Butt out."

I've stomped halfway to my station when Caleb pokes his head out into the hall. "Dude, go easy on

Rachelle."

"I need her to just leave it alone." And that's the truth. I don't need anyone reminding me I'm miserable without Grace. I'm aware of the excruciating emptiness every second of every day.

Shane comes out of the break room and smack into the middle of my exchange with Caleb. His blond spikes contrast sharply with the black hair on Caleb's head.

"You bite Rach's head off again, Ash?" Shane asks.

Great. I'm developing a reputation.

"Can you guys just leave it alone?" Seriously, I'm about to beg.

"Hard to when you're walking around here all Ebenezer Scrooge all the damn time," Caleb says.

I want to punch him.

"Don't you two have work to do, or am I the only one with clients these days?"

Shane throws an arm around my shoulder. "We're just shooting all the business your way so you'll stay occupied and off our cases."

"Asshole," I mutter.

Shane and Caleb crack up laughing.

"Seriously, Asher." Caleb punches my in the arm. "We got your back. So does Rach. Let us help if we can."

And just like that, I feel like worse shit than I did before. I'm pretty sure I've been unbearable the last couple of weeks, and yet the people I work with still care.

"Thanks guys," I say. "Wanna go for pizza later? I could use some company."

"Sounds good, Ash," Shane says. "I'm in."

"Me too," Caleb adds.

"Hey Rach!" I yell back toward the lobby. "We're going for pizza later. You down with that?"

"Only if you apologize," she shouts back at me.

"Sorry. I know I suck."

"You're buying," she calls.

"No doubt," I say.

The small ripple of happiness I feel at the thought of going out for pizza on a Friday night with my friends dims quickly when I think how much Grace would enjoy being with us.

And I know that I said to Rachelle is absolutely true. I suck.

If Grace is hurting as much as I am then I'm the biggest asshole in the world for putting her through this. It's my own fault, and I know it, but I don't know how I'll ever be able to reconcile my love for her with my love for my brother.

Chapter 52

August 6, 2014

Grace

I'M ASSAULTED WITH memories as I walk into Ugly Mug alone. I don't know what I'm doing here other than I couldn't control the compulsion to come here. The lunch Asher and I shared here seems like yesterday, and at the same time seems a million years ago. My eyes cut to the table where we sat, and my heart lodges in my throat.

Asher isn't here. I know this because I checked the parking lot for his car before getting out of my own. I hope Gabe is here, and if I'm honest with myself, I know it's because I wonder if he can give me any insight into Asher's frame of mind.

Gabe isn't running the cash register, so I place my order with the girl working there and take a seat at the counter. I scroll through my email on my phone while waiting for my cappuccino, staring absently at the screen as if I might find the answers to all my problems.

"I wondered if I might see you in here." Gabe's

voice is smooth as he slides the cup toward me. Today's mug is red with yellow smiley faces all over it.

"Hi Gabe," I say, wrapping my hands around the warm cup. "Nice to see you again."

"You looking for Asher?" he asks, leaning his elbows on the counter across from me.

"Not really." I take a sip of the cappuccino and measure his expression. His eyes aren't closed off, so I take a chance and decide to see if he'll dish on whatever he knows. "Although, if you've seen him and you have something to share, I wouldn't object to hearing it."

Gabe laughs as if he appreciates my subtlety. This close, I get a better look at his gauged ears than I had the last time I was hear. The gauges aren't huge. Smaller than a dime, in fact. I find it strangely becoming on him.

"He's been in a few times," Gabe says. "Always brooding and surly. Figured it must've had something to do with you. The way he acts, it must be bad shit."

"Things have been better," I admit, unwilling to go into detail.

"Did you come all the way to Flagstaff for coffee and info on Asher?"

I shake my head. "I'm actually moving here in a couple of weeks to go to cosmetology school. I came up today to drop a few boxes at my apartment and look for a part-time job. I stopped in here for some caffeine and hopefully a friendly face."

"We have both of those," Gabe says. "What kind of

job are you looking for?"

I shrug. "I'm not too picky. I just need to be able to work around my school schedule."

"Which is?" he asks.

His interest in my job search seems odd, but maybe he knows of some places I can apply.

"I'm at school every day until four in the afternoon," I answer. "Sounds like a lot, but I'll be done in about a year."

"So you're looking at working in the evenings and weekends, right?"

I nod and take a long drink of my cappuccino.

"You need a specific number of hours?" Gabe asks.

"My apartment is basically rent free, since it's my aunt's apartment. I just need to be able to kick in a bit on the utilities and have some money for gas."

"I can give you two weeknights from five until eleven," Gabe says. "And one six hour weekend shift, alternating Saturdays and Sundays."

"Are you serious?" I ask, stunned by his offer.

"Absolutely. Most people want more hours than that, so they look somewhere else. But I can use someone who's happy with less than twenty hours. So if that will work for you, you're hired."

"No interview or anything?" I'm not sure why I'm arguing. The idea of working with complete strangers isn't exactly appealing, so coming to work at Ugly Mug, where I'm at least acquainted with one person, sounds like a great idea.

"I'm confident you'll do a good job," he says with a wink. "Plus, it'll maybe give you a chance to run into Asher."

I can't help the smile that crosses my face. "What would I do? I mean, I can make coffee in a regular pot, but I have no idea about those complicated drinks."

"We'll start you at the register," he says. "And you can run food to tables."

"I'd love to work here, Gabe." I finish the last of my cappuccino. "I can't tell you how great this is."

"Glad to have you." He pushes away from the counter. "If you've got a minute I'll get the paperwork for you."

"Sure. I've got time."

And just like that, I have a job.

I only hope Flagstaff continues to be so friendly.

Chapter 53

August 20, 2014

Grace

I FLOP DOWN on the sofa in my small apartment. It's almost midnight, and I've just finished my first shift at Ugly Mug. I don't start school until next week, but Gabe needed me to go ahead and start work, so I've found myself in Flagstaff several days earlier than originally planned.

I'm glad to be out of Greyson, away from the memories, and in a new place where not every corner in every place reminds me of Asher.

Not that it's doing much good keeping my mind off him, but at least my first shift at Ugly Mug had been busy and hectic. I'm going to love working there. My co-workers are really nice. The clientele is friendly and eclectic. And having a manager like Gabe who's willing to work with my school schedule is reassuring.

I look around and take stock of my little apartment. My bed, a full size that Brian didn't take when he moved to California, is against the far wall next to the window that faces the street. A thrift store chest of drawers and a rolling clothes rack stand at the foot of my bed, concealed by a folding privacy panel that looks like shelves full of books.

The kitchen is small, with no room for a table. The counter tops are old school white with gold flecks, and the cabinets are painted white. The almond appliances kind of clash with all the white, but since this place is furnished with leftover stuff from Aunt Becca's kitchen remodel several years ago, I suppose it doesn't really matter.

The brown sofa I'm laying on is another hand-me-down, this one from my grandparents. The leather is worn and faded, but it's comfy, and the two end seats recline. Instead of a kitchen table, which would've taken up way too much floor space, I have an extra-large coffee table in front of the sofa, which is all a girl my age needs. Mom and Dad bought me a new TV that is mounted on the wall opposite the couch.

The bathroom and laundry area is the only part of the apartment that's not part of the main room. Just past the kitchen is a door that opens into a sizeable area with a stand-up shower and all the other bathroom necessities, as well as a stackable washer and dryer. Like the kitchen, this part of the apartment is covered in a dull, beige linoleum, while the rest of the floors are a short, industrial carpet in a similar shade of brown.

I love my apartment. It's simple and small and nothing at all special, but it's mine, and I could not be happier.

Well, unless Asher walked through the door.

Too keyed up to sleep, I grab my laptop and head over to my bed, thinking maybe I'll find something worth watching on Netfilx. Certain I want nothing romantic or drama-filled, I settle on an action film with plenty of violence and fighting. As I prop myself on my pillows and click to start the movie, my eyes land on Asher's drawing where it lays on top of my chest of drawers waiting to be framed.

I try to tune out the vision of the drawing and the feelings it dredges up inside me and focus on the movie. But despite my best efforts, the image keeps popping up in my mind.

My last thought before I fall asleep is of Stella's reaction to the picture. Something about what Asher drew for me made her certain I shouldn't give up on him, and I need to know what it was.

WHEN I WAKE the next morning, it's almost ten o'clock. My laptop is still beside me on the bed, where it was when I closed it after finishing my movie last night. The hours between then and now had been restless, filled with dreams that were nothing more than Asher and me in both real memories as well as imagined scenarios.

It's not difficult to figure out that dreaming about Asher means I miss him. What's curious is how the basket from the drawing kept appearing in random places in my dream. One moment, I'm wearing a shirt with the image of the basket on the front; it's red stripe and black triangles bright against the white background. In another, an actual basket sat on a table between Asher and me as we shared a meal.

I sit up, rubbing my eyes and pushing my hair out of my face. I rewind my thoughts, back to the moment I looked at the drawing. I remember trying and failing to stop thinking about it. I remember wondering what Stella saw in the drawing that made her react so strongly and assure me that Asher and I could work things out.

Slowly, an idea forms, and I can't believe I never thought about it before. The picture he drew is me and the basket. Nothing more. All he ever told me about the basket is that it's Navajo, but just like everything else in the Navajo culture, the basket probably has meaning.

And *that's* what Stella saw when she looked at the drawing.

She knows what the basket means. And it means something big.

I grab my laptop and pull up a browser, typing quickly into the search bar.

Navajo basket.

Just those two words. Nothing more. I figure I'll have to wade through pictures of different baskets or put more descriptive words in my search, but as soon as I hit enter, a string of pictures appear above the list of websites.

And the pictures look exactly like what Asher drew.

I click the one that looks the most like the drawing, waiting impatiently as the webpage loads. When it does, I nearly die.

Navajo Marriage Basket.

Marriage? Hyperventilating is a distinct possibility. I close my eyes and force myself to take a deep breath in order to read what's on the screen without passing out.

The Navajo Marriage Basket is a significant symbol through which the Navajo map their journeys. The center spot of the basket symbolizes the Navajo emergence into the world, and the white coils represent birth. The black triangles stand for struggle and darkness, which finally gives way to the red stripe. The red represents marriage, the blending of blood and the creation of a new family.

Scrambling to the foot of the bed, I reach up to the top of the chest and bring the drawing onto the mattress with me. Laying it beside the laptop, I compare the drawing to the picture on the webpage just to be certain.

There's no denying what Asher drew for me. A Navajo Marriage Basket.

I click a link on the webpage, which takes me to

another site detailing the way the basket is used in a Navajo ceremony.

> *The marriage basket is used during traditional Navajo weddings. The medicineman makes a circle with corn pollen atop the mush, followed by a cross, which he places in the middle of the circle. The basket is then offered to the couple and the man takes the first bite. The woman follows, taking the second bite. The two take turns, taking a bite from each of the four directions, and then from the middle.*

My head is spinning so violently I'm afraid it might explode. Of all the things he could've chosen to use from his heritage, he chose the marriage basket. And the red stripe on the basket is formed by a strand of my hair.

It's significant. It *has* to be.

Why did he never tell me?

But I know the answer. I was only sixteen, Asher only eighteen, when he gave this to me. Way too young to consider marriage, or at least to talk about it. But apparently Asher had considered it enough to create this drawing.

Maybe it was his way of telling me – without actually telling me – how he truly felt.

And then everything had gone to hell when he moved away, his life changing so fast he couldn't keep up, his family not understanding or supporting.

I have to tell him that I know. I search my mind for

the perfect scenario, hoping with every molecule in my body that this will be the thing to bring us back together. For good.

I reach to close my laptop and my tank top inches up, exposing the beautiful white ink just below my waistline. Asher's mark, forever on my skin. And forever in my heart.

I grab my cell phone and dial. A familiar voice answers on the second ring, and I begin speaking.

"I need to make an appointment."

Chapter 54

Asher

E VERY FREAKING THING reminds me of Grace. No matter how many clients I have in my tattoo chair, none of them erase the memory of Grace lying there, trusting me to do my best for her.

I can't look at Rachelle behind the counter without remembering Grace there with her, snacks spread out on the desk and smiles on their faces.

It's the same at my apartment, and especially at Ugly Mug now that I know she's working there. I'm discovering that once Grace has been somewhere, her presence lingers, like a sweet perfume or a soft light. And she's been *all over* my life. So much that I'll never be able to get her out.

I look at the clock. I have some time before my next appointment, so I step out into the hall and peek into Shane's room. He's working on a drawing, but no client is in the chair, so I take the opportunity to pick his brain.

"I can't get her out of my head," I say, dropping

onto his tattoo chair.

Shane looks up and rolls his chair to turn around and face me.

"No kidding," he says, a *well duh* expression on his face.

"She was Adam's girl," I admit. "I never told you that."

"When?" Shane asks, leaning back in his chair and crossing his arms over his chest.

"When he died." I shove my hand through my hair. "All of their senior year."

"That's heavy, no doubt." He rolls closer to me. "Was it serious?"

"Adam never said one way or the other. He didn't talk about her a lot, other than to tell me what was going on at school. He never said he loved her or anything like that."

"What about Grace? What does she say?"

"That it was never serious." I lean over, elbows propped on my knees. "That it was just comfortable and fun, and nothing was lasting beyond high school."

"Well, there you go." Shane nods like that's all there is to it.

"She also told me she broke up with him the day he died."

His eyes widen in surprise. "You never knew?"

I shake my head. "Nobody knew. How could she tell anyone? It would've sounded majorly insensitive. And even though they broke up, she was still sad, so she just didn't say anything."

"What made her finally tell you?"

"I told her I didn't think I could deal with the guilt of betraying my brother with her." I take a deep breath and tell him the rest. How I'd loved her before I left two years ago, but let my stupid pride keep us apart. How I lost my chance with her then and should've never tried to rekindle things after Adam's death. How everything went wrong and it's entirely my fault.

When I finish, Shane is silent for a moment. I begin to think he has nothing to say, but he finally speaks.

"Seems to me she knows what she wants," he says. "And what she wants is you."

I start to argue, but he interrupts.

"Just shut up for a minute and listen. You came in here to talk, so obviously you want my advice. Adam never indicated things were serious. Grace told you outright their relationship was not serious. Even told you they broke up before he died. I think you should listen to her. Believe her."

"I do believe her," I say. "I just don't know how to make myself feel okay about it. How can I really know what my brother felt? What if he was totally in love with her and just never said so?"

"Would she have reciprocated if he loved her? Because it sounds to me like she wouldn't have. Like she's loved you all along."

"She told me that." My voice drops to a whisper.

"That she's always loved me."

"Then what the hell are you moping around here for?" He smacks me on the back of the head.

"I just wish I could know for certain that Adam would've been cool with it. Maybe then I could have some peace about it all."

Shane stands and leans back against the doorjamb, legs crossed at the ankles and hands shoved in his pockets. "I understand that, man. But you're probably never going to get that kind of reassurance. So the way I see it you have two choices. You can feel guilty about your brother *and* be miserable without Grace. Or, you can deal with a little guilt and let yourself be happy with her. Either way, you've got some guilt. That's nothing unique. We've all got things we feel guilty about. But you can choose to be happy at the same time. Simple choice, at least in my mind."

It all clicks into place then, like a puzzle finally completed with the last piece. Shane's exactly right. I don't feel any less guilty without Grace. I'm just miserable and lonely. And I'm a total prick if I think Grace doesn't have guilty feelings of her own to deal with. But she was willing to work through them *with* me, and I just left her to deal with everything on her own.

I leap of the tattoo chair. "I'm going to find her," I say. "Right now."

Shane just laughs as I barrel out of his room toward the lobby.

Rachelle's in her spot behind the counter, fingers clicking away on the keyboard. She doesn't look up when I approach and I wonder if it's because she's just that busy or because she's avoiding me. I wouldn't blame her for wanting to steer clear after the nasty way I've been treating her.

"Rach, can you reschedule my last appointment?" I ask. "I've got to go."

"No can do," she says, eyes never leaving the computer screen. "Person called earlier and requested you specifically. Needs the ink done today."

"Rachelle, I've got to go talk to Grace. I'm going to grovel and apologize and try to put things back together."

Rachelle sighs and looks up at me, her eyes soft and her smile genuine. "And I'm so glad to hear that. Really glad. But this one can't be rescheduled."

I grumble and resist the urge to turn my mean streak back on. "How long will it take?"

She shrugs a shoulder and looks back to the computer. "I don't know."

I stomp back to the break room, pissed to no end that I have to wait another hour or more to go to Grace now that I've finally figured out how to pull my head out of my ass.

I take my phone from my pocket and dial Ugly Mug. I figure I better find out if she's working or not. I secretly hope that Gabe doesn't answer, because if I have to ask him if she's working, he's sure to make some kind of comment.

"Ugly Mug." My hopes are dashed when Gabe's voice comes on the line.

"Gabe," I say. "Asher."

"She's not working so it's safe to come in," he says. So he *has* noticed that I've avoided the place when Grace is there.

"That's not it, Gabe." I might as well be honest since I've decided it's time to stop being such a fool. "I'm looking for her. I have stuff to apologize for."

"It's about damn time," Gabe says. "She puts on a good front, but she's been hurting."

And that cuts me to the quick.

"If she's not at work, is there somewhere else she might be, besides her apartment?"

"No idea. She hasn't started school yet, but that's all I know about her schedule."

"Thanks man."

Gabe laughs. "Good luck."

I hang up and stare at my screen, figuring I can play some mindless game and kill time until my next appointment. Again, I notice the empty spot that used to be the Facebook app, but this time I decide to reinstall it.

Adam's been gone over two months. Surely the condolence messages have slowed down. I'd deleted it because I just couldn't deal with the thousands of notifications, but now I figure I'll just ignore them. No need to read every single wall post. Or even *any* of the wall posts. I'll just post a general *thanks everybody* message and be done.

The app installs, and I log in. I type a quick message and hit post, thinking that if I have to, I'll just deactivate the account and start another that isn't full of sympathy notes about my brother.

I click to look at my inbox messages. There are lots, but way less than the wall posts. I don't read any of them. I just scroll along and try to notice the faces of the people who wrote them. I can tell by the dates I'm getting close to the last of the messages, when a familiar face grabs my attention.

Adam.

It's dated the day he died.

My hand shakes and my thumb almost can't touch the screen to open the message, but somehow I manage. I have to sit down at the table and rest my head in my hands in order to not fall over. Phone laying on the table in front of me, I begin to read.

✧   ✧   ✧

Ash,

Prepared to be surprised, bro, because I'm about to get all mushy and "do the right thing" honest.

I realized a while back that I've never told you what a great big brother you are. You're a really awesome example, and I should've told you that. Yeah, you're only a couple of years older, but that made watching you deal with life and take those big steps all the more important to me.

You didn't let yourself get swept along with the crowd in school. The crowd liked you well enough, but you just refused to get caught up in all that stupidity. Like I was.

I admired you for that. Of course, I wouldn't tell you, because I was so damn jealous that you could just be yourself. So I acted like a dick sometimes. And I'm sorry.

When you quit college and started apprenticing at Resolution, Mom and Dad nearly shit a brick! I knew it was the exact right thing for you. I knew you'd be great at it, and you'd be majorly success-ful. And happy. But again, I was dick and said nothing. I should've stuck up for you. Told Mom and Dad to ease up on you. But I didn't.

But it gets worse. Way worse.

Back when I was still in the height of my dick behavior, I knew you had it bad for Grace. As soon as we moved in next door, you lit up like a freaking Christmas tree, and I knew. You loved her.

I waited all year for you to make your move, thinking once you did, we could finally talk about chicks like brothers do. But you never did. I couldn't understand why you kept quiet. I knew you were in Flagstaff, but damn – you looked at her with your heart all over your face. Last summer, when you were home for a week, you drooled across the driveway at her and never said a damn word. And before I knew it, you were packing up to go back to Flagstaff, and Grace was staring at you with all kinds of longing in her eyes, and you were complete-ly oblivious.

So I asked her to that back to school bonfire. Just so I could one-up you. Just because it made me *feel good. I know, I'm a complete dick. I figured, hey, I know Grace. She's cool. She's nice. Smart. Pretty. It'll be fun. We'll laugh and talk and make Asher all kinds of jealous. I figured I'd go out with her a couple of times then ease off. Then I'd call you and tell you to get the hell on home one weekend and claim your girl.*

But two dates turned into three and that turned into months, and before I knew it, I'd decided to keep her for myself. Not that I loved her. Or that she loved me. It wasn't like that. I stayed with her because it was comfortable. We liked each other.

I knew you loved her. I knew she loved you. And I kept the two of you apart.

But I'm making things right now. I just left her house. She broke up with me. Well, she started the conversation, but it was pretty much a mutual decision. Senior year was it for us. We both agreed it was for the best.

She still loves you, Asher. So get the hell home. And come claim your girl.

I hope you can forgive me, because you're my hero.

MY HEART POUNDS so hard I'm afraid it'll burst right out of my ribcage. I jump up from the table and over to the computer on the other side of the room. I log in to my Facebook account, my fingers having never typed so fast in my life. Once I'm there, I find Adam's message and hit print. The printer buzzes to life, and with every line of ink that appears, my future with

Grace becomes more and more certain.

I wanted Adam's blessing.

Now, I have it.

When the last page prints, I grab it and sprint toward the lobby.

"Rachelle!" I shout, just before turning the corner. "I don't care what you say, cancel that appointment!"

I skid to a stop right in front of the counter. Rachelle looks at me like I've lost my mind. Bing, Shane, and Caleb all step out into the hall to watch the commotion.

"I told you, I can't." She stands up from her seat with her hands on her hips, daring me to ask again.

"I don't care what you said," I say, lowering my voice so she knows I'm serious. "I'm walking out that door in ten seconds whether you cancel it or not, so just know this. I will *not* be here for that five o'clock appointment."

She opens her mouth to snap back at me just as the door to the shop opens, the bell dinging to indicate a customer.

Rachelle's eyes go wide, and she closes her mouth, so I repeat myself.

"Cancel the five o'clock," I say.

From behind me, a familiar voice grabs me by the throat.

"I'm your five o'clock, Asher," Grace says.

Chapter 55

Grace

I CAN'T DECIDE if Asher looks surprised or pissed. Probably a little of both.

The rich colors of Resolution's lobby feel welcoming, even though I have no idea how Asher is going to respond to my presence. When I'd called earlier and asked Rachelle to make the appointment, I thought having the element of surprise would be a point in my favor. Looking at Asher, I'm not so sure.

"Grace?" he asks, his voice shaky and his body rigid. His eyes are full of questions as they search mine. There's a pleading in his expression that pulls at my heart.

Unable to push the word past the lump in my throat, I simply nod.

Asher's shoulders relax. His fists unclench and relief floods his face.

In two big steps he reaches me and sweeps me into his arms.

I throw my arms around him and bury my face in

his neck. He holds me so tight it almost hurts, but no way am I complaining. I feel each breath he takes, my own coming in huge gasps as we cling to each other.

Though it's been only a month since he left, it feels like a lifetime, and now that I'm in his arms again, it's like the lights have been turned on in my heart again.

"You didn't have to make an appointment to see me," he whispers, his breath warm against my ear. "You could've just shown up any time."

"I wanted to surprise you," I answer.

His arms tighten around me. "You don't really want another tattoo, right?"

I pull back enough to look at him, happiness coursing through me when I see happiness shining from his dark brown eyes. "Actually, I do. I have the design in my bag. Let me show you."

I start to let him go to reach into my tote bag, but he refuses to let me go. "We'll talk about it later. Right now, I've got something to show you."

"I bet you do," Shane says, followed by a whistle.

For the first time since I walked in, I'm aware we have an audience. Rachelle is standing behind the counter, hands clasped over her heart and tears in her eyes. Bing, Shane, and someone I assume is Caleb, stand off to the side, all wearing expressions that say *we knew it all along.*

Asher's eyes narrow, and he shoots a *shut up now* look at Shane.

"Let's talk in private," he whispers, and proceeds to

unwrap himself from me and take my hand in his.

As he begins walking toward the hall, I look over my shoulder to Rachelle.

"Hi Rachelle. Thanks for making the appointment."

"No problem," she says, grinning widely.

The three guys step aside so Asher and I can move up the hallway, and even though Asher doesn't look twice at them, I say hello.

"Nice to see you again, Bing." I smile as I walk past. "You too, Shane."

Asher pulls to a stop and turns around. "Grace, this is Caleb." He indicates the one I didn't recognize, with a head full of black hair. "Caleb, meet Grace."

"So glad you finally showed up," Caleb says. "I don't know how much longer we could've tolerated him."

Asher rolls his eyes and laughs, continuing to lead me to his room at the end of the hall. Once inside, he shuts the door and pulls the blinds closed, giving us a little privacy.

"I want to show you the tattoo design." I drop my bag on the tattoo chair and reach in.

His hand on my arm stops me. "And I have so much to tell you. But first things first."

He frames my face in his hands and brings his mouth to mine. Softly at first, as if he's afraid I might disappear. I'm lost at the first touch of his lips, everything in me swamped with the love I feel for him.

The smooth slide of his lip ring sends electricity coursing through me, and when he skims his tongue along the seam of my lips, pleading with me for access, I don't hesitate. I snake my hands around his waist and under the hem of his shirt, pressing my palms flat against the muscles in his lower back. A groan rumbles through him, and he deepens the kiss.

I have no idea how long the kiss goes on, but it doesn't matter. In this moment, my heart is complete, my world is right, and my soul is singing.

"Grace," he whispers, finally pulling back and resting his forehead against mine. He stays there, our noses brushing and our breath mingling, for a long moment. "I love you so much."

My heart stops, then starts again, racing faster than I've ever felt it. Joy, bright and beautiful, blooms in my chest, spreading through my body, from the top of my head to the bottoms of my toes. The words I've wanted to hear from him for two years ring like music in the air between us.

"I've loved you since the day we met, even though I couldn't put a name to it at the time," he says. "Tony Adkins was a first rate asshole, but I'm so grateful for that fight because it brought you to me. I'm just so sorry it took me so long to say it."

"I love you, too." My voice is barely more than breath. "I'm sorry I didn't tell you the truth about Adam sooner. If I had, maybe –"

He cuts me off with another kiss, this one hot and quick.

"Forget about regrets," he says. "We've both got them, but they don't matter anymore."

He reaches in his back pocket and pulls out two pieces of paper, half folded, half wadded, like he'd stuffed them back there in a hurry.

"Before you read this, I want you to know that I'd already made up my mind to come find you. Shane and I talked this afternoon and he helped me see how ridiculously stupid I was being. I asked Rach to reschedule my five o'clock. Of course, she told me that was impossible, and now I know why. I was all kinds of pissed because I couldn't get out of here to go see you, and I wound up checking my Facebook profile for the first time since Adam died. I deleted the app off of my phone because the notifications were dinging in every other second, and I just couldn't deal with it."

I nodded, completely understanding. I'd still yet to log into my Facebook account.

"I looked at my inbox messages," he continues, holding the papers out to me. "And I found this. It's from Adam. Sent the day he died. You might want to sit down."

With shaking hands, I take the papers. I try to imagine what Adam might've written about to him that day, but come up empty. There are too many possibilities to narrow it down, so I take a seat on the tattoo chair and start reading.

My heart aches, reading Adam's words. The flow of the sentences sounds just like him, and I can almost hear his voice saying each phrase. I'm warmed by the feelings of admiration he expressed for his brother, and glad Asher can rest in the knowledge that Adam loved him.

But it's the second half of the letter that steals my breath.

My eyes speed over the words, then go back and read them again. Simple words, yet so profound and important.

> *She still loves you, Asher. So get the hell home.*
> *And come claim your girl. I hope you can forgive*
> *me, because you're my hero.*

These are the words that will free Asher from a lifetime of guilt.

"You were coming to find me before you saw this?" I ask.

He nods. "Shane told me I could either feel guilty *and* be miserable without you, or deal with the guilt and allow myself to be happy *with* you."

"Shane is a smart guy," I say, causing him to laugh. "Now I get what Adam said to me when he left my house that morning."

Asher tilts his head. "What was that?"

"He said, 'Everything will be great now. I'll make sure of it.' He must've gone straight home and sent this message to you."

Asher laughs and shakes his head. "My brother never ceases to amaze me. Even now."

I stand, sliding my arms up his arms and around his neck. Tip-toeing so I'm closer to eye level with him, I give him the rest of my heart. "What I told you the night you left Greyson was true. It's always been you, Asher. And it always will be. You were the first boy to ever touch my heart, the first boy to hold it. And you'll be the last. I'm so in love with you, and I don't ever want to find my way out."

His lips find mine again, and my fingers wind their way into his dark locks. He breaks the kiss, but doesn't pull back, instead trailing kisses along my cheek until he reaches my ear.

"Thank you," he whispers. "For not giving up on me."

Then he buries his face in my neck and squeezes me tighter.

"Can I show you the tattoo I have in mind?" I ask.

"You seriously want new ink?" he questions. "To-day?"

"Today," I answer. "Or sometime in the near future, if we decide to spend our time some other way tonight."

He chuckles, releasing me, and says, "All right, then. Show me."

Grabbing my bag, I pull out the slip of paper I printed and hand it to him face down. The half a second it takes him to turn the paper over feels like a million years.

I hold my breath while he looks.

And when his eyes return to mine, they're wet with unshed tears.

Chapter 56

Asher

MY CHEST TIGHTENS when I see the picture of the tattoo Grace wants.

The basket from the drawing I did for her. The Navajo Marriage Basket.

"You know?" I ask, my voice gravelly and hoarse. "You know what this means?"

"Yes," she whispers.

"When did you figure it out?" Under other circumstances, I might be ashamed of the way my voice trembles, but right now, I don't care at all.

"This morning." She steps closer to me, her eyes never leaving mine. "I showed it to your mom before I left, and she almost cried when she saw it. She told me not to give up on you and that this picture proved to her the two of us could work things out."

"She didn't tell you?"

Grace shakes her head. "I think she wanted me to figure it out on my own. Last night, I had a dream about us, and in every image I saw of us, one of these baskets was there. When I woke up, I knew I had to find out what the basket meant. I looked it up online."

I toss the picture onto the counter. With one hand, I reach out and pull her to me. With the other, I pick up a long strand of her auburn hair and wind it around my fingers. I need to tell her everything. It's way past time.

"When you asked me to draw you something before I moved away, I knew it had to be something meaningful. Something that would convey everything I felt for you. But at the same time, I knew I couldn't just confess my love for you and leave you behind the next day."

"Yes you could've." She lowers her lids, one corner of her mouth turning up in a grin. "I'd have waited for you."

I can't help the chuckle that escapes. "My plan was to get here to Flagstaff, get settled in, find a job, then carve out a schedule of when I'd be back in Greyson. Maybe even figure out some possible times for you to come here. I didn't want to ask you to be mine until I'd made a solid place for you in my life, and I didn't even know what my life was going to look like. Then everything started changing, so fast I didn't know how to get a handle on it, and you know what happened after that." I sigh, still aware of the pain I'd caused her. "Looking back, I realize it was stupid not to be honest with you from the get go, but my intentions were good."

She hooks her thumbs in the belt loops on either side of my jeans and yanks me closer until I'm flush against her.

"It wasn't stupid." She stands on her toes and gives me a quick peck on the lips. "It was sweet. Even if it was unnecessary."

"My thought was that once I had everything in order, I'd come home and tell you about that basket, and what it meant that part of you made up part of the basket. I had this grand plan that I'd tell you how much I loved you and ask you to be a part of my life. Forever."

"Is that what you still want?" she asks, her voice a touch uncertain.

And I never want her uncertain about me or my feelings again.

"Grace, that picture represents you, woven intricately into my life forever." I step back slightly and take both her hands in mine. "I don't have a ring for you yet, but someday I will. And I'll ask you to make it official to the rest of the world, the way it's official in my heart."

I hear her quick intake of breath and watch her eyes glaze with tears. Bringing both hands to her face, I lean down until I can feel her breath against my lips.

"You're it for me, Grace," I whisper. "I knew it two years ago, and I know it even more deeply now."

She wraps her arms around my middle and lays her head on my chest. "You left your mark on my heart a long time ago, Asher, and it's not ever going away."

"I love you, Grace." I press a kiss to the top of her head, then turn my head and rest my cheek there. "I can't even describe how thankful I am to have you back in my life."

"I love you, too." She tilts her head to look up at me. "And this time I'm never letting you go."

"Thank God," I say, and as I lower my mouth to hers, I know in my heart I've never meant anything more than those words. "Thank God."

THE END

A Note From the Author

If you enjoyed this book, please consider leaving a review at your place of purchase and/or any other online review site you frequent. Customer reviews are one of the best ways to show an author you enjoyed his or her work and can be invaluable for other readers as they browse for reading material. This author reads all reviews and greatly appreciates each one.

Turn the page to find out more about *Gabe's Secret,* Book 2 of the Resolution Series.

Gabe Jenkins has a secret...

Nobody knows that Gabe Jenkins comes from money... and from scandal. And he wants to keep it that way. He's perfectly happy managing Ugly Mug, a coffee shop in Flagstaff, Arizona, and leaving his trust fund untouched and his past in Kansas City buried.

That is until Rachelle Taya finds herself in desperate need of money.

Rachelle comes from nothing. The daughter of a single mother who barely scraped enough together to keep them fed, Rachelle knows the meaning of hard work and hard times. The last thing she wants is charity, especially from her friends at Resolution Ink, the tattoo shop where she works as a receptionist, or from Gabe, the guy at Ugly Mug who flirts shamelessly every time she walks in the door.

Rachelle's indifference toward Gabe does nothing to slow down his attraction to her, or his desire to help her. When Rachelle's mom faces a major financial crisis, and her long-absent, no-good father reappears, her world threatens to crash around her. Gabe has the finances to make her problems go away, but that will mean revealing the truth about his family. Will Gabe find a way to come to the rescue or will Rachelle's pride keep her from accepting his help... and his love?

Gabe's Secret

Resolution Series, Book Two

Coming 2015

About the Author

After spending every work day with classrooms full of tweens and teens, then going home to three boys of her own, two of whom fall into the tween/teen category, you'd think that Amy Durham might like to leave the world of teens and young adults behind. Not so!

Instead, she spends her spare moments – which sometimes consist of waiting twenty minutes for her oldest kiddo to get out of band practice – with her laptop and a multitude of teenage characters trying to navigate their way through the twisted, difficult road of adolescence.

You might ask… "Why Young/New Adult Fiction"? Well, because it's what she knows. As a teacher and a parent, Amy is around teens and young adults on an almost constant basis. And while it's true they can be – ahem – challenging, they are also full of life, vision, and dreams. And that's a really cool place to be.

Young Adult and New Adult Fiction allows young readers the opportunity to find hope for the situations they find themselves in, find determination to keep on going, and courage to pursue their dreams. It also allows adult readers the chance to revisit the exuberance of youth, remember the joy and poignancy of first love, and recall how it felt to dream with abandon.

Amy Durham is a wife and mother, an author, a teacher, an avid reader, and a musician. If she weren't writing books, she'd be a celebrity chef!

Contact Amy online at:

www.amydurham.com
amybdurham@gmail.com
www.facebook.com/AuthorAmyDurham
Twitter: @Amy_Durham
Instagram: @AuthorAmyDurham

www.ingramcontent.com/pod-product-compliance
Lightning Source LLC
Chambersburg PA
CBHW070759180626
46818CB00001B/25